I0534888

PACK IN BUSINESS

HER BAD BOY WOLVES: BOOK 3

TESSA COLE

CLARA WILS

Gryphon's Gate Publishing

Pack in Business

Copyright © 2024 Tessa Cole & Clara Wils

All rights reserved. No part of this book may be reproduced in any form or by any means without written consent, excepting brief quotes used in reviews.

This is a work of fiction. Names, places, characters, and events are entirely the product of the author's imagination or are used fictitiously, and any resemblance to persons, living or dead, actual locals, events, or organizations is coincidental.

Gryphon's Gate Publishing
550 King St. N.
PO Box 42088 Conestoga
Waterloo, ON
N2L 6K5

Print ISBN: 978-1-990587-48-1

JANE

"Gone? What? How?" I gasped into the phone as I bolted upright on the couch, sending pain screaming through me. "What happened? No— Wait, just tell me where you are. We'll come to you."

"Don't panic, Jane," Kira replied calmly. "We're looking for her, tracing her scent." There was something in her tone, some hesitation. She wasn't telling me everything.

"But?"

Kira sighed. "It seems my daughter may have taught her how to mask her scent."

Those words didn't make sense to me. If Izzy was masking her scent, that meant she didn't want to be found.

"Wait. Are you saying she ran away?" That wasn't much better than if she'd been taken, but at least she might be okay, just alone.

"It looks that way. Come to the Liberty Gas'n'Go on

West Street in Charles Town. That's where she... ah... left us."

There was more to this story, but I could wait to hear it. For now, I knew enough. Izzy was out there somewhere on her own, having run off, probably because she was terrified of everything going on around her, and this was my fault.

"Coming." I pushed the phone away and rose from the couch, sending more pain racing through my body. The wound on my side was the worst and moving at all seemed to aggravate it. I winced and grunted, stumbling, but Bronn caught me.

"You shouldn't..." Bronn said, his gentle hands urging me to sit back down, but one glare from me and he changed tactics. "At least let me carry you."

I nodded to that, and he picked me up carefully.

A part of me knew he was right. I shouldn't be going out. I was injured and exhausted. It wasn't even nine in the morning and I was done for the day, but I couldn't sit by while my daughter was out there alone.

Tyson led the guys out to their bikes, mounted his sleek, low motorcycle, and Bronn set me carefully behind him. My car would have been preferable, but the pack had taken it. I'd told them to sell it if they needed extra money.

I leaned against my fated mate, savoring the feel of his firm body. He no longer wore his leather vest, but that only meant I got a strong dose of his scent through his plain white T-shirt, and I drank in his aroma of smokey bacon and sea-side air, though that only made me hungry.

I'd had a large breakfast, but apparently fighting for my life and becoming that beast-thing had taken a lot out of me. I was famished again. My stomach rumbled, but that was covered by the bikes coming to life, the throb of the machine beneath me a strange mix of terrifying and soothing.

"Hold on tight," Tyson said over his shoulder. "I plan to break some laws."

"Please do! My daughter is missing, and every moment wasted is a moment she's probably terrified out there."

Tyson nodded then gunned his bike.

I gasped at the raw power blasting us forward, my hair streaming out behind me as the wind stole my breath. I should have been wearing a helmet but wasn't going to stop Tyson to ask. None of the three betas were wearing them, and I didn't even know if the guys *had* helmets, though I seemed to recall seeing some of the pack wearing those minimal skull-top helmets when they'd blasted by my house in the past.

If my riding was going to become a thing in the future, I'd have to ask for one. Right now, I didn't care. I trusted Tyson not to crash.

We hurtled through Shannondale, then turned onto the 115 in Mountain Mission. Crossing the Shenandoah River, we flew past forests and farms to Charles Town and the gas station Kira had mentioned. When I saw the pack, I instantly sensed a strange dynamic. Kira was furious, Rita and Jake were ashamed, the rest were almost fearful.

Tyson took me right up beside Kira, so I wouldn't have to move much or get off his bike.

"Spill, now," I hissed, once we'd stopped.

"We were outside of town on some no-name dirt road waiting for your call." Kira's jaw twitched and her lip curled but it looked like she was angry at herself and not anyone else. "I *saw* Izzy go off with Jake. I thought the girl just needed a little... comfort... you know. I figured I'd give them some space. That was my first mistake."

And probably a mistake I would have made as well. Izzy was scared and upset, but I hadn't imagined she'd run away. I doubted Kira had, either.

"She told Jake she wanted to make out on his bike but didn't want to do it out in the country, so they headed for town," Kira said. "She asked if he had condoms and he didn't, so she got him to stop here to pick some up. She ran in... and never came back out. Jake waited, then went in. When he didn't find her, he raced back to tell us." Kira swept a hand through her steel-grey hair. "It took some convincing, but the clerk told us Izzy came in, bought a can of air-freshener, then asked if there was a back door. The clerk saw a scared girl and a biker outside and gave in, letting her leave through the employee entrance in the back. When we checked back there, we found a pile of Izzy's clothes. She must have changed, then used the spray to mask her scent."

Kira glanced over at Rita with a huff, and Rita's gaze dropped to the ground.

"Luckily, Rita wasn't super specific about *how* to mask your scent, only that it was important. So, even though Izzy bought a supposedly scentless air-freshener, we could still follow *that* scent," Kira added. "But it only goes a few blocks over to the post office. Someone must have picked her up there, 'cause her scent vanishes."

"Wait? What? I thought you said she was on her own?"

"I only just found that out myself," Kira said. "Apologies, alpha."

"And you don't know who picked her up?"

"There was the hint of another scent, but none of us could identify it. It was human."

"Take me there, now!" I called, and the pack was quickly on their bikes and roaring through the city to the post office. I didn't know what I hoped to find, but when I got there and smelled the tell-tale air-freshener, there was something else as well. A scent I knew.

I kept sniffing, wracking my brain for where I'd smelled this before. It hit me suddenly: the scent belonged to Parker Long, Bree's overly large oldest son.

Several things clicked at once. Parker had a thing for Izzy. Izzy had never mentioned she'd been interested in him, but she'd been spending a lot of time on her phone these last few days. I had a sneaking suspicion she'd been planning this — or some escape — and had used Parker's infatuation with her. He had a beat-up old chevy and it seemed like Izzy had met him here and...

Then what?

As much as I felt a tiny bit better that Izzy wasn't with some stranger, I still had no clue where the two of them might have gone!

JANE

I TRIED TO THINK LOGICALLY, BUT THAT WAS VIRTUALLY impossible. Fear squeezed my heart, making it pound a mile a minute, which only made my injuries throb more. It was hard to form a coherent thought while panicked and pained, so I forced myself to take a deep breath and let it out slowly.

What is her long-term plan?

Stay on the run?

No, she has to have some destination in mind, but where?

Is Parker a part of the long-term plan?

Probably not.

I had to admit, I didn't know my daughter nearly as well as I should. I was fairly certain she didn't have a boyfriend or much interest in anyone at the moment, but the truth was, I didn't know. She might have a thing going at school that I knew nothing about. But given what I knew of Parker and how shy he was, I didn't think it was him... except he'd been the one she'd called to pick her up.

So, if Parker isn't part of the long-term plan, then he's just a convenient lift to... somewhere...

It was all conjecture, instinct, but given I had nothing else to go on, I ran with it.

Think Jane, think! Where is she going?

Charles Town had a small bus station, a stop for busses as they passed through, but if Izzy had had Parker pick her up, I guessed she was heading for a larger station where she could catch a bus to virtually anywhere. That or a train station. But which one? Depending on her ultimate destination, she might head in several possible directions.

Trains were more expensive... so busses? If so, the nearest major stations were in Frederick, Maryland to the north-east, or Leesburg, Virginia to the south-east.

Fuck it.

"Kira, take half the pack and head to Leesburg. There's a bus station there, see if you can find her. I'll go with the others to Frederick and the bus station there."

God, I hoped this hunch paid off.

The pack reacted without hesitation, splitting in two as if the groups had already been pre-defined. My betas stayed with me and with us came the Juarez family: Dana, Niko, and Lucas. Petra tagged along as well, driving my car with Milo in the back.

Once again, Tyson didn't spare the rubber as he broke speed laws getting us to Frederick in record time. I was just thankful no highway patrolmen had been watching our route.

When we got there, I was out of my mind with worry. I hurried into the station... or at least, that's what I *tried* to do. Apparently, I'd forgotten I was a physical wreck. I didn't even get as far as swinging my leg over the bike before the pain hit and I nearly fell off the thing. Tyson caught me.

"Easy," he said as I lay in his arms. He lifted me like I weighed nothing and carried me inside.

Okay, being carried everywhere by a hunk of a man was good for my libido, but also *super embarrassing* in public. Luckily, Tyson set me on my feet once we were at the counter, so I wouldn't be forced to talk to the clerk while in his arms.

I pulled out my phone and pulled up a picture of Izzy. I was ashamed to say the most recent one was well over a year old. She hadn't wanted her picture taken these past few years. Still, the image should work well enough. I showed it to the woman behind the counter.

"Have you seen this girl? She's my daughter and I think she might have come through here."

I don't know whether it was the desperation in my voice or the intimidating bikers around me, but the woman hesitated for only a moment before saying, "I really *shouldn't* be telling anyone about who's on the busses, but... yeah, I saw her."

Oh, thank God! I finally let myself breathe a sigh of relief. "Is she still here? What bus?"

The woman shook her head. "Left a little while ago." She looked down at her monitor and began typing. "What's her name?"

"Izzy, Isabella Myers."

The clerk nodded and kept typing for a moment. "Ah... it looks like she's on the bus to... Harrisburg."

"Of course!" Now I knew where she was going. I didn't have any siblings and my parents were both gone. So, I hadn't thought Izzy had family to go to... except my ex-husband had a sister in Harrisburg, Pennsylvania. My ex was a bum, with no fixed address, but perhaps Izzy had hoped her aunt would take her in?

"How long ago did it leave?" We might be able to catch it on the road.

"Twenty minutes or so? It takes the Catoctin Mountain Highway."

I knew the route. I'd been a chaperone for one of Milo's school trips to Gettysburg, which was roughly halfway from Frederick to Harrisburg.

"Let's go!" I called to the pack and instantly I was in Tyson's arms again, carried back to his bike and placed gently on it. Once again, we burned out of there in a hurry. The Juarez family stayed behind to call Kira and let her know we'd found Izzy.

The countryside passed in a blur as I clung to my fated mate for dear life, my heart finally starting to hope that I'd be able to find Izzy and bring her home.

And when the bus came in sight, slowing down to pass through Emmitsburg, I was so filled with relief I cried.

Tyson pulled in front of the large vehicle and waved for the driver to pull over. The man did so and when we'd all stopped, I completely ignored my injuries, running from the bike to the bus and up the steps as the door opened. "Izzy?"

"Mom?" She rose from a few seats back, blinking in surprise.

"Oh, thank God!"

"Mom!" She dashed down the aisle. "You... you're..." Flying into my arms she squeezed me tight. I almost screamed at the pain that elicited. Izzy sensed it and eased off. "You're hurt?"

"But alive."

"And...?" I heard her unasked question. There were too many people around to be specific.

"They're gone."

Izzy's eyes only widened. "You... but how?"

"Later, once we're home, okay?"

She nodded.

"Thank you for stopping," I said to the driver. The large man nodded, seeming a little confused at this strange reunion.

Izzy skipped down the stairs out of the bus.

I took a step to follow, but as my adrenaline ebbed, my pain returned, hitting me hard. My head swam and darkness closed in. I swayed, then fell, blacking out before I hit the ground.

JANE

I woke in my bed with new aches and pains. My head stung and the arm and leg on my right side were sore.

"What?" I breathed. Then came hazy memories of the bus, missing the second step... falling...

I groaned, raising my left hand to my head. There was a bandage around my forehead.

"Rest, you took a nasty spill, but you'll heal." Bronn's voice.

"What time?" I asked.

Bronn understood my extremely vague question. "It's just after five, you've been out all day."

"Fuck."

He chuckled. "Yeah, but you're tough. You'll be okay soon enough. Already that scratch on your side looks a lot better."

I lowered my hand to the bandages around my waist. The area was still sensitive to the touch but felt more like the itchy burn of a mostly healed wound than the agonizing sting of an open one.

"Just rest," he said.

I groaned and closed my eyes to do just that.

Hunger woke me some time in the middle of the night. "Food," I croaked, throat parched. "Water."

"Coming," was the nearly instant reply from Colt.

Soon enough I had a small buffet of meat and bread and fruit with a cup of water and a jug nearby to refill it. I ate indiscriminately, still exhausted and in pain. I didn't care what got in me as long as the ravenous hunger was sated. Colt helped me sit, holding me up, and when I finished, feeling marginally better, I fell asleep in his arms.

Light woke me.

For a moment, I simply lay still as I came awake. Colt was behind me, close and comforting. I couldn't see him, but I recognized the feel of his bulk. His arm, sheathed in tattoos with a stylized bear motif, was draped over me. Bronn was at the foot of the bed as a lion, sleeping, and my alarm said it was ten to seven. The house was quiet and I reveled in the silence.

As I did, I evaluated myself. I still had a bit of a headache, but it was a dull throb, more annoying than painful. The full-body ache from yesterday was mostly gone, replaced with a bit of stiffness. The wound on my side was even more itchy today, probably mostly healed over. This accelerated shifter healing was amazing! Though, I hoped my life from now on wouldn't require it. Brick was gone.

I let that sink in.

Brick.

Was.

Gone.

At first, I smiled, a relieved contentment spreading through me. Yet, the more my thoughts filtered out from that point, the more anxious I became.

Yes, Brick had been dealt with, but things would never go back to "normal." The life I'd had before all this was gone, a memory. I was a shifter now, a wolf. It had been necessary at the time, but now I was the alpha of a displaced pack and I needed to take care of them. My family had gone from three — which had been manageable — to sixteen, and a hungry sixteen at that, which was far less manageable. I had savings and retirement funds, but now I'd burn through that far faster than I'd ever intended. How was I going to deal with all of this?

Everything had happened so fast!

Everything including...

My guys.

They'd bound themselves to me as my betas and they'd shown me all manner of affection, but... had that just been another part of the heightened emotions of the past week? Did they really want to be with me, or had I just been the best alpha-option at the time? Did they really like me or were they just being devoted betas? And the most troublesome thought of all, now that the stress and high emotions of the past week were fading, was: did I really love them?

Creeping doubt claimed my thoughts.

I'd only known them for a week. You couldn't find love in that short a time, could you? The books and movies said you could, and this past week had certainly felt more like some fantasy from a steamy book, thoroughly *unreal*.

With real life now crashing down on me it just didn't seem possible to build a lasting relationship that quickly.

Fighting Brick and being a wolf and having three sexy lovers... it had made sense when things had been immediate and crazy. But with life returning to "normal" would it last? Could it last?

Tyson was fated for me, so there was that. But did that really mean he loved me? Or was it just some trick of biology that was hurling us together. Was *that* real?

I'd had more amazing sex in the past week than any other time in my life. *That* certainly didn't feel real. I'd been with my ex a lot longer and thought he'd loved me. He'd shown me how wrong I'd been. He'd wanted sex, and when I'd started to devote my life to other things, work and kids, he'd bailed for a younger woman.

Were these guys going to do the same thing? My betas were all *a lot* younger than me. Now that I was returning to a life devoted to work and kids — not to mention a pack — would they lose interest in me?

And it was clear I *needed* to spend more time with my kids. The whole incident with Izzy had shown me how much I'd been neglecting them. Would the guys even want to be fathers to my kids, or were they just here for the sex?

All of these thoughts tumbled through my head as a slow-growing ball of disillusioned doubt and dismay formed in my gut.

Needing to be anywhere but here, I slipped quietly

from the bed. Colt shifted but didn't wake. He must have been exhausted.

Had he been up all night, tending to me?

That meant something, right?

I really didn't know and just needed a moment to myself.

I put on my robe over my bandaged form, then tip-toed out of the bedroom.

Tyson lay sprawled in the hall, looking like he'd fallen asleep guarding my door. Was that chivalrous or creepy?

I headed out toward the front room but stopped after a few steps. The sound of movement from Izzy's room made me rethink where I was heading. I knocked softly on her door, whispering, "It's me," then opened it a bit.

"Mom?" she asked, sitting on the edge of her bed, hair rumpled and eyes blinking away sleep.

She reminded me so much of myself at her age, when life had been full of possibilities. Only, Izzy was far prettier than I'd been. Izzy was the me I'd wanted to be: lean and athletic while still being smart and outgoing. I'd only been smart.

I slipped inside and closed the door behind me, leaning against it for a moment, just taking in my daughter.

Her brow furrowed. "Mom?"

"I just wanted to look at you," I said. "Have I told you how amazing you are lately?"

Izzy's eyes went wide. "No, you definitely haven't. What's gotten into you?"

But we both knew.

"I was so scared when I heard you were gone, yesterday," I said, my voice small and tight, and tears welled in my eyes at the memory.

She deflated a little, looking small and meek.

"I'm sorry, Mom." Her gaze returned to me and there was a note of accusation in it. "But I was sure I was going to lose you and I didn't want to be stuck with these strangers for the rest of my life. I thought maybe Aunt Kelly would know where Dad was and I could stay with him?"

I pressed my lips shut. She didn't know her father like I did. The man was a bum. He worked odd jobs and moved around so much I had no clue where he was. His life wasn't stable and he didn't want the kids. She wouldn't have found the home she'd been searching for, but now wasn't the time to say it.

Instead, I nodded. I understood, I really did. "You thought I was going to die."

Izzy nodded, swallowing hard, tears in her eyes.

I sighed and pushed off from the door, going to sit next to her on the bed. She wore an old pair of flannel PJs covered in hearts and stars, PJs she'd loved when she was twelve. More recently she'd wanted to buy something silkier and sexier and I'd resisted. But she was sixteen, growing up, and I wouldn't be able to resist forever. Hell, she'd be gone off to college in a couple years!

I put my arm around her. "I know," I whispered. "I thought I was going to die too. It was some strange miracle of biology that saved me. I don't even understand it."

"Yesterday, while you were resting, Colt told us what happened, and Kira told us what she knew of dire wolves." Her tone was soft and a bit unbelieving. "It wasn't much, only that they're some rare mutation that happens when a shifter survives repeated trauma, near death. She thinks, because you nearly died on your first shift, then nearly died a couple times when training, then nearly died fighting Brick that it just... happened. Apparently, they're tougher and stronger and generally better at everything."

Ah. So, I wasn't special... just a survivor. Still, I'd have to talk to Kira about this *strange mutation*. Even if a part of me never wanted to think of that monster ever again.

I sighed. "I'd throw it all away just to be normal again. Just to be a woman struggling to be a good mother."

"You're a good mom," she said softly as she wrapped and arm around me, brushing my wounded side, which, thankfully didn't bother me much. "You did what you had to, to protect me, us, everyone." She leaned into me, resting her head on my shoulder.

"Thank you for understanding, but I know now, I've not been giving you what you need," I kissed the top of her head. "It wasn't smart of you, running off yesterday, and I'm still a little upset about that, but I can understand why you did it." I drew in a heavy breath. "But please don't ever do anything like that again, okay? Talk to me. I know I wasn't free for talking much this past week, but I *will* be. I want us to be able to talk about anything."

"Even sex?" she said with a breathy laugh. Almost instantly she added, "I never did anything with Jake that one time. Well, we got naked and stuff, but I didn't even kiss him. I just made a lot of noise and made him masturbate into a condom so it would look like we... you know."

"I know." And as much as I hadn't liked it, I added, "I'm glad you were smart and safe, even while trying to push my buttons."

She leaned into me. "Yeah. I just... everything is so fucked up!"

I should scold her for swearing but wasn't up for that fight right now. Hell, I'd been swearing far too much lately. Also, she was right.

"I know," I said with a heavy sigh.

"Are you going to keep..." She hesitated, pushing away from me a little to look me in the eye. "You wanted straight talk, right? Well, here it is. You making out with those guys *all the time* is just really— It feels like I'm living in a whorehouse! I mean, I know you're a woman and you have, like, needs and shit. And I know you haven't had a guy in your life at all since Dad left. And I want you to find someone special, Mom, but wow, I don't want to *hear* you fucking."

My jaw was tight, lips pressed together. I couldn't figure out whether I was angry or about to laugh. If I was angry, it was at myself for not thinking of my family while I'd been... galivanting with the guys.

Okay, maybe I was also a bit angry at Izzy for insinuating I was a whore. But I also couldn't really deny much of what she'd said.

"I'm sorry about that." I swallowed hard. "I don't know what will happen with them. I... really do want to have a lasting relationship with someone, but you're right. It can't just be all loud sex. I'll try to be more considerate if I do decide to keep seeing them."

Her brow furrowed. "You're thinking of *not* seeing them? Aren't they your betas or something?"

"I don't know anymore. Now that I've had a bit of time to think, I'm... reevaluating things."

"Oh." She blinked, her expression confused.

I leaned into her, bumping her shoulder and giving her a bit of a squeeze with the arm still around her. "If I do keep seeing them, one of my requirements is that they need to be in this for more than just me. I have a family. You and Milo, and they need to start being the sort of dads you deserve."

Izzy grimaced. "Going from no dads to three... that's definitely not normal, Mom." But then she sighed. "But anything is better than none, I guess." She looked down, reluctantly accepting.

"No," I replied softly. I put a finger under her chin and lifted her face to look at me. "Izzy, this is important, *very* important, and a lesson I didn't learn until far too late. Having no man in your life is *far* better than having the *wrong* man in your life. Your father was definitely the *wrong* man. He didn't care about me, or you, or Milo. He was selfish and lazy and not good for us. *You* are what's most important in your life. You don't need the validation of a man. I... I was weak and I thought I did. It took your father leaving for me to realize how wrong I'd been. And I have to admit, the way Tyson and Colt and Bronn treat me, makes me feel special. And that's what you need to look for, someone who truly cares about you. But it's more than even that. Find someone who sees and appreciates how strong you are on your own, and is strong on their own, and wants to work with you to be a team. I'm hoping that's the sort of men my betas are, but I really don't know them yet. I don't even know what they see in me. I—"

"I do," Izzy said softly. "You were badass even before you became a wolf. You've always been there for me and Milo. Remember when I had that nasty flu a few years ago? I missed over a week of school and when I went back, I failed that history test." She smiled. "You went in and yelled at Mr. Laraneidas and demanded he let me catch up and rewrite it? You said that my failure was his failure because I was an otherwise great student and the only reason I'd failed was because he hadn't given me the time to learn the material." Her smile grew. "And he said I should have been studying at home while sick. Then you cut him a new one saying I'd been feverish for six days and in the hospital for two of those, and if he expected me to study in that state, then he must be a fucking moron."

I was fairly certain I hadn't used those exact words, but... I did recall that fight with her teacher. "I remember."

"You've always had my back, Mom. And then these bikers came along and I was terrified, but you... you did what you had to, to protect me and Milo... twice. And one of those times wasn't as a wolf. You're strong, Mom. I want to be just like you when I grow up."

My heart nearly melted at her kind words.

"Just find a man who actually respects you and loves you," I advised. "Don't make the same mistakes I did."

She nodded. She licked her lips and looked away. "So does that mean I'm off the hook for yesterday?"

I sighed. "Sort of."

She looked back at me confused and I grimaced.

"I'm not going to ground you or anything, because something tells me things are still going to be complicated and 'abnormal' for a while," I told her. "And I know that's been throwing you for a loop already. Your punishment is to live with all these changes and try to adapt like the rest of us. It's a very adult punishment. Welcome to my life, every day."

She laughed. "I think I can live with that."

Oh, we'd see. "No tantrums, then?"

She smirked. "No promises."

Yeah, that's about what I expected.

"Now you should get ready for school. It's still a school day, right?" I was fairly sure it was Friday, but not entirely certain.

"Yeah... I guess."

"You want normal? Go to school. That's normal." I rose. "I'll let you have the shower first, I need coffee."

As I reached her door, Izzy asked, "Are you going back to work?"

Fuck! Work!

I hadn't been in in over a week. The trouble was... I was so thrown at the moment I'd probably be a complete basket case for a day or two. "I don't know."

But I should at least call them.

Izzy didn't push the issue and I left her there to get ready for school. Tyson was up, and in the kitchen when I got there.

"Coffee?" he said, indicating the machine in the middle of brewing.

"Oh, yes," I said with a long sigh, leaning heavily on the counter.

Work...

I had enough to worry about with the pack! *Everything* seemed like too much work right now. I hadn't thought about my job in days.

I shook my head and frowned. I'd take today and the weekend to get myself sorted, then go back in on Monday.

Now... I just had to tell my boss that.

TYSON

Jane winced as her boss yelled on the other end of the phone. With my enhanced hearing I would have heard him anyway, but his raised voice was making it very easy to understand him.

"*...you just vanished, Jane! Disappeared at the worst possible time. The Regency account was on the rocks as it was, and I had no clue where you were with it. I've had to scramble all week to catch up and they're still complaining. You'd better be here first fucking thing Monday morning and ready to hit the ground running because you've got a hell of a lot of catching up to do! Understand me?*"

"Yes. I do. I'll be there."

"*You'd better be. Let me make this clear. You're on thin ice, Jane. I shouldn't be doing your job for you. If you're so much as a minute late or take one more sick day this year, you're gone.*"

"I understand. I'll be there bright and early Monday."

Jane hung up and huffed a sigh so heavy she seemed to deflate. She slumped heavily into one of the dining room chairs, elbows on the table, head in her hands.

I brought her a cup of coffee. "Here," I said, setting it beside her. I didn't want her to know I'd overheard that. "Everything okay?"

"It will be," she said, sounding tired and completely defeated. "I just need to make sure I'm back to work on Monday." Then she let out a harsh laugh. "I can't believe..."

"What?" I asked. I didn't really know how to comfort someone. I tried stroking her back and while she tensed for a moment, she thankfully relaxed into my touch.

"My boss was just saying he shouldn't be doing my job for me, but *I'm* the one who does *his job for him*! That's what he's really mad about. He lost his lackey." She sighed again. "But he's still right. I should have been there and I wasn't."

"Ah," I said. That was the most diplomatic thing I could think to say, since I mostly just wanted to punch her boss. But I couldn't. I couldn't be that kind of a man anymore, because I'd happened to overhear another conversation that morning that I probably shouldn't have.

I'd woken when Jane had gone into Izzy's room and heard everything she'd said to her daughter.

"I... really do want to have a lasting relationship with someone, but you're right. It can't just be all loud sex, and I'll try to be more considerate if I do decide to keep seeing them."

If she decided to keep seeing us?

That *if* was burned into my memory. And that had only been the beginning.

"...Now that I've had a bit of time to think, I'm... reevaluating things. If I do keep seeing them, one of my requirements is that they need to be in this for more than just me. I have a

family. You and Milo, and they need to start being the sort of dads you deserve..."

But the three of us knew shit-all about being fathers. None of us had good role models. There were few things in this world that scared me, but the prospect of being a father was one of them. I was terrified I'd end up like my own father, a brutish tyrant of a man.

"Find someone who sees and appreciates how strong you are on your own, and is strong on their own, and wants to work with you to be a team. I'm hoping that's the sort of men my betas are, but I really don't know them yet. I don't even know what they see in me..."

I'd thought we'd proven ourselves to her, but she was right. We'd only been together a week and there was so much we didn't know about each other. I'd hoped that would all come in time. Now I didn't know if we'd get that time from the way Jane was talking.

"Just... find a man who actually respects you and loves you. Don't make the same mistakes I did..."

Mistakes?

Plural?

To my ears, it sounded like her husband had been the first mistake and the second had been Colt, Bronn, and myself. Because we *had* rushed things... by necessity... sort of. I mean, other than her heat, we hadn't *needed* to sleep with her this past week.

I'd thought that had happened organically, but I was beginning to see just how much we betas might have been taking advantage of a woman who was going through a trying time. What she'd needed was comfort. And the only *comfort* we knew how to give was the sexual kind. The heat had started things off on a super-sexy note and we guys had just continued on that path, but never thought to see what she truly needed.

We'd made mistakes. We'd fucked up. And now Jane was *reevaluating things*? I was terrified of what that might mean.

Brick had been dealt with, the threat was gone, but it was clear she was still at her wits end. And now, she had to rush back to work next week, like nothing had happened, while taking care of her kids *and* this pack? That was a lot of pressure on her.

I wanted to ask her what I could do to help, but right now wasn't the time. She was still tired and healing and clearly upset. So, I'd just *be* helpful.

"Ah... hey, now that things are calming down a little, the pack was talking last night and we might use the last of Brick's money to clean up your yard a bit. It's the least we can do."

"Thanks," she said, her tone weary. "Brick's money's almost gone then?" It sounded like she was hoping it would have lasted a lot longer.

"Yeah. We were going to clean up and re-seed your lawn and stuff, but with the house repairs and the fence and the back yard and the food..."

I watched her deflate a little more with each of the things I mentioned.

Fuck, this wasn't helping.

"Hey, look, you rest, okay? We'll take care of things for you today, for as long as you need." I rubbed her back a bit harder. "We're here for you."

She nodded, head still in her hands, shoulders

slumped. "Thanks, Tyson." Then she sat back in her chair — which meant I couldn't reach her back anymore — and picked up her coffee, holding it in both hands and sipping from it.

I'd tell the pack we needed to be careful around Jane, not ask too much of her. Instead, we needed to start pushing ourselves a little harder. If we were bringing in some money, that would be less stress on her, I just had no clue how we'd do that. We'd thrown around a few ideas the other day, but none of them seemed like things we could implement quickly.

And implementation wasn't my strong suit. I'd been raised to be an alpha, to make decisions and give orders. But I wasn't the alpha, I was a beta. Betas made things happen, figured out *how* to do things. And *that*, I was learning as I went. This past week, it had been easy: train Jane and make sure she survived. That had been all we'd cared about. But now, I had no clue how to ease Jane's burden. How could a pack make money without stealing? How did they live a settled domestic life?

Like being a dad.

What did I know about being a dad? Mine had thought regular beatings were good for a kid. For that matter, what did I know of being a husband? Brick had never been a husband. He'd been a sperm doner, then an abusive tyrant to Kira and his kids.

He'd been royally messed up.

And now, I was royally messed up.

All I knew how to give a mate was sex. I knew how to make Jane blissed-out with orgasms, but what did I know of love? What did I know of kindness and affection and all the other things that made a couple and a family work?

The more I thought about it, the more I could see Jane's point about needing to reevaluate things, and the less I was liking what she might find when she did.

The pack started to filter up from the basement as Jane's kids emerged for breakfast. I got to work preparing things for everyone, realizing we were out of half the things we needed. I was already falling down on the job. Still, we got the kids off to school and I got the pack organized, seeing to groceries and repairs and other duties.

Jane went back to bed, claiming a headache.

I gathered Bronn and Colt and told them what I'd heard, as well as my newfound fears. Yet, that only made them worry. They didn't have solutions, only the same issues I had.

After a morning talking it over, we decided that our task as Jane's betas was simple: figure out what she needed before she did, give it to her — or the pack — and make sure she didn't have to worry about a thing.

And since one of her primary concerns was money, we needed to somehow turn the pack's vague job ideas into money-making businesses, fast. And at the same time, figure out how to be the mates and fathers Jane and her kids needed.

No big deal. Just all that important life shit that none of us knew a fucking thing about.

Even my mom couldn't help us with this.

We were on our own.

JANE

I'D TAKEN A COUPLE IBUPROFEN BEFORE GOING BACK TO BED that morning and when I woke again at around eleven, I felt pretty good... physically. Emotionally, I was still a wreck. My dreams hadn't been pleasant, wolf fights and yelling matches with my daughter. Though, the worst dream had been my betas leaving me after I told them I wanted more than just sex and they turned out to be just like my ex-husband.

I got up and showered, hoping that would make me feel better. That involved taking off my bandages, and I was shocked at what I saw.

The last of a few scabs came away with the bandage for the wound on my side, while the faint yellow-brown mottling of old bruises covered most of my torso. Some of the color on my arms was a bit more prevalent, but they didn't hurt. My head — looking in the mirror after I removed that bandage — had a scabbed-over cut which ran into my hairline. I touched it tentatively and it was still a bit sensitive, but otherwise okay.

I luxuriated in a long, hot shower, hoping that would make me feel more human, and thankfully, it did.

After that, I did a slow tour of my house. All the damage Brick and his crew had done the night of my shift — less than a week ago, but what felt like a lifetime — was repaired and repainted, and I couldn't even tell where some of the damage had been. Whatever else the pack could do, construction was definitely up there on the list. When I checked out the new back door, I paused to survey the back yard.

It had been leveled — probably more even than it had been before the pack had arrived — and a few of the pack were repairing the fence. Petra was helping Niko Juarez and Jake put up the last few boards, but what really caught my attention was the conversation she was having with Terry, my neighbor, through the remaining gap.

They were both smiling and laughing, to the point that I began to wonder if there might be something sparking there. I hoped so, for Petra's sake. She deserved a good man like Terry after the horrors she'd been through.

I checked out the front yard next. It too had been meticulously leveled, and Dana Juarez was leading a small group who were spreading grass seed.

As I watched, a truck pulled into my driveway. I was curious who this might be, but then Bronn, Brutus, and Lucas Juarez got out, surprising me. My first thought was that they'd stolen the truck. It was an older model, but it looked like it was in good condition.

But then I looked around and couldn't find a few of

the motorcycles. Bronn reached me as I surveyed things and must have seen my confusion.

"We sold Ginny's old bike," he said. She'd taken Brick's when Brick had taken Harley's. "As well as Brutus' and Lucas'. Got a good deal, too. Traded him the bikes for that old truck and this." He handed over a wad of cash. "That's a little less than six thousand."

I blinked. "You sold your bikes?"

Bronn shrugged. "We don't need them now, do we?" His tone was level and earnest, his dark eyes somber. "We're here to stay, Jane."

Oh... wow.

"And if we need a ride," Bronn added, "the truck seats up to five, so we should be good." He smiled, like he had more good news. "And that mechanic might be looking to hire a few apprentices, too."

"Thank you, Bronn, this will help a lot." Not just the money, but the extra vehicle, and potentially some income from another source.

Lucas and Brutus were unloading a massive load of groceries and Bronn stepped inside with me to give them room.

"You... okay?" he asked, voice hesitant. There was something in how he was asking, some deeper question.

"This is all just a lot," I said as I sat on the couch. "The pack is one thing, but trying to integrate you into society isn't going to be easy." I leaned forward, elbows on knees, sliding my hands through my hair to clutch at the back of my head.

"We'll help any way we can," Bronn said, but he didn't sound convinced about that.

He sat beside me and put a tentative hand on my back, rubbing slowly. Tyson had done something similar that morning. It was so different from the heated closeness we'd shared before.

They seemed to be pulling away, and I couldn't figure out if that was good or bad.

I sighed, deciding it was time to get things out in the open.

"Look, there's one way you can help." I sat up a little and met his dark gaze. "If you're going to be with me, that means you'll need to be there for my family as well. And not in some amorphous 'they're a part of the pack' way. You and Tyson and Colt need to start thinking about how to be good fathers for my kids."

Bronn nodded, not seeming surprised. Perhaps the guys had already thought of this?

"Yeah," he said with a sigh. "We'll work on that, but we may need a little help here and there. You have to remember, we didn't have the greatest father figures growing up."

Right.

Colt's dad was Tank, a despicable, lecherous monster of a man. Tyson's father was Brick, a horrid and brutal tyrant. But Bronn? "I thought you said things in your pride were okay... before Harley took you."

Bronn bobbled his head in a yes-and-no gesture, grimacing. "My father wasn't a brute like Tank or Brick, but still, pack life isn't the same as human life. Both of my parents were... distant, having other important duties. I was raised mostly by a coalition of females and taught to fight by both sexes, but I never really knew what it was like to have a father who was there for me."

"Ah." This was going to take a lot of work on their end. "But... do you *want* to be fathers?"

"Yeah, of course!" Bronn's reply was instant, almost too fast. "Your kids are great. We all want to protect them. But beyond that, we don't know much else." He raised his brows. "How... would you describe the father you'd want to see in your kids' lives?"

Now *there* was a question. The first answer that came to mind was: *not my ex*. So, I gave it more thought.

My dad had been kind and generous, but not often around, away on business. That was something, I supposed.

"Present," I said. "There for the kids when they need them. I know it's impossible to be there all the time, even I can't do that, but as parents, if they're in trouble, or if they really need us, we drop everything and go."

Bronn nodded.

What else?

I went with the basics. "Also, kind and generous, but firm and setting a good example of discipline. We need to give the kids what they need, but not everything they want. That makes kids spoiled and entitled. And we need to know when to say "no" and the right way to discipline them when they stray from acceptable behavior."

Bronn gave a breathy, mirthless laugh. "I can't say the three of us are the best examples of acceptable behavior all the time," he said.

"I guess that's something to think about, then," I replied somberly. "If you're uncertain, check in with me. I think we've lost the fight against swearing, but that's a relatively minor hill. Mainly, we don't want our kids hurting others physically or verbally. We want them to be confident enough to not be provoked into fights, able to turn the other cheek and walk away from toxic people."

Even though I'd done the exact opposite of that with Harley. Still, I hoped they'd never have to go through anything like that.

"And if they need to fight?" Bronn asked.

Yeah, that was the problem. By killing Harley I'd shown my kids there were times when you needed to fight back. It was a lesson I'd never hoped to demonstrate to them, but I had.

"I think, I'd want them to know enough of fighting to protect themselves, or others, if needed. But, if possible, fight in such a way as to do minimal damage, subduing threats while letting authorities deal with those who are truly violent."

Bronn nodded, but he had a skeptical look on his face. I waited to see if he'd say anything, but he didn't.

"What is it?"

He sighed. "It takes *a lot* more training to learn how to fight in a..." he pressed his lips together, bobbling his head again, looking for words, "...non-violent way than it does just to fight like everyone else. Hell, I'm not even sure I know how to do that."

"Oh." I hadn't thought that would be a problem. Well fuck, another impossible thing to add to the list.

My mind spun. It took me longer than it should have to recall how we'd gotten to fighting. Right. How to be a good father.

"I think a good parent listens to their kids, really hears what they're saying and even what they're not saying. Knows what they need beyond what they *say* they need." Now I was getting into territory even I struggled with, but we might as well get it out there.

"That's deep," Bronn breathed in a low whisper.

"For now, try to imagine what Tank or Brick would do and do the opposite. That's probably the easiest way to start."

Bronn nodded for a moment, then asked, "What's the opposite of beating on a kid when they do something wrong?"

Fuck me. "Talking to them in a civil tone and letting them know what they did was wrong, then determining a suitable, *non-physical*, punishment."

He nodded to that. "Got it. I'll let the others know."

"Thanks, Bronn."

"Anything else you need?" he asked.

Yeah, I needed to know where the four of us stood in our relationship, and what came next, and how to process and handle all of these mixed-up emotions.

"I think that's it for now, thanks."

He leaned in and kissed my cheek. "Let me know if there's more," he said softly, then rose and went to help Lucas and Brutus put the groceries away.

"Oh, there's more," I whispered, barely voicing the words because I knew how keen shifter hearing was. "So much more."

BRONN

OH, THERE'S MORE. SO MUCH MORE.

I was certain Jane hadn't intended me to hear that, but lions had even more sensitive ears than wolves.

Fuck. What more was there?

Tyson had told me and Colt about Janes *reevaluating* of things, but what did that mean? Weren't we already giving her everything she needed? Well, okay, she'd explained about the kids, that was one area where we needed work, but what else? We were already helping out around the house. Hell, we'd completely repaired her house of all the damage from the night of her first shift. And I knew money was going to be a constant issue, but we'd just sold three bikes to get that truck and give her more cash to work with.

One thing I was certain of: I would never let any harm come to Jane. But what *more* was there? And why wouldn't she just tell us?

Something had changed in Jane since fighting Brick.

She was secretive and withdrawn. I didn't like this side of her.

Once I was done putting away the groceries — the fridge was overstuffed, we might need a second one soon — I looked back at Jane. She was still on the couch, head in hands. Something was wrong, but she wasn't telling us what.

I went to see Tyson and Colt. They were in the basement, brainstorming about how the pack could start making money. I caught some of their conversation as I came down the stairs.

"...the trouble isn't doing the thing itself, it's marketing. How do we let people know to find us out here in the middle of nowhere? You need the internet and shit, and none of us have any clue about any of that!"

Colt sounded like he was at his wits end. He looked over to me as I turned the corner at the bottom of the stairs, and his amber-brown eyes were filled with frustration.

"This is so much more complicated than we thought," he said to me.

"It gets worse," I said. Then I quickly outlined my conversation with Jane around fatherhood and her *there's so much more* comment.

"She's feeling overwhelmed, pulling away," Tyson said, pretty much pinpointing what I'd seen of her upstairs. "Fuck!" Then he looked to me. "How'd the sale of the bikes go?"

"We got a used four-door Toyota Tundra and about six thousand in cash. That should last Jane a little bit."

"Not Jane, *us*. We need to start thinking as a unit." Tyson sounded agitated, desperate.

"And your plans for work?" I asked, then quickly supplied, "The guy who sold us the trucks might be looking for a couple mechanics, no questions asked. I figure Lucas knows a bunch and is young enough to learn without questioning things."

"And Winnie was interested in that stuff as well," Tyson added. See if they're willing to give it a go."

"Will do." I'd add that to my list of things to take care of.

"As for our other plans... things aren't shaping up as well as we'd hoped," Tyson said with a heavy sigh.

I nodded. "I heard... marketing."

"Exactly," Colt bit out. "The only one here who might know something about that is Jane, but the whole point of this is to take things *off* her plate, not add to it." Colt shook his head, a defeated look in his eyes. "Who thought we could ever live a normal life?"

"Jane did," Tyson answered. "She believes in us. We can't let her down. We need to show her we can adapt and are willing to work to make a new life for all of us."

"Fuck. Right. Shit, yeah." Colt swore more when he was frustrated.

"We can't give up," I said, stoic. "Jane needs us."

Steps on the stairs silenced us, but it was Kira who came around the corner, a smile on her face.

"As we suspected, the woods here are perfect for wilderness survival training. The long narrow swath of forest means there are lots of places to be lost in nature, but you're only ever a mile or so from a road. There are dozens of good places to camp and..." she only now seemed to notice our dour state. "What?"

"That may be the case, but how do we let people know to come here, that we're offering anything?" Colt bit out.

Kira's brow knitted, her face clouding. "Oh... huh."

"And how do we do it, without exposing ourselves to the outside world as a whole," I added.

That was another concern for us wolves — and now Jane too — the risk of being discovered. We'd have to be really careful since one drop of blood from any of us onto the open wound of a normal person could be disastrous. Sure, that wasn't likely to happen, but roughing it in the wild would increase chances of a scrape or cut, so...

Kira, however, wasn't quite thinking along those lines, when she answered, "The business can be in Janes name, we'll just run it for her."

"But do we get paid? And what about taxes and shit?" I added. Because that was also a concern. As much as we all had IDs and such, we'd never paid taxes on the stuff we'd stolen. We'd tried to minimize our contact with government in general.

"As long as Jane has the money to take care of us, we don't need to get paid. We'll volunteer for her," Colt supplied.

That... could work.

"One problem at a time," Kira said. "The woods will work for wilderness survival. That's a win. Let's take that and run with it." She looked around at us. "What else do we have?" She didn't wait before going on. "We know the hunting in the woods is decent. There's game there, we just need to be careful not to wipe it all out. So, selling meat and products is still an option. From what I hear, that stuff can get a pretty penny since it's not common and such. And we wouldn't need anything special to sell it, just a spot in town or on a major road."

She had a point.

Apparently, we needed to be thinking more like Kira.

Tyson realized this too. "We could use your help figuring this out, Mom."

She smiled. "Of course you do. You're men."

"We're young," Tyson corrected.

"That too."

So, the four of us put our heads together to plan out how we could make things easier for Jane. Kira had a way of making any problem sound reasonable and looking through her eyes we began to figure out a few things.

Yet we still hit a few snags. First, it would be easier if the people in this little community of Jane's knew we were wolves. That would make our lives in general a lot easier, since we wouldn't have to worry about shifting. Yet, it would require some fence mending with families we'd pissed off, and by *we* I meant Tank mostly.

Second, we needed someone, either within the pack or outside, to help us with marketing and things like websites and all that stuff. Petra knew a little bit of business, but she was still in a pretty fragile state. We weren't sure we wanted to put that sort of weight on her.

Third, it was going to be a lot of work, and some of it wouldn't happen quickly.

Still, we were feeling good about our plan. So good that Colt proposed a party, to help lift everyone's spirits.

We'd tell Jane our plans and celebrate our new lives as well as defeating Brick. Hopefully that would bring Jane out of her funk.

Because this withdrawn, upset Jane was making all my protective instincts kick in. All I wanted to do was hold her, make her feel better. But something told me that wasn't what she needed or wanted. And, since she wouldn't *tell us* what she needed or wanted, I didn't know what to do.

I wished there were some miracle *thing* I could do to make everything better, but there wasn't. We'd do what we could for Jane and hope that eventually she'd open up to us and tell us what more she required.

I couldn't bear the thought of losing her. Jane was one of the few bright and shining things in my life.

I couldn't lose her.

I wouldn't lose her.

COLT

THE PACK CROWDED INTO THE FRONT ROOM OF JANE'S house. A small feast had been prepared by Kira, Bronn, and a few others, and now we sat around, eating and talking and laughing. Well, Jane wasn't laughing. She wore a forced smile and was being kind, but I had a feeling she wasn't enjoying this.

At first, I hadn't understood why Jane struggled with this attention and celebration, but I was starting to understand a few things. My first clue had come when I'd recounted her fight with Brick for the entire pack. I'd looked over at her afterward and seen the pained, sick look on her face.

I'd thought she'd like to relive her victory, but it was clear she didn't. That's when it sunk in. She *wasn't* like us. I'd known that peripherally, especially those first few days, when she'd struggled to understand our ways. But then she'd worked so hard to fight and become a wolf. I'd thought that had made her one of us… but it hadn't.

She still had human sensibilities, which included an

aversion to aggression. She'd fought only because she'd had to. That was it. She didn't want to relive it, didn't want to think about it. It was something to be forgotten, put behind her.

And that's when more things began to fall into place for me. She'd talked a lot about changing the pack, helping us live a civil life, peaceful and free. *That* was who she was. She wanted a sedate and serene life, ensuring her pack was safe and financially secure.

And as the evening wore on, I began to see why she might have been pulling away from us betas. We'd been serving her as if she were an alpha bitch, gratifying her sexually and carrying out her commands to the pack. That may have worked while she'd been training and terrified for her life, but now she'd want something else, something more. She wanted us to be lovers and fathers. She wanted kindness and compassion and under-standing and a partner to help her live the life she envi-sioned. And we'd never really asked her what that was. She'd told the pack what she wanted for all of us, but no one had ever asked her what *she* wanted.

When Jane politely begged to retire early, claiming a headache, the pack accepted this without question. However, while she was having a quick shower, I gath-ered Tyson and Bronn and told them of my realization.

"Fuck," Tyson hissed. "You're absolutely right."

"We assumed we knew what she wanted: sex and training because that's what she needed this past week but now..." Bronn nodded slowly.

"Let's have a talk with her after her shower," I suggested. "Let her know we've realized we may not be approaching things correctly and ask her what she wants."

Tyson and Bronn nodded.

We were in her room, waiting for her, when she came in after her shower. She took one look at us and sighed. "I'm not up for anything tonight, guys, okay? I'd like to sleep alone."

There it was, exactly as I'd suspected.

"We understand," I said. "Could we just have a few minutes to talk though?"

She nodded, looking like she expected this to be a harrowing experience, and moved around us to get to her dresser. The three of us, wanting to give her some space, shifted to the other side of the room.

Tyson and Bronn looked at me to start. I wasn't great with words, so blunt honesty it was.

"We realized we may have fucked up," I said simply. "We gave you what you needed this past week, when things were dire and immediate and intense, but now your needs have changed and we haven't stopped to ask you what *you* want? What *you* need?"

She'd started to take her bath robe off so she could change into her sleep clothes but stopped at my words. The robe had slipped down a little, exposing her slender neck and smooth shoulders, not to mention the top of her back and arms. Clutching the robe closed in front, she turned to us.

She seemed surprised at first, then her features clouded a little.

"I don't know what I want anymore." She took a step back to lean-sit against the low dresser with a huff of a breath. "Everything is so confusing. I don't know how to be a wolf, but I can't go back to being what I was. And now I have this pack to care for and my kids, who really need me right now." She grimaced. "And I have to go back to work next week. If I don't, I'll lose my job, which I desperately need to pay for everything this pack needs, but how am I supposed to concentrate on anything? My mind's filled with thoughts of wolf this and pack that, all running a mile a minute and spinning around, not actually settling anywhere or going away." She'd been staring at the carpet but looked up then. "Can you help me with any of that?"

I didn't know, but it was good to hear her talk and know where she stood.

Tyson answered. "Why don't you let us worry about the pack?" he offered.

She seemed to deflate a little. "I try. I do. But that doesn't stop me from worrying."

"It's what makes you a great alpha," Bronn whispered.

"Yeah, but it takes up so much of my time and thoughts, that being a great alpha means I'm neglecting the rest of my life!"

I nodded. That was the core of this, I think. Being an alpha wasn't ever going to go away for her, and she was such a giving and sympathetic person that she really wanted to care for each and every one of us. That was actually very un-alpha-like. Most alphas lived to gain power and take for themselves, their betas were there to enforce and keep the pack in line. Alphas didn't *care* for their packs, they *used* them. But not Jane. She had thirteen extra people in her life to be concerned for now. That had to be crushing her.

So, how could we beta's help?

I figured I'd asked her, "What do you need from us? How can we help you?"

"I don't know!" she blustered, throwing up her arms...

...But she'd been holding her robe closed and the release and movement pulled the robe open. She was naked beneath. I could practically hear three cocks going rock hard at the sight of Jane in all her glory, because she was fucking *hot!*

Being turned, and hours of relentless training, had left its mark on her. She was leaner, muscles defined on her thighs, abs, and arms. Her breasts were perkier and slightly smaller, but still full and heavy. Her hips were full and round, which made her narrower waist stand out even more, giving her an ideal hour-glass figure.

"And *that's* not helping!" she shouted, pulling her robe closed again. "I can smell your fucking arousal, guys. I'm pouring my heart out here, but one look at my tits and you all get this horny-hunger in your eyes, like you want to eat me!"

Oh fuck.

But how could we *not* get aroused seeing such a perfect, beautiful, sexy woman?

"Sorry, Jane," I said lowering my eyes. "You're beautiful." I stopped there. It wasn't an excuse, I just hoped it might ease her tensions. "And we can still think while our cocks are hard. We do want to help you, but if you don't know what you want, then we're floundering too."

"We've been trying to anticipate your needs," Tyson said, a bit more tactfully. "But if the real problem is your swirling thoughts, then..." He cleared his throat, slightly awkwardly. "There is only one way *I* know to help you clear your mind."

She huffed. "Yes, I know, sex. The trouble is, it clears my mind for the duration of however many orgasms you can give me, but by the time it comes to me actually *doing* something, all the worries and anxiety return. And it probably wouldn't be polite to have you fucking me while we were trying to organize the pack or at work, or..." She shook her head. "I can't believe I'm actually saying any of this."

"Would it ease your mind to know that we're your partners in all of this?" Bronn said softly.

Yes Bronn! That might work!

"Are you though?" she asked, seeming confused. "You're my betas, my second in command. I'm the head and you're the arms. The arms can't really help with head stuff."

"That's how betas *usually* work," Tyson said. "Perhaps with you, we can be different, just like you're being a very different alpha."

"And not just with the pack, but your kids," I added. Technically, we considered them part of the pack, but I didn't think Jane did yet. "We'll learn what they need and be your partners to help raise them."

"And with income as well," Bronn added. "Like we told you at the party, we have a few ideas we're going to start implementing to make more money for all of us."

"We're in this together," Tyson said. "We'll be whatever you need. If you need partners, we'll be partners, four heads. The pack can be the rest of the body."

She sighed. "Really?"

We all nodded.

"Really," Tyson said.

Another sigh and she even smiled a little. "That would be great. Though, I still don't know exactly what that looks like." She looked away, her smile fading. "You have to understand... I've never had a real partner. My ex was a lazy slob. He expected me to take care of him as well as the kids and everything else. At work, *not only* did I have to do *my* work, but also the work of the men around me just to be considered an equal. I've never had anyone who wanted to step up and *do* things for me, or *with* me." She gave a soft breath of a laugh. "And I have to admit, you have been *doing* a lot around here. The house is repaired, the lawn is tended, the fence is mended and you sold some of your bikes to help bring in a little money. I'm very thankful for that, if I didn't already say it."

"I knew," Bronn said simply.

She nodded. "I guess, I just need to let you know what I'm thinking." She shrugged. "I don't know how easy that will be for me. I've *never* done it before. It might take some time. Be patient with me, okay?"

"Only if you can be patient with yourself," Tyson said.

She scoffed. "Yeah, that's not going to happen anytime soon."

Tyson looked around at the three of us as the silence stretched after that. He spoke softly into the deepening quiet of night. "I know you don't want sex, but would it comfort you to have one of us close to you tonight? Holding you? Sleeping nearby?"

She considered that for a moment. "Yeah, it would. Just one though, okay?" She looked over at the three of us. "Colt?"

I stood a little taller. "Yeah, whatever you need."

Tyson looked at Bronn and nodded toward the door, and the two of them stepped out.

Jane and I looked at each other for a long moment, then I turned my back and began to undress.

I heard her soft breathy laugh. "Thank you," she whispered.

Once I was naked — I couldn't sleep with anything on — though tonight I wished I could, I sat on the edge of the bed, facing away from her. I heard the rustle of cloth and the shifting of sheets, then that same soft laugh.

"Okay," she said.

I lifted the sheets and slid under them, lying next to her, but not touching. "Just... let me know what you need," I whispered.

"Just... hold me?" she said, sounding so small. "No rubbing or caressing or pressing too close, just... hold me like I'm your favorite stuffy in the world."

"Stuffy?" I asked, what in hell was that?

"Stuffed animal."

"Like taxidermy?"

She laughed. "What? No, like the soft plush toys that kids have."

"Oh! Is that what they're called?"

"You really did have a rough childhood, didn't you?"

"Yeah." I didn't want to go into details, now wasn't the time.

"Did you ever have anything dear to you, but not in a sexual way? Something you'd want to keep close to you at all times, hold dearly?"

"Yeah." I understood now. "When I was a kid, I had a keychain of a stallion. At night, I used to hold it in my hand so tight I'd get bruises. I'd rub it for luck and try to remember my mother, who named me."

"Jesus, Colt! Now *I* want to hold *you*!"

I chuckled. "Why don't we try that. You hold me like you would a... stuffy, so I can see what it's like."

"I'd like that." She shifted over to me. "You're too big. Do you mind if I just hold your arm?"

"Go ahead."

She wrapped both her arms around one of mine and held it tight, pressed to her. I felt the softness of her chest through the sheer silk of her nightgown. Fuck! That was sexy. I balled my hand into a fist so I wouldn't be tempted to touch her, especially since my hand was pressed against her thighs.

I instantly started thinking about roadkill to stop myself from getting aroused and took long even breaths. That seemed to work.

She rested her head on my shoulder. "Like this," she said softly, snuggling closer, curling around my arm. "Thank you, Colt." Then she relaxed, her breathing slow and even.

It took me a little longer to find sleep. I wanted to get used to this, to being close to her and feeling her amazing body pressed to mine, without my cock going rock hard. I wanted to be there for her forever.

I didn't know if I was in love, but I knew that seeing her smile made my heart burst with joy and seeing her in pain was like my own personal hell. There was nothing I wouldn't do for her. And this, just being close and peaceful together, was actually really nice. I could get used to this.

Maybe this was love? This selfless give and take?

If so, then I was all in.

That thought finally allowed me to rest.

JANE

I WOKE UP WITH MY BODY STILL WRAPPED AROUND COLT'S arm. He'd shifted in this sleep, rolling off his back to face me, his other arm draped over me casually. What wasn't so casual was the log of rigid flesh pressed against my calves. I had my legs pulled up and, with him facing me, his cock rested perfectly in the divot between my shins. And since it was Colt, his morning wood was rather spectacular. He must have been having one sexy dream.

My dreams had been more on the sexually frustrating side. The betas... and my ex for some reason... had been taking turns with me, all getting off but leaving me wanting.

Hence, I was seriously craving an orgasm.

Luckily, I had a sexy beast of a man next to me. *And* it was a beta's duty to serve his alpha, wasn't it?

"Colt," I whispered, stroking his cheek.

He gave a long shivering sigh. "So soft," he mumbled. What was he dreaming?

"Colt," I said a bit louder, shimmying my body against his.

He gave a long grunt, his cock swelling before his eyes blinked open. A lazy, sleepy smile spread across his face. "Hey gorgeous. I just had a sexy dream about you."

I shouldn't have been surprised, but I was. "Oh?"

"Yeah, you were in a giant bunny costume, or you were a life-sized plush bunny, either way, you were so soft and fluffy and sexy as hell."

Curious. I'd unpack that later, right now, I was in desperate need of a release.

But as much as I'd felt compelled to wake Colt, I really didn't want him to do much. Some greedy part of me just wanted to use that glorious body of his to get off. "Stay very still," I whispered. "I need something from you." Reaching down I wrapped a hand around his thick shaft. "And I'm going to take it. Do you mind?"

Colt drew in a heavy breath. "Use me," he breathed. "I'll always be here for anything you need."

That's what I'd wanted to hear.

I stretched out a little, shifting my legs and body down so I wasn't curled into a ball next to Colt. I pulled my nighty up to my waist and shimmied closer to Colt, his heavy shaft now pressed between my thighs. With a low sigh, I draped my top leg over him and began rocking slowly, using his rock-hard erection to rub my clit.

Colt moaned softly, not moving, still and steady. Good, I wanted to take a little bit of something just for me, selfish as that was.

It didn't take much before my body began to sing with steamy heat. Colt's erection slipped over my damp folds as I ground on him harder and harder, seeking my release.

"Gods, you're so fucking wet," Colt mumbled. Yet he remained unmoving.

I *was* soaked. I needed this so bad. Every push against him and I opened a bit more, gliding over his rigid length.

Then the combination of his pressing erection and my hungry opening met, and his tip slipped inside me, pressing and full and so very much what I'd needed.

"Fuck," he hissed low and throaty and sexy.

I unleashed a groan driven up from deep within me, a long, low sound behind my lips. I shifted my hips forward so he was pressing to just the right spot inside me and shivered with bliss.

I was so close to a peak, trembling and ready for my release. Unable to control myself I jerked on that heavy tip, but that caused it to slip out. I keened. Colt did move then, though it was barely more than a slight shift. Yet the motion rammed his cock into my clit.

I came, shuddering, convulsing with clipped, breathy cries as I fast-rocked my hips over his wet tip to prolong the orgasm.

And when I was sated, I slowly pulled away from Colt, shifting my nighty down again.

He slipped onto his back, a massive grin on his face. He didn't seem to mind not getting off.

Good.

The room billowed with the scent of our combined arousal. I rose and went to my newly repaired window. Opening it, I let the chill autumn morning air cool me.

It was just before dawn, the sun not quite up yet, but the sky lightening more and more. I loved this time of day.

Perhaps… today would be a better day?

I hoped it would.

It had certainly started off right.

"How you feeling?" Colt asked from the bed, voice soft, concerned.

I sighed. "I'm okay." It was the truth. I still didn't really know how I felt about… *anything*, but right now, I didn't feel awful, and that was something. I turned and leaned my ass against the edge of the dresser, crossing my arms over my chest.

Changing the topic, I asked, "So, me as a bunny, huh?"

"You're *always* cute, but this was *extra* cute," he said with a chuckle.

I laughed. "Is that your kink?" I asked, feeling just a little lighter after that compliment. "Furries?"

"Furries?" He seemed surprised. "Is that… a thing?" He laughed. "No." Turning his head and looking away for a moment, he seemed to consider it. "I'd say my kink is kind and compassionate women who just want to be held, but who are also a sexy beast when they want to be." He looked back at me with a warm grin.

A pleasant heat shivered through me.

Then Colt shrugged. "Either that or knees. Knees are *so* sexy!"

I laughed, as he'd intended. "Knees, huh?"

He shrugged again, then sobered. "Actually, I think I just want a woman who can see past my size and my scars and my... past... and love me for the scared boy inside who doesn't know how to live in this harsh world."

Well, fuck. That was a lot to take in.

"Mommy kink?" I asked, partially joking, but also not... because I was just a little turned off by that. It was too much like my ex.

"No, I don't need someone to take care of me, just see that I'm more than what's on the outside."

And the simple fact of admitting that made me start to truly see Colt, because he was far more than just his huge, scarred body and dangerous, criminal past. He had a truly kind heart, buried deep in there.

"I think I can manage that," I said softly.

He smiled, and there was genuine affection and trust in that smile, not the heated hunger I'd seen when I'd accidentally flashed my betas last night.

"I know," he said, blithe and open. "That's what I love about you."

And there was that word.

Oh, we'd all thrown it about the last week or so but had any of us really meant it or had we just been caught up in our passion?

"You can't mean that," I whispered, my fears finding a voice. "It's only been a week. You can't fall in love in a week. I don't care what the movies and books say."

Colt didn't refute that right away, and for some reason that meant so much more than if he'd just quickly insisted on his love. He actually thought about it.

"Well, first..." he said slowly, "...I don't think love works how any of us expect. It might take years, or it might take days. I guess I want to believe in those movies and stories." And that was his soft gooey center, his kind heart, showing through. "Second, what I love *about* you, is your willingness to accept me. Whether that means I love you or not...?"

He took another long moment and I waited with bated breath.

He sighed. "I know this much. You remind me of someone I loved."

He'd mentioned her before. Then and now, I sensed he carried a great deal of pain in relation to this other woman, whoever she might have been.

"You're kind and gentle and giving and also strong and determined and fierce," he said. "I love *that* about you. And whether or not I'm *in love*, I want nothing more than to love you the way you deserve."

I had no clue what to say to that. It soothed my fears, while at the same time made me freak out just a little that this man was already so committed.

Was I that committed?

Could I say I wanted nothing more than to love him? Or did I just want his amazingly sexy body and the comfort of his protection? I didn't know.

I swallowed as the two of us remained where we were, gazes locked for a long time. Then he drew a deep breath and began rolling out of bed. That broke the moment.

Our scent of arousal no longer filled the room, but it clung to me. I closed the window and slipped out to have a quick shower. By the time I returned, Colt was dressed. I quickly dressed and together we went out to join the pack for breakfast.

After breakfast, the guys outlined their plan for the

pack to make money. They'd given me an overview last night at the party, but this was everything they'd come up with so far.

Bronn started. "I've already called the mechanic who we sold our bikes to. He said he might need some help, so we're sending him Lucas and Winnie as apprentices. They'll both be making roughly twenty thousand a year."

My eyes went wide, mouth gaping. Those two kids would help this much? An extra forty grand would go a long way in helping out.

Bronn smiled at my astonishment.

Tyson took things from there. "You've also mentioned how well we did fixing-up your house. We figure we could make a go of that, doing renovations and such. Those most skilled, and most inclined, would be Petra, Nico, Cassie, and Jake, with Colt supervising them." He hesitated for a moment and I knew he'd be asking for something from me. "I... was hoping that perhaps we could speak to some of your neighbors to see if they need anything redone to start things off. Offer a reduced rate to get some good word of mouth going and some promotional pictures."

"You want me to ask around?" I confirmed.

"If you're willing. They'd probably accept it better coming from you. But if you want, we can reach out ourselves."

I thought about this. "Does anyone in that crew have a head for business?"

Tyson responded. "Petra apparently was taking some business courses part time before..." Before Tank had abducted her.

That was perfect! I wanted a way to help Petra and Cassie find some strength within themselves and this would work wonders.

"Okay, here's the deal," I said. "Colt can run the crew from our end, but I want the public face of the crew to be Petra and Cassie if they're willing. I'll take them around and introduce them to the neighbors and see if they need any work done. In public, everyone defers to their judgement. That's the deal.

Colt nodded with a smile, clearly approving. "We can do that. I like it."

"Good." I was starting to get a little excited. "What else?"

Tyson continued. "Brutus loves being a wolf and is actually good with animals, so we thought he could do the dog training. We'd throw Rita in with him to help with the business end of things and keep him in line."

I nodded and Tyson kept going. "That leaves me, Bronn, Kira, and Dana. Kira really wants to help out with the kids. Since school isn't an option for us, she wants to continue Jake and Winnie's education a little. But she'd also make sure your kids are looked after if you're not home. She's toying with the idea of a daycare as well, for any small kids in the neighborhood, but we're less certain about that."

"The rest of us would start up a survival camp and ethical hunting adventure. We'd take small groups out into the woods and teach them how to survive in the wild and how to hunt and use every part of an animal. We'll also be able to sell meat and products we make from those trips."

Tyson sighed. "The trouble with the dog training and camping stuff is... how do we let people know about it? We don't want to put any more pressure on you, but if you know of anyone who could help us with a bit of branding and marketing, then we could talk to them and get things moving. We can use the money Lucas and Winnie are bringing in to pay for any start-up costs."

"This is great," I said with a wide smile. They had a well thought out plan. "Run with it. Do it. Yes!" I gave them my permission to begin. "I'll take Petra and Cassie around to see if any of the neighbors need work done on their houses." As for marketing, I did know someone, but I wasn't sure how much she'd want to help. Debbie Coles — the woman who I'd recently discovered was a witch — did freelance marketing. But she also seemed to hate shifters. Still, I could reach out to her. Perhaps a paycheck was a paycheck and it didn't matter who it was coming from? Because other than her, I didn't have any other contacts. Though... Terry, next door, and the Khan's, might know some people as well. I'd check with them if Debbie fell through.

"I'll look into the marketing and branding thing," I added, which was all I could promise for now.

The guys were ecstatic and went to work right away starting to flesh out their plans and working on numbers and I left them to it.

TYSON

I was thrilled at how Jane had responded to our business ideas. I didn't think anything could bring me down from that... but then, once the three of us were outside in the fresh air to develop things a bit more, Colt turned to us.

"We need to talk." The usually jovial man was far too serious.

And there it was. Instantly my mood faltered.

"What is it?" I asked, concerned.

"Jane... and love." I didn't understand what he meant, but he quickly went on. "This morning, Jane said something that got me thinking, and I think it's something we should all be thinking about, especially you, Tyson."

Okay, now I was worried.

"I said something about how much I loved her, and she said it just wasn't possible," Colt explained. "She said: you can't fall in love in a week. It made me think, was I really in love?" He sighed. "I *want* to be. And the way I feel, it's a lot like what I felt for Tasha, but... hell, I don't even know if *that* was love. I think it was... but..." He shrugged.

I nodded, following so far. The trouble with the three of us was simple: we'd never really known love. Colt had probably come the closest with Tasha before Tank had killed her. But that meant we didn't really know what love was supposed to feel like. I knew, theoretically, it was more than sex, about trust and respect and caring... but... was that it? Was there more?

Bronn grunted, his brow furrowed, gaze lost and searching.

"The more I think about it," Colt continued. "The more I'm wondering... did Jane say that because she's not in love with me? With us?"

I was about to instantly refute that when Colt held up both hands.

"Wait a sec," he said. "I think I know what you're going to say and I'll get to that. I'm not saying she doesn't appreciate us or that she isn't *interested* in us. I'm saying... is it *really* love, you know? And Tyson, I know you're fated, and she feels that too, but that's why I said you really need to take this seriously. Because if she starts thinking that all she feels for you is just some trick of biology, I don't know what she'll do with that. She may try to fight it. The fact that you're fated means you want each other, you want to fuck and take care of each other, but is *that* really love? Are you truly emotionally invested with all your heart, or just doing this because your body and mind are yelling at you that you have to?"

Fuck. He was right.

"So, what do we do?" Bronn asked.

Colt shrugged. "No clue. With Tasha... we were young and only together for a couple months. I *think* that was love, but since I've no other reference point, I can't be sure." He sighed. "I think we all need to take a step back and really try to understand what we're doing and thinking and feeling. And yeah, I know we're all shitty at touchy-feely stuff, but if we want to be right for Jane, and her kids, I think we need to start figuring that shit out."

"You're right," I said with a sigh. "Let's give Jane her space for a bit. Let her think while we do the same. If she asks for one of us to be with her, we can do that, and we can still show her how we feel, but I think taking a step back is the right call."

The other two nodded.

"I need a bit of time to think about this," I said. "I'm sure you do too. We know what we have to do for the pack-work project, so let's split up and start on that."

We went our separate ways. Bronn needed to tell Lucas and Winnie about their new jobs, so he headed back inside. Colt would talk to his construction team and start working out the equipment they'd need. I was supposed to be scouting possible survival camp locations, but as soon as I stepped into the quiet sanctuary of the woods, all I could do was think about Jane. Not only what Colt had said, but about her kids and how she wanted us to be father figures to them.

I'd been kicking myself for not seeing she needed that. Being fated for her clouded my mind. It meant I needed to be near her, giving her everything she needed in bed and in life. I could protect her, I could care for her, try to provide for her... but her kids?

How had I missed that they're a part of her too, and a huge part at that? It only made me think about Colt's words even more. What other blind spots did I have? Was being fated truly love or just messed up biology? At the moment, I was leaning toward biology and that... didn't have great implications.

"Fuck," I cried out at the trees.

What do I know of love?

I'd never loved anyone before. I'd fucked and I'd had friends and tended to the pack, but I was fairly certain I'd never truly loved. At least Colt had some vague frame of reference with Tasha. I had nothing.

"Tyson?"

I spun at the voice, not fully registering who it might belong to until I saw Jane's son there behind me.

Fuck! What was he doing here? I had no clue what to do with the kid. No, not *the kid*, he had a name... and it was... Fuck! I had so much on my mind I blanked for a moment.

Oh, right, Milo.

I tried to hide my mounting panic.

"Oh, hey kid." *No, use his name, you dumbass!* "Ah... Milo. What're you doing here?"

I should *not* be this afraid of a scrawny teenage boy, but I was. What did I say? This was too soon!

"Just walking. You?"

"Ah... thinking... and walking."

Milo laughed. "You seemed to be doing more thinking than walking."

The kid was probably right.

I wanted to tell him to go away, that I had important

things to think about, but that wasn't what fathers did... was it? But then... what did I say?

I stood there, probably looking like an ass, not saying anything.

But then I took a good look at the kid — *Milo!* — and I was pretty sure he hadn't noticed my awkwardness, because he seemed pretty awkward himself. He was looking around at everything but me and sort of swaying a little.

"Hey... Tyson? Could you... ah... teach me how to fight?"

Fuck me! What do I say to that?

I mean *I could*, but I was almost certain Jane wouldn't want me to. That *might* be something fathers did with sons, but I had the distinct impression it wasn't what Jane was hoping we'd do with her kids.

So instead, I asked, "Why?" Which led to other questions. "And why do you want to be a wolf? Why did you run out that day? How did you know about us?"

He was on the spot now. He kept swaying on his heels while staring at a nearby tree. "I may have seen Lucas and Jake shift, when I snuck out one night. And... who *wouldn't* want to be a wolf? You're strong and tough and nobody will mess with you. I just..." He shrugged, humming and hawing for a long moment. "I started high school this year, and well... when I left middle-school I was one of the tallest in my class, but now... I wanted to try out for football or baseball or something, but compared to those guys I'm still a shrimp and I've no muscles at all and... when I did try out, some of the guys teased me and pushed me around and said nasty things."

"And you want to fight them?" That didn't seem wise.

"I don't know! I just wanna be bigger!" He kicked the dirt. "My Mom's okay and all, but maybe if my dad had been around, I'd have started sports sooner and be stronger and shit."

Ah.

"You don't need to be a wolf to be strong," I said, desperately hoping I was doing the right thing. I looked around, spying a log that would work for the idea which was slowly forming in my mind. "Come here," I said, going over to the fallen tree.

Milo followed, still sulking a little.

"Can you lift that log?" I asked. "Not the whole thing, just one end?"

Milo looked at me. "I dunno, maybe?"

He wasn't getting the point. I showed him what I was thinking, standing at the end of the log and picking it up in both hands. Once it was at chest height, I adjusted my hands so my thumbs were under it. "Like this." It was easy for me. It wasn't a large log. "Then you lift it over your head, like this." I pushed the log up until my arms were straight above my head, forming a rough triangle made with my body, the log, and the ground. "Then lower it slowly back to your chest." I did so. "Then squat with it." I crouched down, then up. "Then lift it again. Can you do that? Try it."

I dropped the log and Milo went to it.

He *was* pretty scrawny, but he hefted that log well enough. I'd picked the right size it seemed, as it was just a bit of a struggle for him. He got it situated in his hands, then proceeded to do as I'd shown, lifting it over his head then back to chest, then squatting with it.

"What now?" he asked.

"How many of those do you think you can do? Ten? Twenty? More?"

He was already shaking just a little from standing there holding the log.

"Maybe... fifteen?" he guessed.

"Try it."

He did.

I had to admit, the kid had spirit. He pushed through and managed to do twelve, shaking and straining, before dropping the log. He fell back on his ass at the same time, sweating and groaning.

I knelt next to him. "You okay? How do you feel?"

"Sore," he groaned. "And sweaty. And I can't stand up. My arms and legs feel like jelly. I'm so fucking weak!"

"But you won't be, if you keep doing that," I said softly. I chuckled. "Not tomorrow though. If you think you're sore now, it'll be worse tomorrow and probably the day after too. But once you've recovered, come back out and do that again. And keep doing it until twelve is easy and you're not sore. Then try fifteen, then twenty, then thirty, and so on."

A curious and defiant look came to his face. "How many can *you* do? I wanna see."

I chuckled again; I'd walked into that one. "Sure, ki— ah— Milo. Let's see what I can do." I rose and went to the log, lifting it. "Oh, and when you can do lots of lifts with this log... find a bigger one. This one's a little on the easy side for me, but let's just see how many I can do, okay?"

Milo nodded, smiling intently, eyes lighting up.

I began. The first thirty were a breeze. The next fifteen or so were not as easy. I started sweating after seventy. By the time I hit eighty-five, I was shaking, but I was determined to make it to at least one hundred.

Except as I rose out of the squat on my ninety-seventh rep, one of my legs slipped on the mossy forest floor and I came crashing down, falling onto my back and laughing.

"There," I panted. "If you can ever do a hundred with this log, you'll have beaten me."

"That's..." Milo's eyes were so wide. "Yeah, sure, I can do that. I'll keep working on it." He got up slowly, having recovered. I stood, my muscles a bit sore. I'd be fine in a few hours with my advanced healing.

"Thanks, Tyson," Milo said. "You're cool."

I laughed and smiled. The kid's praise meant a lot to me. Was this what it was like to be a dad?

Maybe?

I decided I could scout possible camp sites later. Perhaps I'd spend a bit more time with Milo. "Anything else you need?" I asked.

He looked away, hedging for a moment before saying, "How do I talk to a girl I like?"

I laughed. "Got me, I'm still working on that one."

He looked up at me confused. "But you and my mom are... like... totally doing it, right?"

Wow... awkward. Luckily, this one was easy to answer. "We're fated for each other. Has your mother told you about that?"

"No. What's that mean?"

"It means we're drawn to each other. We want to protect and serve each other, be near each other and..."

"Fuck?"

"Heh, yeah. So... it just sort of happened for us. But honestly, I still don't know how to talk to your mom about serious emotional stuff. That's hard for anyone. Best advice I can give is be honest and be yourself and just tell her. And if she says she's not interested, don't bug her."

"Yeah, my mom said something similar."

I'd given him the same advice Jane had? Maybe I *could* do this father thing.

"Thanks Tyson. Oh... there is something else. Mom gave me the task of talking to everyone in the pack about what it's like to be a shifter. She said I had to get all the good and the bad so I can make up my own mind to become one... when I'm fifteen. So... what's it like?"

That was a *much* easier topic. I gave it to him straight. There were a lot of up-sides: strength and healing and running as a wolf. But then I told him about the burden of the curse and the feral pull that's always there, just below the surface. I also told him about obeying your alpha and betas — even if that alpha is your mom and you're not a kid anymore — and some other drawbacks.

"This curse... it's not a good thing to have," I said as I ended. "Your mother did it only because she had to. *You* have a choice. If you just want to be strong, do those exercises I showed you and you'll get there. There are humans stronger than I am." Not many, but it was probably true.

Milo had a right to know. "I don't know if it was the curse or just how we lived, but we did some bad things before your mother tamed us. Things that could get us thrown in jail. I don't think you want to be that kind of person, do you?"

Milo shook his head, clearly not liking what he was hearing. "No, I guess not, but maybe that wasn't the curse, just... your upbringing?"

He sounded like he wanted that to be true. It might be. I honestly didn't know. What I feared was that the curse predisposed a person to violence and evil.

"Maybe," I said. "Maybe not."

He nodded. "Well, thanks Tyson, I guess." Then he ran off back toward his home.

That left me standing in the woods, wondering about the curse. Was I irredeemably evil? If I was, then what did that mean for Jane? Would *she* change over time? And if I was cursed, could I really love someone?

I hoped so.

Fuck. Talking the kid out of becoming a wolf had really messed me up. I doubted myself, how I felt. Was I right for Jane? The more I thought about it, the more I convinced myself that the fated bond was all that was keeping us together: biology, not love. Because how could a vile thing like me love someone...

...and how could anyone love a vile thing like me?

JANE

I DREW IN A LONG BREATH BEFORE KNOCKING ON THE Coleses' front door.

"Just a warning," I said to Petra, who'd come with me. "Debbie is a witch and doesn't like wolves."

Petra, the poor thing, seemed to shrink even more into herself. I'd seen her starting to come out of her shell these last few days. She'd seemed happy when helping with the rebuild around my house and I'd seen a definite smile on her face when she'd been talking to Terry next door. But now, she seemed her old, submissive self.

It was one of the reasons I'd brought her, to help her grow and find her strength. I'd told her about the plan for the construction business and how we wanted her to run it. She'd been quite surprised and shocked that we'd chosen her. If she was going to be facing other neighbors to ask for business, she'd need to get used to this type of thing. We weren't here for Debbie's business specifically, but still, I hoped Petra would learn something from this encounter. Now all I had to do was convince Debbie to help us.

The door opened. "Oh, hey Mrs. Myers," Kathy said with a grin. I was glad she'd answered the door. It gave me a chance to thank her.

"Thank you for the potion you gave me. It helped me fight off the nasty wolves who were the real threat. I'm in your debt."

Kathy beamed. "Glad to help. You here to see my mom?"

I nodded. "Is she here?"

"Yeah, one sec," Kathy said. Though before she turned away, she whispered to me, "She's still not fond of wolves. She may not like you being here."

"I know," I whispered. Then louder, "But this is business related so I'm hoping she'll hear me out."

Kathy shrugged then turned to a door, just to the right, inside the house. She knocked on it lightly. "Mom. Someone is here to see you." That was diplomatic.

Debbie appeared from what looked like a small office to one side at the front of the house. She saw me, then sighed, moving to the front door and mostly closing it, shielding herself behind the door as she spoke.

"I thought I told you not to come back?" She said, accusing. Not the best start.

"Debbie, I know you aren't fond of wolves," I told her, "but I have two quick things to say, if you'll let me."

She didn't look like she wanted to, but she relented. "Go on."

"Thank you. First, I wanted to let you know that the nasty wolves, the ones who were behind all the horrible things that happened around here, are gone. I drove them off. The rest of the pack are good people who are trying to find a new way to live, in peace with everyone." Debbie scoffed at that, but I saw how her gaze drifted over to Petra, pregnant and submissive, behind me. There was a certain sympathy in that look.

Good.

"Second, I'm hoping that wolf or not, you might be willing to help us with some marketing we need. It would be a purely business relationship, you don't have to like us to take our money, do you?"

She sighed, clearly not liking this. "No, but it does mean I'm less likely to do so." She stepped out from behind the door a little. "I'm listening. What do you need?"

This was progress.

"These people want a fresh start, living a normal life. To do that they need to work. They've come up with some ideas, but a few of them aren't going to get off the ground without some help. They'd need some branding advice, and at least a simple web presence and ways to get the word out."

"What are the businesses?" Debbie asked.

"Well, a couple of them thought they'd try dog training."

Debbie scoffed. "You sure they aren't going to eat the dogs?"

I made a sour face. "No, Debbie, they aren't. But as wolves, they can work with hard-to-handle dogs and assert some dominance to help them learn how to behave. It would be for the most difficult dogs."

Debbie matched my sour face as she sighed. "Seems simple enough, I can work with that. What else?"

"A few others would like to take small groups out into the woods and—"

"Fuck no!" Debbie said, backing off. "You want me to help wolves lure people here so they can devour them in private in the woods?"

"Wolves don't eat people!" I said disgusted.

But then I remembered someone mentioning what they did with their dead. The gruesome practice of eating their bones so no one would ever find their DNA. I'd have to change that. Yet another thing on my never-ending *To Do* list. Still...

"They want to teach people survival training and ethical hunting."

Debbie shook her head. "Yeah, no. I'd need to trust you a whole lot more than I do now to support that."

I sighed. There was one other item, and it couldn't hurt to ask while we were here. "Petra here, and a few others, made some repairs to my house and did a fantastic job. They'd like to start up a small reno business." I looked back over my shoulder and Petra was nodding, doing her best to smile, though it seemed a sheepish, slightly terrified thing. "So, if you wanted to help with that, we'd appreciate it. Also, if you need any fixes done around the house..."

"I'm not letting any of you in here." That was fair. "But... I *could* do the marketing for the dog training and reno businesses. Let me do some figuring and send you an estimate. Is that all?" She backed up behind the door again.

I did have one question. "Why... don't you like shifters?"

Debbie's face went hard. "Simple. Shifters are evil and unnatural, end of story. Now good-bye." She closed her door.

I sighed, shaking my head. As I turned to leave, Petra spoke, hesitantly. "Witches and Wolves have a bad history," she said, her voice mousy, soft and a little squeaky.

"Oh?" I prompted.

Petra nodded as we began the walk across the cul-de-sac back to my place. "I only know what Kira told me, but apparently, the first witches were taught by fae. Fae are protectors of nature and shifters are unnatural, so... they've always been at odds. The two sides have been waging a quiet war that humans never knew about."

"Ah, I see," I said.

And with that, Petra seemed to shrink back within herself. It might take this woman a while to come out of her shell.

Hoping to bring Petra back out, I changed the topic. "Tyson says you have a business background or something?"

She brightened a little. "Yes, sort of. I took some night courses while I worked at a diner. I was most of the way through a business administration program when..." she clammed up again.

When Tank found her.

Hoping to steer her away from that train of thought, I asked her, "How many more courses would you need to complete it?"

She blinked up at me. "You think I could? I just left. It's been almost a year."

"Why not? Or you could start over and get an associate's degree at APU in Charles Town."

"You think so?" She didn't seem to believe it.

"Yes, I do. I'll support you, so will the pack. I want to make this business work for you, Petra."

"But..." She rubbed her belly. "What about...?"

"Kira likes taking care of children. She can help out if you're studying or working. The whole pack can help raise them."

She smiled, just a little, a faint and fleeting thing as she looked at her belly. "Thank you," she said, voice so quiet I could barely hear it.

I wanted to ask her if she'd thought of names for the child, but... that might lead down a dark path. It was Tank's child after all. Given how far along she was, I didn't think abortion was an option at this point. But there were still things we could all do to help.

I stumbled over my words a little to say, "If you... wanted someone else in the pack to... adopt it. If you don't think you're ready for a child... then we can work something out."

"No," she said. And when she looked up at me, her eyes flashed with determination. It was the first spark of real strength I'd seen in the woman. "This is *my* child. *Mine!*" Her words were heated, possessive. "I always wanted children, but never thought it practical and hadn't found a man... and then..." She faltered for just a moment before that fierce protectiveness returned. "This is my child. It doesn't matter who the father was. I'll raise them right."

I smiled. So, she had claimed this child, making something good of all the evil that had happened to her. Good. "I'm glad, Petra. And we'll all help you raise it."

She nodded. "I hope it's a girl," she said, resuming her softer tone.

For her sake, I hoped so as well. I couldn't imagine what Colt might have been like as a kid, but a little bear shifter boy seemed like a real handful.

"Me too." I reached out and rubbed a hand across her shoulders. She flinched at first, then warmed to me.

"You're a good alpha," she said with a nod.

I blinked. Many people had told me something similar, but it wasn't until now, hearing such a genuine and heartfelt sentiment from Petra, that it truly sunk in.

Perhaps... I could do this after all.

JANE

PETRA AND I SPENT SOME TIME PRACTICING HER PITCH. I wanted her to be the one talking to the neighbors about the reno business, if she was up for it. She wasn't sure she could do it, but I'd seen the determination in the woman when she'd talked about her child. I knew there was mettle in her and I meant to bring it out. So, we spent the rest of the day Saturday working on that. Cassie helped and the two of them seemed to lend each other strength. They had a decent little spiel by that evening. We'd take it around to the neighbors tomorrow to see what they thought. I'd go with them for support, just in case they needed me.

That night I asked Bronn to stay with me, nothing sexual, just sleep beside me. He accepted gladly.

Tyson smiled and didn't seem upset that I hadn't picked him, but we both knew he was desperate. I knew because *my* fated link was practically begging for him. I hadn't been around him all day and the pull just to be near him was intense. And more than just nearness, my core ached to have his knot locked inside me. I could resist the draw, but it made me feel unfulfilled, like I hadn't eaten enough dinner, only it wasn't food I was hungry for. I had the feeling that by the end of another day like this, it would be far worse. I didn't know how long we could actually be apart.

For tonight, I tried not to think about it, focusing on the man in my bed: Bronn. The trouble was that all my guys insisted on sleeping naked, which meant cuddling with them without it becoming heated was hard.

So, like I'd done with Colt the night before, I asked him just to lay there, then snuggled close next to him, clasping his arm to me with my head on the pillow beside his and one leg just edging up over his.

"Is this comfortable for you?" I asked.

"Yes, of course. Whatever you need."

I need you... I think...

Fuck I don't know!

Why don't I know?

Bronn was as gorgeous as any model, a sinful delight of dark, muscled skin. Not to mention how generous and giving and patient and sturdy he was. Why wouldn't I want him? But the biggest question in my mind was still, *why in hell does he want me?*

After lying awake for far too long, with doubts and fears running through my head, I decided to ask him.

With my heart pounding so hard I thought it would bash its way out of my chest, I whispered, "Bronn, are you awake?"

"Yeah. What's on your mind, sweetness? I can feel your heart racing. What's wrong?"

What *was* wrong? Everything! In no universe should a man as beautiful as this want to be in my bed.

"Why...?" The word barely squeaked out, just a breath of air, I hardly heard it. "What do you see in me?"

He stiffened for just a moment. Fuck. I'd put him on the spot. Yet he sighed out a long breath a moment later, relaxing.

"Colt said you and he talked about love." I should have known my three betas would talk. "You want to know if I love you?"

Yup. But saying it was a lot harder. My heart pounded against my chest so hard I vibrated, my mouth dry.

"Yes," I managed to say, again barely a breath, but he heard it and nodded.

He lay there for a long time, not saying anything, while I freaked out on the inside. What did his silence mean? Could he not say it? Did he not know? Was he trying to find some way to let me down easy? *What?*

"I'm a simple man," he began. "I don't have a lot of fancy words." He rolled his head to look at me, but we were too close and he was just a blur in my vision. "So, I'll say what I feel, okay?"

I nodded.

"I know you may not see it, but I think you're fucking sexy." His low, sure tone sent a zing of liquid heat straight from my hammering heart down to my pulsing core.

"Really?" I mean, yeah, I worked out and I'd certainly blasted away a bunch of the fat on me this past week with the crazy training and shifting, which had literally taken a lot out of me physically. But I was still plain-Jane Myers with my brown hair and brown eyes and...

"Hell, yeah," he breathed. "Even before you became a wolf and got all toned, you had great legs and arms, round hips, and a perfect pair of tits. But more than your body, you... you have a kind face and there is this look you get in your eyes when someone compliments you. It's like they're actually sparkling. And you've got a big heart, a giving heart."

"My heart turns you on?" I joked, not quite believing him.

"Yeah, in a way. It means you love freely. You take care of people, you want to protect them, and you'll do whatever it takes to do all of that. Your giving heart makes you *fierce* when you need to be, and *that's* sexy."

"Oh."

"Also, there's something in your scent. I can't describe it, but it calls to me like no one's ever has before. Your scent drives me wild, and I just want to hold you and sniff you forever."

That was... interesting, and not entirely bad.

"And you're more than just sexy," he whispered, a bit reverent. "That same heart of yours, it makes me want to be near you, to protect you while you help others. It... it makes me want to give you what you give to others, so you can get something back for all the tenderness you put out into the world."

He drew a long breath. "I want to be near you, and I feel this sort of pull when I'm away from you, to get back to you. I want to serve you, not just as a beta, but as a man. My heart hurts if I think of you in pain. I want to shelter you. I... I don't know if that's love, because I've never known love and I've never felt this way for anyone before, but... yeah..."

"And you really mean all of that? You're not just saying that to get into my bed or because you're my beta or whatever else?"

"I mean every word. And you don't need to believe me. Just wait and see. Long ago, before I left my pride, my mother once told me, *words are just air. They fade as soon as they're spoken. It's deeds and actions that matter and last.* So... I'll show you how I feel. It may take some time, but I'm never leaving you, Jane. I'll always be there for you."

Wow.

My heart's rapid pounding turned to a frantic fluttering of uncertainty and anticipation. I still didn't know *why* Bronn wanted to be with me, but he'd certainly convinced me he wasn't going anywhere. And I really didn't know how I felt about that. I really wanted him to remain close, to hold me and be there for me. I wanted his warmth and caring, and his sexy-as-sin body. I wanted all of him.

Because I believed his words.

I don't know if it was his proclamation that he'd show me, or just how earnestly he'd been, but I trusted what he'd said.

It occurred to me that perhaps I'd never really felt true love either. Perhaps I was freaking out now because this *did* feel far too real and deep, and I had no clue what to do with that.

I shifted over to kiss his forehead. "Thank you, Bronn, that means a lot."

"You feeling better?" he asked.

"Probably enough to sleep. I... I may need reminding of all of this from time to time."

"I'll tell you every morning and every evening and any time in between if you'd like."

I gave a soft laugh. "Ah... that seems a bit much, maybe just if I'm looking down?"

"Done."

And my heart finally settled.

As I dozed, finding the edges of sleep, it occurred to me I hadn't given him anything in return for his words. So, drowsy and soft, I whispered to him, "I think you're sexy too, and I... I hope what I feel is love."

He gave a contented grunt, then rolled his head to kiss my forehead as I'd done for him.

Then, finally, I slept.

The next day, Petra, Cassie, and I made our rounds of the neighborhood. The first stop, as usual, was the Khans. Melody opened the door and beamed when she saw me.

"Jane! So good to see you. And who are these lovely ladies with you?"

"This is Petra and Cassie," I said. It only occurred to me then, I didn't even know their last names. I hoped Melody didn't ask. "May we come in?"

"Of course, deary, what's this about? Come in. Sit!" She directed us to her living area.

We'd decided Petra and Cassie would give their pitch, but it was probably best if I did the introductions.

"The last time I was here, I mentioned how I was reforming that group of bikers. Well, as part of that I'm trying to help them find new career options. Petra and Cassie are forming a renovation company."

"Shining Stone Construction," Cassie burst out.

I stared at her, blinking. This was new.

"Sorry," she said with a grin. "We only came up with the name last night."

"Shining Stone?" I asked, curious.

Cassie's grin grew. "It's our names. Cassie — at least in part — means 'shining' and Petra means 'stone' so... Shining Stone."

Shining Stone it was.

"How lovely," Melody added.

I turned back to our host. "Part of the troubles at my place involved a night when the more raucous members of the gang did some damage to my house. Those people have been dealt with and are no longer around. And we found out that the rest of the crew was quite adept at putting things back to rights. They did windows and doors, even mended some floors and ceilings, oh, and repaired my fence. So, if you're willing to listen, Petra and Cassie would like to give a little pitch about what they do."

"Yes, of course." Melody beamed. "I love to see women being industrious, especially in what are normally male dominated professions. Do go on."

I sat while Petra and Cassie stood. I watched them, fingers figuratively crossed.

"Thank you for seeing us," Petra began. Her voice was a little soft, but in this small space it was loud enough. "We at Shining Stone Construction are just starting out, looking to help our neighbors with simple construction projects or repairs around the house."

Cassie picked it up from there. "We understand you

may be wary to hire a new company, so we're offering a significant discount for anyone who helps us out while we're getting established. We'd charge you only for materials, plus a small daily amount."

Petra continued. "That amount will get you both of us, plus our crew of three others. We'd dedicate ourselves to your project and strive to complete it quickly and with minimal disturbance to your life."

Cassie took over. "At the moment we can handle carpentry, as well as simple plumbing and electrical work."

Petra finished. "Please let us know if there is anything we can help you with. Thank you for your time." They both looked at each other with a smile, then sat back down.

"How wonderful," Melody cheered. "Well, you know... I've been thinking for some time that I might want to redo our kitchen. Could you handle that?"

I was a bit surprised to hear Petra answer instantly. "Yes, of course." Good for her, no hesitation. I had no clue whether they could do a kitchen, but they *believed* they could.

"Oh, and Jay, my husband, has been grumbling about lack of space in the garage. Perhaps a small shed?"

"That would be easy, yes," Cassie said with a smile.

"Wonderful!" Melody said with a clap of her hands. "I'll discuss the details with my husband when he gets back from town and we'll call you." She whispered conspiratorially, "But don't worry, it's not like I need his permission. I just want to let him know before I say yes. So, consider me in!"

Wow.

This is why I loved Mrs. Khan, always so willing to help her neighbors.

"Oh! And I'd be happy to let my friends know how it goes, once you're done," she added.

"That would be great, we really appreciate this," Cassie said. "We don't have business cards yet, so just call Jane and we'll be there to work out the details."

"Done!" Melody chirped. "I'm sure you'll do a great job!"

And that was it... we had our first contract.

I hoped the rest of the neighborhood was as considerate.

JANE

TERRY COOPER WELCOMED US INTO HIS HOME AND THE girls gave their spiel. I watched Terry, who never took his eyes off Petra, even when Cassie was speaking. When they finished, he sat back.

"Ah... well..." he hedged. He was probably trying to think of a kind way to let us down. He'd already had some minor updates done to his place and I hadn't really expected him to 'buy in' to the business. "I've been considering adding a guest room," he said after a moment.

Oh... that surprised me.

He shrugged. "I just haven't been sure if I wanted to use up space in the basement or add something on to the back of the house. Any thoughts?"

Petra and Cassie looked at each other, conferring in hushed tones for a moment before Petra spoke. I'd noticed she'd been a bit more alive and animated during her part of the speech this time and suspected I knew why. Even now her eyes seemed to light up a bit when she looked at Terry.

"It depends on a lot of factors," she said. "Adding a room to the basement would cost less, but you'd be losing space down there. An addition to the back would require a lot more work and would cost more but would be adding to the footprint of the house and would increase your resale value considerably."

He nodded. "Why don't you run some numbers and give me an estimate for both options so I can figure out which I'd like." Again, his eyes never left Petra's.

She blushed. "Yes, we can do that."

Oh, the two of them had it bad.

When we left, I let the girls go on ahead and stayed back to chat with Terry.

"So... Petra, huh?"

He blushed. "Is it that obvious?"

"It's Goodyear blimp obvious, yeah." I lowered my voice a bit more. "She's pregnant, you know?" It seemed obvious to me, but perhaps he hadn't noticed. "You ready for another kid?"

He smiled, rolling his eyes. "Yeah, I'd noticed." He shrugged. "And I wouldn't mind having another kid around."

I shook my head. I'd just assumed that most men — especially a single dad of two kids — wouldn't want a baby in their life, especially not another man's child. But then, Terry always had been a bit more compassionate than most men. I hoped he and Petra would get together, they both deserved to be happy.

"You're a special kind of guy, Terry," I said with a grin.

"But if you're going to date her, be careful. Her previous guy was a brute who didn't treat her well at all. She's probably still got some hidden scars from that. You still interested?"

He nodded. "I'd like to talk to her more, at least."

I smiled. A good start. "I think she might like that." I reached out and patted his shoulder. "I'll see what I can set up."

"Thanks, Jane," he said, beaming.

I shook my head as I left. So far today was going really well.

But... our next two houses weren't so cheery.

The Herrera's at least let us in and heard the spiel, but they were standoffish the entire time and didn't want or need anything redone. Though... there was a bit of an odd connection made while we were there. Elena Herrera was pregnant, late in her third trimester, and she gave off a sort of sympathy toward Petra. Still, their run-ins with the pack before I'd taken control hadn't been pleasant and they politely refused and asked us to leave. Still, that hadn't been as bad as it could have been... nor as bad as the Pearson's were.

James Pearson answered the door. He still had some healing wounds from his fight with Tank. As soon as he saw Petra and Cassie, he went off.

"What are *they* doing here?" He looked around quickly to see if there were others. "They're part of that gang, aren't they? Where's the others? Why did you bring them here?"

I quickly cut in while he was taking a breath to continue his tirade. "Mr. Pearson, I have been working to reform these folks. Those that assaulted you have left and are not returning. The rest are good people and these two were hoping to talk to you about an opportunity—"

"I'm not interested in anything they have to offer," he barked at me. "And frankly, I can't believe you'd take those thugs in. I want nothing to do with them." He seemed like he was about to slam his door in my face, but he quickly added, "Are they going to be with you for long?"

"Yes, they have nowhere else to go. We're trying to figure out the best place for them to—"

"Fucking hell," he cursed with a roll of his eyes. He gave a harsh laugh. "If they're staying, I'm not sure I want to remain in this neighborhood anymore. I came here because it was supposed to be safe and quiet, but clearly, it's becoming a haven for bad sorts. I'll be having a talk with the Khans about this, you can be sure. Now leave me alone!"

He slammed the door in our faces.

Wow.

I mean, after what had happened to him, I didn't blame him for being upset, but...

I sighed then turned to the two women. Petra looked a little shell-shocked, Cassie just shook her head.

"I don't blame him," Cassie said. "That's the response I expected *everyone* to give."

I stared across the rounded end of the street at the Rosses' place. Would they let Petra and Cassie in? The Rosses were fae and had been willing to let me in, but... they'd known me before I was a shifter.

Perhaps I'd see what Petra and Cassie wanted. "The

next house has a couple fae living in it. They were kind to me, but it's up to you whether you'd want to go there."

Petra didn't look convinced, perhaps still reeling from Mr. Pearson's vitriol.

Cassie shrugged. "Why not, who knows?"

I smiled. "That's the attitude."

We crossed through the park to knock on the Rosses' door.

Fern and Iris did indeed let us in and heard the girls out. Afterward, they turned to me.

"It's wonderful what you're doing with these folks," Iris said softly.

"It's clear you've been a good influence on the pack." Fern nodded.

"Has anyone else taken you up on your offer?" Iris asked.

"The Khans would like a kitchen reno and a new shed," Cassie quickly piped up. "And Mr. Cooper is considering a guest bedroom."

The two fae ladies looked at each other, as if they could communicate just through their gazes. Hell, perhaps they *could* for all I knew.

They turned back and Iris spoke. "We'll wait and see how that goes," she said to Cassie. Then to me, "And we'll see how the pack does under your leadership."

Fern continued. "If everything goes well and you've proven these shifters can be different, we may wish to have a second greenhouse built out back."

"That seems fair," I said quickly. Petra and Cassie nodded.

As we left, the two fae ladies kept me behind as Petra

and Cassie moved on. "It really is a wonderful thing you're doing with them," Iris said.

"I hope it lasts," Fern added.

I smiled. "Me too. Thank you so much."

"And those others?" Iris asked.

"I... ran them off."

Fern gave a vicious little smile. "Good girl."

As I left, I heard Fern whisper to Iris, "Did you see it? The change in her aura?"

"Yes, dire wolf."

"And...?"

"It might be nice to have one protecting us instead of attacking us for once."

"True." Fern's tone was hesitant. "We'll see."

"Oh, don't be a fuddy-duddy, I'm sure everything will be fine!"

I smiled as their voices faded. Fern might still need some convincing, but Iris was fully on board. Good to know.

We skipped the Coles, since I'd already talked to Debbie.

The Jacobses had a similar reaction to the Pearsons, with a little less vehemence. Yet the overall message was the same. They didn't like that the bikers were staying and they were considering leaving. It was a shame, but I guessed not everyone thought these folks could be reformed. Hell, if I hadn't become their alpha, *I* might not have wanted them around either. It was all a matter of perspective.

Next door to the Jacobses, only Erik Holt was at home, as usual. His mother was at work and his father was a truck driver, off on some long haul. I didn't think he'd want to hear us, and probably had no say in any renovations anyway, so, we skipped that house.

Which brought us to the Longs.

Bree let us in with open arms and gladly listened to the two women, but shrugged when they were done.

"I can't really afford any work right now, even at a reduced rate," she said, "and I don't need anything done that badly either. Sorry, ladies."

"Thanks for listening," I said and began to rise.

"Sit your ass down, I wasn't finished!" Bree admonished me and I sat down again with a grin.

"Yes?"

Bree addressed the two others. "I'm a teacher at Washington High School. If you have any information I could give out, I could see if any of the teachers or staff there need any work done."

"We don't have any information," Petra said. "But we can get you something, what would work best, a flyer or poster or pamphlet?"

"I don't like putting up posters, too impersonal, maybe just a small flyer I could keep in my purse? I'd prefer to talk to people and try to sell you folks, especially given this deal you're offering."

Petra spoke up quickly. "The deal was just for those in this community." She seemed to consider for a second. "But... we'd be willing to extend it to a couple others who are friends of friends."

"A couple? Just two?" Bree asked.

I looked over at Petra, curious at this as well. She gave a small smile. "Scarcity breeds immediacy. I remember that from one of my courses. If we're just a new construction crew with a reduced rate that *anyone* could have, then we're not *that* special, but if only the first two people get our reduced rate, it might prompt people to speak up sooner."

Bree laughed. "Ooooh, I like this one, Jane."

Petra blushed.

"Sharp as a tack, you are. Sharp as a tack! I'll let them know that."

Bree pulled me aside as we left. Petra and Cassie were chatting excitedly on their way back to my house. "It's a good thing you're doing with them," Bree said softly. "I don't know how you're doing it. I'd never be able to just take people in like that, especially so many! You're a saint Jane, a frick'n saint!"

I wanted to tell Bree about the pack and the wolves and how I was their alpha and had no choice in the matter, but I didn't think she was ready for that quite yet.

"Thanks, Bree, that means a lot. It's hard but rewarding. And they're giving back to me in ways I'd never expected."

"Like those three sexy hunks of yours are *giving back* to you," she said with a waggle of her eyebrows.

I laughed. "Yeah, like that."

"I can't even find one man," she said, frustrated. "Not that I'm really looking. But dang woman! Three? If you ever get tired of one of them, send him my way, okay?"

"I'll… consider that," I said. "And you'll find someone someday, if that's what you want. I thought you were happy on your own." It was something we'd said to each other a lot when we'd both been single mothers.

"I am," she said reluctantly. Then she lowered her voice. "But sometimes a woman wants some *real meat*, you hear me?"

"Loud and clear." I understood entirely.

We said our goodbyes and I returned home. But Bree's comment about *real meat* had gotten the fated part of my brain and body desiring just that. I'd been growing more and more distracted as the day wore on, thinking about Tyson and wanting to be near him. And right now, I wanted nothing more than a thick slab of his *meat*. Still, I waited until after dinner to drag him off to my room.

JANE

THIS WASN'T GOING TO BE A SEDATE OR QUIET MAKE-OUT session. So, before I disappeared for the night, I warned my kids, "I'm going to have some private time with Tyson. I suggest putting in some earphones for a while." I hoped that was subtle enough.

"Eww, Mom!" Izzy groaned.

Milo shrugged and went to his room.

Once in my room with the door closed, Tyson pushed me up against the wall, his lips smashing against mine. We opened instantly and his tongue licked long strokes into my mouth.

Our agitated impatience made things awkward, I wanted his naked body pressed to mine, but we had to get our clothes off first. Our hands moved of their own accord, knowing what to do. Mine slipped under his shirt and began pushing it up and off, managing to get access to his chest and abs. But the shirt wouldn't go any higher than his arms as long as his hands were on me, and he didn't seem to want to let me go.

His large hands pushed up my shirt, stopping at my chest, crushing my bra and breasts. I'd never been one for rough fucking and bruising caresses but being fated had changed all of that. My body knew it would heal and his savage massage was only making me that much hotter for him.

His fingers curled around the fabric of my bra and tore it away, shredding the cloth. The jarring movement and ripping noise made searing heat explode in my core as I was wracked with the shivers of a near orgasm. Yet, some practical part of my mind didn't want to replace my clothes after every fuck with Tyson. We were cash strapped as it was.

I had to distract him before he ripped my shirt off. One of my hands dove into his jeans and squeezed his cock. Both of us could be rough.

"No more ripping," I gasped around his lips and tongue.

Tyson gave a long groan into my mouth as I increased the pressure on his cock. Then he relented. He stepped back, giving me room, and we spent a frenzied moment stripping.

I managed to get my top off in the time it took Tyson to shed everything. Shifters knew how to get out of their clothes quickly. Then he helped me, pushing my pants and panties down over my hips, and crouched before me. I stepped out of the pooled clothes, except, as I lifted my legs, Tyson seized them, putting them on his shoulders. I spread my arms out on the wall behind me for support and Tyson drove his face into my apex.

I let out a long cry as his tongue lashed over my folds

and clit, even as his mouth latched onto me, sucking hard. My hips bucked into his face, my body and soul on fire, needing this contact. It must have been something about being fated that got me so turned on so quickly. I'd gone from zero to a hundred in a matter of seconds, and I felt like I'd die if I didn't release the blazing heat building in my core.

I fisted my hands in Tyson's long, thick hair, pressing him hard against my pussy. His tongue slid inside me, adding moisture where none was needed. I was so close! When he shifted his mouth slightly and his teeth raked over my clit, I came hard.

I hoped he could hold his breath, because I wasn't going to let him up for air until I was done flooding his mouth. Burning pleasure roared through me. I was sure I was screaming, but I was barely aware of anything other than my driving need and the relief — scant though it was — of this first release.

When I finally pulled back, Tyson did indeed gasp. With a groan, I slipped one leg off his shoulder for support and leaned heavily against the wall.

Tyson growled, the look in his smoldering dark blue eyes when he looked up at me was feral.

"Mine," he snarled.

"And you're mine!"

He removed my other leg from his shoulder and stood, his hands grasping my hips to lift me. For a moment, I thought he was going to fuck me right there against the wall, but instead he turned and with a step, threw me onto the bed.

I landed, bouncing, thrilled at his strength. My gaze

dropped to his cock, his knot already swollen and dark red.

"Knot me," I begged him. I wanted nothing more than to feel that huge plug filling me.

"No," he said with a wicked grin. "Once we're locked, that's it, I can't fuck you like I want to. I want to feel my dick sliding through your hot, wet pussy first."

I hadn't been one for talking dirty before, but now, I practically came at his words. Mostly because I wanted the same thing he did.

He grabbed my feet and pulled me toward the edge of the bed, then roughly rolled me over and positioned me with my knees on the edge of the bed and my ass in the air.

"Fuck, you smell so fucking delicious," he purred.

"So do you," I purred back. His smokey bacon and sea-side air was tinged with deep, heady sweetness.

Then his cock parted my folds, pushing in until his knot pressed against me. I squirmed against his hold and pushed back, wanting all of him, but he pulled out then slammed back in.

The impact shuddered through me, making my soul sing and my nerves spark with electric need. As much as I wanted his knot, I loved feeling his shaft moving inside me. Mewling and moaning, I couldn't even speak as he thrusted harder and faster.

"Gods, fucking, yes," he breathed.

Fuck yes, indeed.

I arched my back, pleasure rolling through me in great, building waves. Once we were locked, he wouldn't be able to thrust, just grind and rock, and this drawn-out tease was amazing.

"Knot me!" I cried out, on the cusp of a massive orgasm. I wanted to come with him once we were locked, and I sucked in sharp breaths, trying to stay in control.

"Don't hold back," he gasped. "I want to feel you come on my cock. I want you to gush all over me, and then I want to make you come again."

How can I say no to that? Not that I could speak. I grunted and just let myself go.

Tyson bent over me, sliding his hands from my hips, up my sides to find my breasts pressed into the sheets. He pulled me up until I was on all fours and roughly kneaded my tits while he continued thrusting into me. His cock surged deeper, his knot opening me, thrilling me, teasing me, and never fully entering me. Between that and his hands, I lost it.

Body-wracking pleasure consumed me, rushing over my skin and burning through my veins. I bucked back so hard his knot did slip inside me, but he pulled it back quickly before I could lock around him, and I let out along screaming whine as I came, gushing around his length.

He drew himself out entirely and my whine escalated at the loss of his hardness in my grasping pussy. But then he returned, not with his cock but with two fingers curling inside me to press just right. He savagely fingered me, spiking my pleasure and making me squirt wildly over his hand and the bed and... Holy fuck! I'd never been this wet before, never had such an extreme release. My orgasm wouldn't stop. I bucked and shook and screamed as he extended that transcendent moment.

And just when I started to come down, my own juices dripping down my thighs, he drove his cock all the way inside me, his knot popping into place. He grunted as I locked around him and squeezed him hard.

"Yes!" he hissed. His hands lifted my torso until I leaned back against him, still kneeling on the side of the bed. "Fucking, yes!"

He jerked himself up into me, unable to move much, but given how he swelled inside me, I didn't think it mattered. He was close.

With one final, hard convulsion, his cock pulsed with his release, unleashing his heat inside me. My orgasm redoubled, especially once his hands slid up to my breasts, crushing and tweaking my oh-so-sensitive nipples.

I couldn't speak, only let out long, very un-lady-like grunts of raw pleasure.

"You're so fucking hot. So fucking amazing," he breathed in my ear.

And with our fated desire peaked, I believed him implicitly.

As usual, once we were locked, we stayed that way for some time, surfing waves of bliss as they rose and fell. One of his hands slid down to rub my clit as I began to cool, which spiked my heat and swelled my pleasure once again. His releases came and went, the sensation of yet another flood inside me always surprising. But that was the effect of his knot. I was supposed to keep him locked until he'd drained himself.

And when we did finally come down together, his knot shrinking, we collapsed onto the bed in a heap. He laid behind me, clutching me close, desperately, and I snuggled back against him, our fated bond demanding as much skin-to-skin contact as we could get. With a groan, I swiveled my head back over my shoulder to find his lips and we drank deeply of each other until we were exhausted and he slowly drew out of me.

This wasn't the end, and we both knew it. This was just a lull as we regained ourselves.

Always intuitive and attentive, Bronn snuck in with a tray of water and small bites of food. "Thought you two might need this," he whispered, setting it down, then leaving.

That!

Little gestures of kindness and giving, selflessness...

I loved *that* about my guys.

I wasn't sure I knew much about love, but this conscientious pampering was something I could get behind. And that only reminded me of all my concerns and worries about my betas.

Tyson must have sensed my mood shift. He kissed the back of my shoulder, then disengaged from me slowly.

"Want to talk?" he asked softly.

Except I heard trepidation in his voice and got the feeling he didn't want to talk. Still, he'd opened that door and I decided to step through.

I rolled over to face him. He was *very* close, too close. I shifted back a bit. Perhaps looking at him had been a bad idea, because our fatedness pulled at me. Seeing all his solid muscle and those dark eyes, and the fall of his thick dark hair... it almost entranced me back into his arms. I'd end up back there eventually, no matter how this conversation went. It seemed so... inescapable. Not that I wanted to escape it, but...

I sighed. "It's hard talking to you," I said.

"The fate bond?" he guessed.

I nodded. "It just confuses everything."

"Or makes it clearer?" he offered. "Strips away the questions and concerns and lets us be together."

"Perhaps." I considered that for a moment, then shook my head. "No, it's not that simple. If we were truly in love and together and in tune, then I don't think we'd have come crashing together as desperately as we just did."

He nodded at that. "You're probably right."

"The bond makes me want you, desperately, and that clouds how we both really feel."

"And how *do* you really feel?" he asked,

"That's just it! I don't know, because the bond keeps getting in the way. You're sexy and dedicated and you've been good to me, but... do you love me? Do I love you? I don't know. Do you?"

Wow, had I really just asked him that? I held my breath, hoping his response didn't shatter my heart.

JANE

Tyson grunted but didn't respond right away. He rolled onto his back, looking up at the ceiling.

Colt hadn't answered right away, neither had Bronn. As much as the waiting freaked me out, I liked that they didn't answer immediately, that they took the time to think about it. A quick answer would have felt false.

Tyson sighed. "The trouble with me — with *all three of us* — is simple. We wouldn't know love if it slapped us in the face. We've lived hard lives and are only now allowing ourselves to feel something other than rage and fear and hatred."

He met my gaze again. "The bond makes things simple for me. I know you're my home. I will always come back to you, be there for you, help you, protect you, serve you and desire you. I don't know if that's love, but it's a far cry from what my life was before and... and I really like this new feeling. I like that I can talk to you about anything and not feel ashamed or less of a man or anything. You're soft and caring and warm and loving, and I just want to fall into you and let you surround me while I surround you, and we slowly become one."

Wow.

I'd read a lot of professions of love in my romance books, and that had been up there among the best. I didn't think he'd actually been professing love, but this was the truth of his soul, and it was pure and radiant and heartwarming.

I felt like I needed to respond in kind, with honesty and purity, but I wasn't sure if he was going to like it. Still, I pushed myself to do it.

"When I look at you, Tyson, I see... danger. Maybe it's because of the life you used to lead, but you're so strong and big and..." I shuddered as those words made my fated side want to ride him like a prized stallion. My core flooded just thinking of it. I pushed that down for a moment, so I could go on. "You sure as hell look like a bad boy, even if you aren't one anymore. The fated bond means I'm drawn to you like a moth to a flame. I keep waiting to get burned, but I haven't... yet. You've been nothing but caring." I sighed, here was the bad bit. "Still, I can't help feeling that one day you're going to defend me a little too hard and kill someone and... that's not the kind of protection I want. I want to be surrounded by softness, just like you do. But you're *not* a soft place for me to land." My voice got throaty and husky, the fated pull almost taking over. "You're very... hard." I *had* to reach out and stroke his thick, bulging bicep, heavy shoulder, massive chest.

He didn't seem upset at this. He nodded, as his body

responded to my touch. We were quickly losing our window of sanity.

"I know," he said softly. "I wish I could be soft some- times. But I have no clue how."

"Learn from me?" I offered, even as I inched closer to kiss where my hand had just caressed, lips pressing to his chest. Hard muscle flexed against my mouth, and I licked his nipple, drawing a low throaty moan from him.

"I will. We all will," he whispered. Then he kissed the top of my head. His body was trembling as he held himself back, trying not to overpower me. "Maybe it's time to see if our bond can be... soft," he said, voice strained.

Gods, he was going to try to hold himself back?

I didn't think that was possible. I was quickly getting lost in our bond and his body.

He remained on his back, submissive, as I moved closer and kissed down over his rock-hard, chiseled abs. He was practically vibrating beneath me, yet his hands, when they reached for me, weren't insistent or hard. He stroked my hair and rubbed slow circles on my back... even as I kissed lower.

My hand found his erection, sliding over it, exploring, feeling the silken smoothness over his rigid length. His knot was barely there, but pulsing, and I explored that odd, slowly swelling ball, drawing another throaty groan.

Oh, yeah. I loved that sound.

Unable to help myself, I darted out my tongue and licked his heavy tip, tasting our combined releases.

Another groan rumbled from him, the sound vibrating through my body, reigniting my own desire, and

I ran my hand up his length and wrapped my lips around his tip.

"Fuck," he breathed, a tremble rolling through him. Somehow, he managed to keep his hands gentle, one on my head combing through my hair and the other sliding to my cheek and tilting my face up.

Our eyes locked. His gaze was soft, filled with sweet love with a flicker of raging desire. I didn't know what he saw in my eyes, but for a moment, his restraint faltered. He bucked up, thrusting into my mouth. His cock slid through my lips, tapping the back of my throat before quickly retreating.

His eyes rolled up, head tilting back, and he released a shuddering breath, then a grunt of determination as he regained control.

I was *so* turned on by his ability to restrain himself, even as a part of me ached for him to lose control.

It was time to test my lover.

I mimicked the thrusting he'd just done, my mouth diving over him, my throat opening until I'd taken him deep, my lips pressed to his knot.

"Gods!" he gritted out.

I backed off quickly, enough to breathe, but I kept bobbing on his length. The burning need for him to lose control and unleash himself on me grew stronger than my desire for him to remain soft and restrained.

I'd been raised Catholic, taught to save myself for marriage, but I'd also been a curious and rebellious teen. My compromise had been to save my virginity by pleasing my boyfriends with my mouth. I'd gotten really good at blow jobs, and I used all my teasing knowledge now, unable to help myself.

My hand slid down over his knot, my thumb and middle fingers encircling the top of his sack, rubbing over that odd, yielding flesh gently as my pinky teased his ass. My head bobbed viciously, every third thrust pushing him as deep as I could go. My cheeks hollowed, sucking on his hard flesh, and yet still, his touch was tender.

His hand on the back of my head didn't push or guide, just swept through my hair as my head rose and fell. His other hand fisted the sheets at his side, white knuckled, showing his desire. His head tilted forward and he found my gaze again, the raging passion in his dark eyes evident. I didn't know how he was holding back.

I couldn't speak, but I hoped through our locked gazes he got the point. I wanted him to come, to lose control and take his pleasure.

"Jane! Oh fuck, yes! Jane!" his voice escalated, rising higher. Then finally, the hand on my head fisted my hair and held me in place as he gave three hard, quick thrusts into my mouth.

The last lunge drove him deep into my throat, my lips spread wide over his knot as his release pulsed into me. I knew he wanted to stay that deep, but he forced himself to retreat, allowing me to catch my breath as he filled my mouth.

"Holy damn mother of every fucking god!" he breathed as his cock pulsed the last of his release in my mouth. I hollowed my cheeks to suck it down before popping off him.

"I think you've proven you can be soft," I said, approving.

"It was the most exquisite torture." But he grinned. "I want more."

I raised a brow in question.

He sat up and pulled me to him. His lips found mine in a gentle, yet insistent kiss as I adjusted my legs, straddling his lap. I could tell he wanted to be hard, faces pressed breathlessly close, but he kept his contact light and affectionate. I wasn't so gentle, biting his lips, sucking them into my mouth, my tongue lashing into his.

I didn't know how he did it. Our fated bond raged through me. It didn't help that my pussy was positioned right over his knot. I rubbed myself over him furiously.

The orgasm came as a soft spike of pleasure and I gasped into his mouth. He drank my bliss down with a moan, his hands tenderly stroking through my hair, over my face and neck and shoulders. I ran my hands up into his thick, long hair, combing through it, pressing my body to his as my orgasm ebbed, leaving me wanting more.

When his lips left mine, we pressed our foreheads together.

He whispered, hot breath on my lips, "I know sex isn't love, but since we're being forced together, perhaps I can show you a little love through my sex." Then his lips nibbled at mine. I wanted hard kisses, open and devouring, but he kept his contact light. Then he moved off my lips to my cheek and chin.

I whined a little at the loss of his lips, my mouth

empty, biting my own lip. I rubbed my core on him again, but this time, it wasn't enough. I needed him inside me.

"Soon," he said, as if sensing my thoughts. His lips caressed me, covering my shoulders and the tops of my arms, then — oh blessed God, yes — over my breasts. He lingered there, but again, didn't try to devour my soft flesh with hard sucking or raking teeth. He kissed and licked softly, finding every sensitive inch.

It was utterly divine.

His hands slid down under my thighs and lifted me a little. I shifted up onto my knees and his cock sprang free from between us. His kisses gently pressed to the underside of my breasts and over my belly as I brushed my folds over his tip, unleashing a wave of steamy bliss.

"Yes," I moaned, my need turning feral. "Enough of this! Stick your fucking dick in my pussy!"

He chuckled, his hands sliding up to my ass. "You have control. We go at your speed."

God, he was amazing!

And my speed was super-sonic at the moment. I dropped myself on him, taking him fully inside me, knot and all.

A long, low, insistent moan rattled in my throat as my core locked around him.

"That works too," he hissed, his restraint clearly being tested. "Take me, my alpha."

He kissed the top of each breast, then up to my lips for a long, deep kiss.

With a groan, he slowly laid back. His hands caressed me all over, sliding from thighs to shoulders as I finally got to ride my stallion. And I rode him hard, a desperate gallop, grunting and moaning and rocking myself on him, grinding my clit on his pubic bone as I leaned forward, hands on his shoulders.

"Fuck me!" I demanded. I wanted to feel his gyrations, his rocking thrusts, or perhaps his hands claiming my breasts. He just smiled, his fingers sliding up my sides into my hair.

"You're beautiful when you're domineering," he whispered. His voice trembled with his effort to hold back.

I loved it and hated it at the same time. I was so close to an orgasm and I knew just the right touch from him would set me off. Grabbing one of his hands, I pulled it down, out of my hair, and dragged it to my breast, pressing his rough palm hard against me. He got the hint and kneaded me softly, before pinching my nipple with just the right amount of pressure.

I grunted, my body bucking and shuddering in time with my racing heart as I took my pleasure from him, a tremulous orgasm rippling through me. But it wasn't enough!

"Yes," he whispered, desperate. "More. Take more."

"Make me!" I didn't know what that meant, but I wanted him to be more active in this.

"Deal," he said with a chuckle and gave a single, hard rock of his hips, which spiked my orgasm to new heights. I sat back on him, my hands combing up through my hair, lost in lust.

His knees came up behind me, supporting me, and I leaned back on them as his hands moved over me.

My pleasure was his clay and he reshaped it with every assertive press of his hard palms and fingers. His hips rocked, shifting his cock, locked inside me as my sheath clamped down on him, trying to squeeze a release out of him. I didn't know how he was resisting, even while driving me mad.

I think I lost my mind, then.

I became a being of raw pleasure, going by feel: pressure and sensation. Every brush of his fingers around my breasts sent shivers through me. His hand carved a path of sizzling passion over my belly and through my curls. His thumb slid over my clit in slow, shudder-inducing circles.

I didn't know if I had come down and was finding a new orgasm, or whether this was some new height, building on the last, and I didn't care. I was in heaven and I couldn't stop coming on this amazing man.

Distantly, I heard his grunting, labored breathing as he neared his release.

"Yes," the word escaped my lips, a blessing and permission.

He took it, sitting up suddenly, and all his hard planes crushed against me. His arms, like iron bands, encircled me, trying to compress us into one being. His lips found mine in a desperate kiss as he shuddered and convulsed, his heat blooming inside me.

He was right, sex wasn't love.

But I'd never felt more loved than I did in that moment.

JANE

SEX WITH TYSON HAD STARTED EARLY, GONE LATE, AND been *very* distracting. That, combined with how exhausted and blissfully relaxed I'd been when I'd finally gotten to sleep, meant it was a knock on my door that woke me, *not* my alarm.

Because I'd forgotten to set my alarm.

"Jane? When do you need to be at work?" Colt whispered.

Work?

Work!

I shot up and looked at my alarm. It was seven twenty. I had to be at work at eight. And it was an hour's drive on a good day!

"Fuck!"

I couldn't afford to be late, today of all days. I flew out of bed, rushing to dress. I didn't have time for a shower, despite how much I needed one. I'd also not have time for breakfast, despite how famished I was.

Bursting out of my room I looked at my kids' rooms.

Were they up? Their bus usually came around now, if not sooner.

"Are they up?" I asked.

"And gone," Colt answered.

"Why didn't you wake me sooner?" I barked at him.

"Thought you'd do that yourself." He shrugged.

Yeah, I should have.

"Fuck!"

I had my boots and jacket half on as I flew out the door. I got two steps before realizing the new truck in the driveway was blocking my car. For an instant I actually thought about driving over the lawn, but the pack had done such a good job cleaning it up and seeding it and...

"Bronn!" I shouted inside. "Move your fucking truck!"

There was a distant curse, then crashing. A moment later, he came running out wearing nothing but jeans — bare chest and bare feet, in the middle of October — to get to his truck.

I got to my car and followed him out of the driveway, zipping out of our small back-woods community heading for Reston, Virginia. I knew I must have forgotten something and, luckily, it hit me before I'd gone too far: my computer.

"Fuck!" I did a far-too-fast skidding U-turn and assaulted the gas pedal to get back to my house. I stopped out front, ran inside, grabbed my computer — oh, and my purse, with my wallet and work ID, which I'd also forgotten — before running out again.

I broke all the speed laws that morning, thankful that no cops were waiting in the bushes to pounce on me. Still, with my over-sleeping and traffic on the 267, I was ten minutes late. I ran inside, ducking behind cubicles, hoping my boss hadn't noticed.

But he was waiting for me at the door to my office.

He took one look at me and sighed, shaking his head. "You're late... and *this* is how you show up?" he gestured to me. I could only guess what I looked like, a frazzled mess of a woman. "Sorry Jane, I'm guessing you had something going on in your life this past week, but things have been rough here too. I'd hoped you'd be here nice and early with at least some make-up on or something, but this...?" He shook his head. "You're fired, Jane."

"No, wait, please, I need this job!" I was desperate and already at my wits end.

He raised a brow, his gaze sliding over me in a very un-boss-like way. He stepped in, too close.

"Oh?" he breathed, his pungent coffee-breath hot on my face. "And what would you be willing to do to keep it?" His hand came to my hip, then slid up to brush the side of my breast as he licked his lips.

Wow. Creep much?

This was why I'd never progressed higher in this company, despite that I — and my team — practically kept my department afloat. Despite the fact that I was five times the worker my boss was, I'd been suspecting for some time that he'd been keeping me down. He knew he had a good thing going, since I did the majority of his work. And every now and then I'd catch him looking at me the wrong way. I'd never be able to prove sexual harassment, especially since this man's brother was the head of HR.

"You're a fucking creep," I shouted, and pushed him

away. Then, because I was fired and it didn't matter, I slapped him. But I'd forgotten my strength, now that I was a wolf. My hit knocked him into the wall. He collapsed to the floor, stunned.

I really wanted to kick him in the nuts but didn't want him to call the cops on me, so I just stalked out.

Then, I alternated between yelling and crying as I drove home.

I was screwed.

So.

Fucking.

Screwed.

I had a pack to take care of and no job. What a great start to the day... and the week... and the rest of my fucking messed-up life!

I couldn't go home, not right away. I stopped in Shannondale, getting out of my car to sit by the river. I couldn't process any of this. Everything from the past week came crashing down on me in an instant. Everything including the truly magical moment with Tyson last night.

In the span of a few hours, my life had gone from magical to unmanageable. I wept hot, bitter tears, blubbering by the waterside. I'd thought things had been looking up. Brick was defeated and gone. The pack was making plans and exploring opportunities. I'd been confused and uncertain, yes, but I realized now... I'd still been mostly happy amidst all of that.

But now...

With no job, how was I supposed to provide for my pack?

I could try to find a new job, but there were no guarantees I'd find anything in Reston or closer. And I couldn't move. I couldn't take the pack away from the place they'd been starting to call home and all the plans they were making. Let alone cause more upheaval in Izzy and Milo's lives by moving. And yes, there would be some income from the pack soon, but not enough. The extra funds Lucas and Winnie would bring in as apprentice mechanics had seemed significant when added to my salary, but on its own, it wouldn't support the pack. And it shouldn't be up to them to do it. They were barely more than kids!

I could try to work remotely. I'd done that during COVID, but I doubted many firms would want to hire me as such, so I'd end up freelance, having to scrape and scrounge for clients. It just wouldn't work.

Nothing would work.

I was lost.

Given over to the depths of sorrow, I finally dragged myself home a little after noon. I still hadn't eaten anything and I was starved, especially after last night's sexcapades. But what right did I have to eat our food if I couldn't help to buy more?

I closed the front door behind me, dropped my things, then flopped on the couch, burying my face in pillows.

"Jane? Why are you home? What's wrong? What happened?" It was Cassie.

"Jane?" and Petra.

Fuck!

I could have broken down in front of anyone else, but I was trying to show these two what it was to be a strong woman and escape your past. So, I dug down deep, finding some last shred of tenacity and stopped my tears. Sitting up slowly, I smiled, or tried to.

The two of them were kneeling next to the couch, close and worried.

"I'm okay," I said, betrayed by my sniffles. "I... I was fired from my job today." I plastered on that forced grin again. "But that's in the past now. I need to move on. Anything interesting happen here?"

I could see the concern in the two women's eyes, but also an understanding that I wanted to talk about something else.

"Mrs. Khan called and confirmed she'd like to go ahead with the kitchen and the shed," Petra said with a smile of her own. "We were just looking up some things and putting together our estimate for the job."

"That's wonderful!" I said and meant it.

I sat forward and wrapped an arm around each woman. I pulled them close and took strength from the success of the pack. It wouldn't bring in the money we needed, not enough at the reduced rate they were offering, but it was a start. Something occurred to me then. I was an accountant and there seemed to be a lot of "running the numbers" going on. I was really good at that. Pulling back to look at them, I offered, "I can help you, if you'd like!"

They smiled.

"Sure," Cassie said. She was probably just humoring me, but still it felt good to be needed.

My stomach rumbled. I gave a half-hearted laugh. "But first I need to eat something, I'm ravenous!"

So, the three of us prepared lunch and ate while working. They looked up materials and called suppliers, hunting for the best bargain on cabinets and flooring and other materials. I compared numbers and began a breakdown of costs. It felt good to be working with them on this.

Maybe... this could be my new thing?

It wouldn't be lucrative, not right away, but there were going to be several businesses running out of my house and they'd all need an accountant. A part of me knew it wouldn't be nearly enough to support us, but I ignored that part for now, liking the idea of helping my pack in that way.

I was *maybe* starting to feel a *teensy* bit better, when there came a knock on my door.

I rose and answered it, smiling.

My smile vanished in an instant.

There, looking every bit his vagrant-self, was my ex-husband.

COLT

"Tyson!" I heard Jane shout.

My first thought was: *Tyson's not here, he and Bronn went to scout camping locations in the woods.* But Jane needed someone. I was in the basement with Jake, teaching him some fighting techniques. He understood when I bounded for the stairs.

My alpha needed me.

My second thought was: *Why is Jane home so early? Shouldn't she be at work? But perhaps that's why she was yelling?*

Reaching the top of the stairs, I raced across the kitchen to the front door, which Jane was holding open. A shabby looking man in rumpled clothes — looking like he was coming down off a high — stood on the front step.

Jane seethed. I could feel her anger radiating off her like a blast furnace.

I had no clue what was going on. My best guess was Jane wanted someone to toss this man out.

"You want me to get rid of him?" I asked.

The man's eyes went wide, then wider still as he took me in. Jane turned and her eyes went wide in a different way as she noticed I wore only jeans. I'd been helping Jake in various types of combat, including while shifted, and hadn't bothered to put on all my clothes.

"He's huge!" the man said.

Jane turned back to him with a large grin. "Yes, he is. Oliver, meet my new boyfriend, Colt. Colt, this is Oliver, my *ex-husband*. He's not wanted here, please escort him back to his car."

So, this was the moron who'd left Jane. From everything I'd heard, he'd never treated her well and had run off with some younger woman ten years ago. I couldn't believe anyone would be so stupid as to leave this wonderful woman, but I guessed this guy was only interested in getting his dick wet and even though Jane was hot, he'd wanted someone younger, which was just idiotic.

"Happily," I said with a grin and stepped forward around Jane.

"Whoa there, big guy! I don't want a fight," Oliver said, stepping back, which made him slip off the front step and fall on his ass.

"Then leave!" Jane said vehemently behind me as I loomed over the man.

He didn't look like much. Perhaps once he'd been handsome, but now he was scrawny and balding and looked used-up. Jane definitely deserved so much better than this ass.

"I need some money, just a bit, then I'll go!" the man

said, crab walking backward onto the lawn as I took another step froward.

What a fucking low-life, disappearing for years, then coming back to ask for money?

"No Oliver. Not again. Not this time," Jane said, her tone firm. "You picked the wrong day, in so many fucking ways." I didn't know what that last bit meant and my mind was stuck on something else.

...Not again. Not this time...

Was this a common thing? Would Jane really give this oaf anything? I certainly wouldn't, but... this was Jane. She had a large heart and a kind soul. Well, this man wouldn't be taking advantage of that any longer.

"Go," I barked at him, letting just a hint of a roar rumble through my voice.

"Ahhh!" Oliver shouted and threw his hands up over his face, like I was about to attack him. He wasn't worth it.

"Go!" I roared again, and this time he rose and bolted for his car.

Good.

I turned back to Jane. "That's your ex?"

"Not now, Colt." She sighed and with it, seemed to deflate, small and weary, features clouded.

My heart shattered to see her look so defeated.

I went to her, lifting her in a tight hug. I kept her pinned to me with one arm, kissing the top of her head, while I walked inside and closed the door with my other hand. Then I put both arms around her and gave her another squeeze before letting her down.

"Thanks," she said with a heavy sigh. "I needed that."

"You're home early." I raised a single brow in question.

"Don't ask," she said, and the gloom returned. "I'll tell everyone later. I just want some peace and—"

"Jane? Alpha? He didn't leave," Cassie said. She was looking out the kitchen window.

"What now?" Jane asked. We both joined Cassie at the window.

Oliver was in his car, but he wasn't leaving. He was on the phone.

"Fuck," Jane said, sounding utterly defeated. "Fuck my fucking fucked-up, shitty life!"

I turned to her slowly, shocked. I'd never heard Jane swear quite like that before. I wanted to ask if she was okay, but it was clear she wasn't. Then I wanted to ask what she needed. But, if I was a good beta, I'd just know. I should be able to help her without asking.

"I'll get rid of him," I said, heading for the front door.

"Colt! No!" Jane called after me. "He's not on my property. I don't want to escalate things. Just... leave him be."

I nodded, but now I had no clue what to do.

So, the group of us watched him. He didn't leave. And Jane's comment about not escalating things seemed to possess some magical foresight... because twenty minutes later, we heard sirens approaching.

"I'll kill him," Jane muttered. "He didn't..."

But it appeared he had. Three cop cars stopped outside Jane's house, around Oliver's car and he got out and began speaking with them.

"No." Jane hissed. "No way is he going to poison them with lies." She headed for the door. I knew it was probably a dumb idea, but I followed. I had to, I was her beta, I had to protect her.

And yeah, just as I suspected, as soon as the cops saw me... several guns came out.

"Stop there!" one of them called.

Jane froze, then looked back over her shoulder. There was a moment of blinking confusion, then she saw what the cops saw: a large, half-dressed man. Put a white undershirt on me and I'd be the picture of urban abuse.

I raised my hands slowly.

Jane sighed and rolled her eyes, then continued forward.

"That's right, Miss, you're safe now," a female officer said as Jane approached them.

"What did this lying asshole tell you?" Jane said, deadpan, pointing at Oliver.

That caught the policewoman off guard. "Ah... sorry?"

"See, it's just like I said!" Oliver interrupted with victory in his voice. "My ex-wife's clearly being used by that brute." He looked around. "Her yard is usually much nicer than this, and there are motorcycles over there. She's a hostage in her own house!"

I sighed. I had no clue what the little man thought this would get him. Perhaps it was nothing more than petty vengeance? What a fucking bastard.

"That's not the case at all," Jane said, still calm, but with an edge of anger in her tone. "There's no threat here. I'm in no danger. I promise you, Colt takes *far* better care of me than Oliver ever did. Yes, he's big, but he's a teddy-bear and wouldn't hurt a fly."

I smiled and waved a hand in — what I hoped was — a friendly manner.

"I'm sorry officers," Jane continued, "but you've been the butt of a *prank* pulled by my vindictive ex-husband here."

And slowly the officers lowered their weapons, just a little, as their gazes swung to Oliver.

"Is this true?" the female officer asked Oliver. She seemed to take a long look at him. "If so, then lying to the police is a misdemeanor."

Oliver was suddenly sweating. His plan had backfired, though I didn't really know what he'd expected to happen.

"No, I was genuinely concerned for her!" he shouted. I doubted that was true, but he blabbered on. "Take a look at this place, something happened here, and who do all those motorcycles belong to?" He pointed to the line of bikes at the edge of the driveway.

"Miss? Can you explain that?" an officer asked Jane.

Jane drew in a long breath, perhaps giving herself time to come up with a good answer. She'd been telling the neighbors she was reforming us bikers, but I wasn't sure how well that would go over with the cops.

"My boyfriend's extended family happens to be visiting at the moment," she said. "I don't think it's a crime for them to ride motorcycles. It's a hobby of theirs." She laughed. "I don't like the noise they make, but it's not like they're riding them up and down the street. In fact... Petra! Cassie! Can you come out?" I glanced back over my shoulder, keeping still, not giving the police any reason to fear me. The two women came out. "Cassie is Colt's... sister, and Petra is his cousin."

I supposed Cassie could be related to me, we were both blond.

"My house *is* a bit of a mess right now," Jane continued. "But you try sleeping a dozen guests for a few nights and see how yours looks." She laughed again. "This is all a misunderstanding."

The female officer approached Jane and whispered. I wouldn't have heard if it hadn't been for my enhanced hearing. "You can be honest with me, are you in trouble?"

Jane shook her head, smiling. "No, only from that jerk." She tilted her head to Oliver.

The officer sighed, nodded, then called to the others, "Nothing here guys."

Those who had guns out, put them away. One of the male officers came over to Oliver. "If this was a prank, it wasn't funny, sir. Luckily, we can't prove that. Please ensure our services are actually required before you call nine-one-one next time, got it?"

Oliver nodded.

The police got in their cars and left.

Oliver glared at Jane and me.

"You're lucky I didn't try harder to turn that on you," Jane spat the words. "You're a loser and a freak. If you ever.... *ever* come around again, it better be because you have your act together and you want to get to know your kids, because there is no other reason you should ever show your face here again, got it, Oliver!"

"Bitch," he snarled.

"That's alpha bitch to you," she returned in a far better snarl.

He flinched back, confusion and a hint of fear in his eyes. "You're...crazy!"

He stumbled to his car. I was surprised the hunk of rust even started, but it did, and he was gone a moment later.

I let out the breath I'd been holding.

"Fuck me," Jane breathed, vehemence still lingering in her voice. "I did *not* need that today!"

The anger and frustration in her voice startled me. What surprised me even more was the shimmer that cascaded over her. She was close to shifting. I'd never seen her this out of control.

"Let's go inside," I said. I didn't really feel the cold and I knew she wouldn't either, but it was a cool October day and we were all just standing in the yard. "You can tell me what's gotten you all riled up... other than your bastard ex, that is."

"Colt..." I looked back at Petra, who was shaking her head.

Should I not have asked?

"Today is just the *fucking best day ever!*" Jane growled, storming into the house. "First, I get fired, then my ex shows up and calls the fucking cops! What else could go wrong?"

Ah.

Wait...

"Fired?" I knew I shouldn't have asked the instant the word was out of my mouth.

"Yes! Fired!" Jane spun on me from the doorway,

unleashing all her fury. "I was ten fucking minutes late and my bastard boss fucking fired me... then, as if that wasn't enough, he insinuated I could get my job back by doing some — probably disgusting — sexual favor for him! And now I can't provide for the pack and I have no clue what I'm supposed to fucking do!"

"Jane, I'm sorry, I..." I stepped in to hold her, thinking that would help, but she batted my arms away with stunning strength.

"I don't need sympathy. I need a solution. So, unless you have one, I think I'd like to be alone!" She spun and charged inside. I watched her go, heading for her bedroom. She slammed her door so hard I flinched.

"I tried to warn you," Petra said.

She had.

I nodded and we all went inside.

"She hadn't told us about the part where her boss was a creep," Cassie said. "That's just... sick." She sighed. "Any ideas what we can do for her?"

"Give her time," I said. "This is all fresh and new and it hurts a lot, I'm guessing. But love and kindness and time will help. She's an accountant, which sounds boring as fuck to me, but I'm pretty sure they're always in demand. She'll find something else."

Cassie nodded.

We stood around in silence for a moment before going back to what we'd been doing. I wanted nothing more than to be with Jane, comforting her, but I'd give her some space. I just hoped that was actually the right thing to do.

JANE

I WAITED, HOPING COLT WOULD IGNORE MY PLEA TO BE alone. I couldn't believe I'd blown him off like that. I'd just been so angry!

I hugged a pillow, curled up on my bed, crying. I wanted someone to come and hold me and tell me everything would be all right.

But no one came.

I sulked in my room all afternoon, my mood only getting darker. I berated myself for my silly idea about being the accountant for the pack. It would probably be a few years before their businesses really took off and we'd run out of money long before then. My savings were significant, but something told me I'd burn through them — and my retirement fund and the kids' college funds — quickly enough with so many people around.

My mind loved crunching numbers. Even while wallowing in self-pity, I could do it with ease. With sixteen people in the house, even with the income from the two apprentice mechanics, we'd still be running a deficit of over ten thousand dollars a *month*! Hell, even *with* my job, I wouldn't have covered that!

The numbers confirmed it. We were doomed.

What sort of alpha couldn't take care of their pack?

I was a failure as an alpha, as a mother, as a woman...

And it was clear my betas didn't really love me. I was in pain, and where were they?

Where was Colt? I'd told him I wanted to be alone, but didn't he know that meant I *didn't* want to be alone?

And what about Bronn? He was usually so attentive and sensed what I needed, but he was nowhere to be found?

And Tyson? We'd had something last night, but had it just been great sex and nothing more?

I felt so completely and utterly alone, even in a house filled with people.

Eventually I heard the door open and Milo and Izzy's voices. They were home from school. God, I couldn't face them. I'd have to tell them why I was home early and I just... couldn't right now.

I hoped they'd think I was still at work and do their own thing. But then the door to my room opened. I curled up tighter into a ball, ashamed to face them.

Yet, the voice that spoke wasn't either of my kids.

"There's something you should know," Rita said, voice hushed.

Fuck! What now!

Anger spiked through my morose melancholy.

"What!" I hissed, sitting up and whipping around to face the woman.

I was sure I looked a complete mess, but Rita didn't bat an eyelash. She was intent on her report. "I saw something today, at the kids' school."

I waited for her to go on. She and Brutus were keeping a discreet eye on my kids while at school, watching the school grounds from a distance. My kids were part of the pack now and would always be taken care of.

She sighed. "It may be nothing, but I was making my rounds of the campus when I saw a bike go by in the distance. I can't be sure, but it looked like Ginny." She shrugged. "Those four may not have gone too far."

"Fuck my life!" I bellowed, throwing up my arms, then slamming them back down on the bed. "Of course they're still around. Why would they leave, when they could make things worse for me?"

"Ah... yeah," Rita said. "Well, we'll keep a closer eye on the kids just in case. Just... wanted to let you know."

I waved her out. She left and I slumped back down on the bed again.

Could things get any worse than this?

I was certain they could.

And, not long later... they did.

I'd been trying to rest. If I was going to spend all afternoon in bed, I might as well have a nap. But just as I was beginning to doze off, the hard pounding of rock music blasted through the house. Soon after, the loud revving of an engine could be heard over the horrible racket. I knew exactly who and what this was: Erik Holt, the kid across the street, was working on his hot-rod car.

Well fuck him. He'd pissed off the wrong woman on the wrong day and I'd had enough!

I leaped out of bed and tore out of my house. I may have ripped my bedroom door off its hinges, but I didn't stick around to check. I marched over my lawn, across the street, and up his driveway. The kid was in the garage. A large stereo system at the back was pumping out the music and the garage acted like an amplifier, focusing the blaring noise directly at my house. Erik was working on something at the front of the car, the hood up. Once within sight of the grease-stained youth, I laid into him.

"Turn off your fucking music, you ignorant delinquent! And stop revving this fucking car or I swear I will tear it apart piece by piece until there is nothing left!"

Eric was big, over six feet and built strong. He had nothing on my guys but was still imposing in most circumstances. He looked shocked for just a moment before indignant arrogance took over.

"You can't tell me what to do in my own house!"

"*You* don't own this house!" I shouted back.

"My parents do, *not you*, so go fuck yourself, lady." Maybe he'd had a bad day too, I didn't know, but I certainly wasn't going to take that language from him!

"I swear I'll tear you a new one, *boy*..." Rage rippled through me. There was a pinch of pain, which I hardly noticed, then I was looking down at him, not up. A deep roaring rumble slurred my words as I continued, "...if you don't give me some peace and quiet!"

Erik yelped, stumbling back, crashing into a tool rack and knocking tools everywhere as he fell. His eyes went wide with terror and a dark spot grew on his jeans as he wet himself.

I didn't care. He hadn't turned off his music yet, and it was giving me a headache. I turned to his stereo system, on a table at the back of the garage and lashed out at it. My massive clawed hand shredded it. The music stopped instantly.

Wait... claws?

Without the blaring noise, I heard the low rumble of the car, but also... my own rolling growl.

"Jane! Stop! You'll kill him!" Tyson's voice reached through my hazy thoughts as he placed himself in front of me, arms out as if to stop me.

Why was Tyson so small? He didn't even come up to my chest.

Bronn was here too, picking up Erik, "Get inside kid, you didn't see this. Go!" Even Bronn looked terrified.

I looked down at my clawed hand, covered in fur and bone... then the rest of me... which was the same... also my shredded clothes, which lay in tatters around me. And only then did I realize...

I'd shifted.

Not into my wolf, but a dire wolf hybrid. And I wasn't just a man-shaped wolf, I was a *scary-as-fuck* man-shaped wolf. Bone armor covered me, and from it, bony spikes protruded off my elbows, shoulders, knees and probably all sorts of other places.

I was a fucking monster!

Then, as my own confused terror mounted, the form fled. There was hardly any pain as I reverted to myself, shaking like a leaf and buck naked.

Tyson bundled me in his arms, holding me close. "I hope none of the neighbors saw that," he breathed.

Oh God!

But... no, I was at the back of the Holt's garage and no house — other than mine — would have a good angle to see in here.

"What happened?" Tyson asked. "Are you okay? I've got you now." And he did. He held me tight, finally giving me the comfort I'd desperately needed all afternoon. Yet, he was shaking as much as I was, sounding confused and horrified. And his fear — fear of me — broke me entirely.

I wept, heavy sobs, burying my face in his chest.

"Fuck me," Bronn whispered as he returned. I couldn't see him, but I heard him moving around, probably gathering up my shredded clothes. "Here, put this on for now."

I pulled my face away from Tyson's chest and glanced, bleary-eyed, at Bronn. He'd taken off his shirt, offering it to me. I just stared at it, in too much of a state to do anything with it.

Bronn and Tyson carefully pulled the shirt on over me. It covered me to the tops of my thighs, which was good enough, if far from decent.

Tyson picked me up and carried me, hurrying back across the street to my house and my room.

Bronn set my door back in its frame, muttering something about fixing it later. Then he left me with Tyson and went back out to the front room.

Though he tried to be quiet, my keen hearing caught Bronn telling the others, "She wolfed-out on that kid across the street, her hybrid form, and since she's a dire wolf it was fucking huge and scary as hell."

That was *not* what I wanted to hear. I wept harder as Tyson cradled me, trying to tell me everything would be okay.

But how could anything be okay ever again?

BRONN

I'D NEVER SEEN JANE LIKE THIS.

She didn't come out of her room for dinner, so I took her some food. Tyson was still with her, and when I entered, he turned to me with a look of pure bewilderment. Jane was curled up on the bed, softly whimpering. He stroked her back, making soothing noises, but seemed at a loss for how to help her. She was still wearing my shirt. It looked like she hadn't progressed passed flopping into bed.

I don't know what to do! Tyson mouthed the words at me. Jane would be able to hear anything we said.

Shifters weren't generally known for their comforting and soft nature, and Tyson specifically had been raised to be brutal and hard.

I set the tray of food down on her bedstand and shrugged, I didn't know either. Especially since I now had a better idea of what Jane's day had been like.

Tyson and I had been returning from scouting the forest when we'd seen Jane march across the street. We'd followed her and seen her go full-on monster. Her dire wolf hybrid was truly a nasty-looking thing.

I had no clue what that kid must have thought. I'd taken him inside, where he'd fainted. I prayed he wouldn't remember what had happened after he woke up.

After we'd returned, Colt had filled me in on the rest of her day. Cassie had gone across the street to try to talk to the boy, but apparently, he'd still been in shock. It would be a waiting game to see what he did with what he knew.

None of this was good.

I left and returned a moment later with Colt, who replaced Tyson, looking after our distraught alpha, then I took Tyson outside to tell him the full story.

"Fuck me," he hissed, voice low. "It sounds like one truly awful day was all it took to get Jane's mid-form to come out." He shook his head. "What are we going to do about that kid?"

He answered himself. "If Harley were alive, we'd kill the poor sap to keep our secret safe. But there's no way we can do that." Tyson was vocalizing his thoughts. He did that sometimes, to work through things. "Perhaps... we could try to convince him he was on drugs? Bad food messing with his head? But... his radio is still all torn up and claw-marked. That's not going away. Unless we take it, but we're not the kind of pack that steals things anymore! Fuck! Things are a lot harder when you have to play by the rules."

There was something else Tyson needed to know. "Rita thinks she saw Ginny in town today."

"Fucking hell!" Tyson threw up his arms. "Can't we catch a break?" He sighed. "Anything else?"

"That's all I know."

He shook his head again.

"I have an idea about the kid," I said. It had been brewing in my mind as Tyson had been speaking.

"I'm all ears."

"We can't kill him, but we can threaten him. It's not a great compromise, but we can tell him that monsters *are* real and he needs to keep his mouth shut or the monsters are going to return for him." I didn't like it, but it seemed the only option to me.

Tyson nodded. "Do it. I don't like it, but it's better than killing the poor bastard."

I nodded and jogged across the street. The garage was still open and we hadn't locked the door from the garage into the house. I let myself in and found the kid — though he was as big as any man — still cowering in the kitchen.

"Don't hurt me!" he begged, arms up before him.

Perhaps I could threaten him in a mostly friendly way?

I knelt. "I'm not going to hurt you, kid." I waited for a moment until he lowered his arms enough to peer out at me. "And, if you keep your mouth shut about what you saw, no one will hurt you. You just found out the hard way that there are strange things in this world, but that's a secret you have to keep. Tell *anyone*, and there won't be any place you can hide. You saw that thing. It was part wolf, and now it has your scent. It can track you down and find you wherever you may go. You understand me?"

The kid nodded quickly, desperately.

"Are you going to tell anyone?"

He shook his head vigorously.

I smiled. "Then we don't have a problem. We just want to be good neighbors, got it?"

Another quick nod.

"Good." I stood and offered a hand to help him up. Reluctantly, he took it. I dusted him off, then smiled. "And when you work on your car out there, you're going to keep the noise level down, right?"

Another nod.

"Great." Then, hoping to maybe help the kid recover, I asked, "You a mechanic?"

Another nod.

"We've got a few mechanics in our crew too, if you need anything, let us know, maybe we can help. Good neighbors, remember?"

Another nod.

"Good."

The kid still wasn't speaking, but he looked a little less pale and sick. I took that as a good sign and left. That had gone better than I'd hoped.

As I crossed the street, I saw Jane's neighbor, Mrs. Khan, hurrying over to Jane's house.

I picked up my pace to return to Tyson, who was still waiting outside, as Mrs. Khan got there.

"Oh! Hello there!" she said to us. "Ah... sorry to bother, but is Jane available?"

"Had a rough day. Went to bed early," Tyson said, quickly.

Mrs. Khan nodded. "Oh, I see, well, can you tell her I

asked what she's thinking of making for the Halloween party? We don't want to end up with a situation like last year when we both made jack-o-lantern pumpkin cookies, now do we?"

"Of course not," Tyson said easily.

"Good, yes... well, just ask her to let me know. Thank you!" Then the older woman took a long look at both of us, sighed, and headed home.

Halloween party? I mouthed to Tyson as we went back inside.

He shrugged, shaking his head, looking more than a little tired. "No clue, but..." He blew out a breath. "It may be a chance for the pack to prove we're not monsters."

I winced at that word, and Tyson's lips tightened. Jane might have heard that. He hadn't said it in relation to her, but I had a suspicion that word had slipped out because of what we'd seen earlier.

"Fuck," he hissed and flopped onto a couch.

I sat on the other end, shaking my head. I understood how he was feeling. We were all walking on eggshells, concerned about Jane. But when he spoke next, he surprised me, apparently our thoughts had diverged.

"I mean... we're fucking cursed! How can we ever integrate with these people? We're not meant to live normal lives... not after everything we've done. It just seems wrong."

Ah. So that's why he'd been so quiet and pensive all day.

And yeah, we'd done a lot of horrible things in the past, but it had been at the command of Harley and his brutal betas. Still, the internal scars of that life lingered.

It hadn't been as bad for me as it had been for Tyson. He'd had to prove himself worthy of being a brutal alpha nearly every day. I'd been the lowest of the low in the pack, which meant I'd done things others didn't want to, often disgusting drudge work, but rarely had I done anything truly objectionable to others.

I sighed. "Jane wants us to be different, so we'll be different. It's that simple," I said. "She's willing to overlook our past, so maybe everyone else will too?" I didn't think we'd be that lucky. Not everyone was as kindhearted and compassionate as Jane. Still, it was a hopeful thought.

"The other day, she asked me if I'd ever killed anyone and how many. I... I didn't know what to say. I've got the blood of dozens of people on my hands, Bronn. What do I do with that?"

"I don't know," I told him. "But I *do* know you didn't want to kill any of them. You were just doing what you had to." I knew that didn't help much. "We were tools, weapons Harley used against his foes."

"And against a lot of innocent people," Tyson said softly. "Like that kid across the street. Anyone who knew what we were and wasn't turned..."

"It was awful, yeah, but it was still Harley," I said. "I know we can't ever forgive ourselves for what we've done, but... we've got to try to at least come to terms with it, so we can move on and be the better people Jane believes we can be."

He nodded. "I know, but that doesn't make it easy." He sighed heavily. "Then there's this whole... being a father thing." He wasn't looking at me. I followed his gaze to the dining table where Milo sat, doing his homework. Izzy chatted with Winnie and Jake in the kitchen.

"How would you have wanted to be treated, as a kid?" I asked.

"Not having to lie and cheat and steal and kill would've been nice."

Agreed. "Anything else?"

He shook his head. "Milo found me in the forest on Saturday. I... I helped him work out a little. He wants to be strong. I don't even know if that was a good choice or not."

I laughed lightly. "You know we're overlooking a really easy resource on all of this." I raised my voice. "Hey, Milo and Izzy, can we talk to you two for a moment."

I hoped this worked.

Milo quickly ditched his homework and ran over to jump into a plush chair in the living area. Izzy looked less interested but said a few more words to the others then came over, standing a bit off, closer to the dining table.

"Yeah?" she asked.

Okay, here goes. "Your mother and... ah... and us, the three of us, Tyson, Colt, and I... We're all getting close. And your mom would like us to be more... ah... like fathers to you and Milo. And I know that might be awkward. Trust me, if it feels weird for you, it's weird for us too. But I'm curious to know what you'd want... in a father?" I looked from Milo to Izzy, making sure they knew the question had been for both of them.

"Yeah, awkward," Izzy said with a huff of breath.

"Someone who protects us, but also teaches us to protect ourselves," Milo said quickly.

I looked at Izzy. "Is that what you want too?"

She shrugged. "Yeah, I guess. I mean, it would be nice to be able to take care of myself." From the way she said it, I had a feeling she'd had some situations in the past where she might have wanted to be able to defend herself.

"Okay," I said nodding. "What else?"

"Someone who spoils us and gives us everything we want?" Milo tried with a mischievous smile.

"Yeah... no. *That's* not happening," I said with a laugh.

He shrugged. "I had to try."

Izzy gave another huff. "Someone who leaves us alone but is there when we need them."

"And what are some situations when you might need us?" Tyson asked.

"I don't know!" she said waving her arms.

But Milo replied, quietly, "When we... when we're hurt. When our homework is too hard. Congratulating us when we do things right, and not being too harsh when we do things wrong. When we want to play catch or just... be with you. When parents are needed for school things. That sort of stuff."

"Yeah," Izzy said, subdued. "Sounds about right."

I smiled at Milo. "Thanks Milo, that was really insightful." He beamed. "Though, I don't know if any of us will be much help with homework. Our education wasn't the best. Sorry."

"But," Tyson added quickly, "if you kids want to know how to defend yourselves, we can definitely do that. We're already doing that with our pups."

"And don't call us pups," Izzy said. "For one, it might

freak out the neighbors, and two, it makes us sound cutesy, which we're not. We're kids, teens, almost adults."

"True, thank you," Tyson said with a nod.

"You can call me pup, if you want," Milo said with a shrug.

Here was the challenging part. "We're still learning this, and... we might need a bit of help. We may not always know when you need us, even if it seems obvious to you. Are you two okay being honest and open with us?" I asked.

Milo shrugged. "Sure."

Izzy was more circumspect. "Open and honest? It's not like all of you have been open and honest with us."

I nodded. "You're right. But we'd like to change that. If there is anything you want to know, ask us. Just understand, we may have secrets, just like you do, things it's not easy for us to talk about."

"Do you love my mom?" Izzy asked directly.

Well... fuck.

"I can't speak for Bronn, but I can tell you that my situation is unique." Tyson drew in a long breath. "Your mother and I are fated for each other. That means we're drawn together, sometimes even if we don't want to be. It's confusing and complicated and doesn't help when we're figuring out how we feel. But I can say this... your mother is kind and loving and caring and generous. I want to love her and I... I think I'm getting there. I don't know if she loves me either, but since we're fated, we both know we can't be with anyone else, so we're working on it, every day."

Izzy nodded. "Well, at least that's honest." She looked at me.

I sighed. Where to begin. "So, I'm a lion shifter, just in case you hadn't known, and for us there's something in the scent of another, which can draw us to them. I found that in your mother. Her scent calls to me. I want her to be my mate, and like Tyson said, there is a lot about her to love. She's kind and giving and smart and fierce. I *think* what I feel for her is love, but I can't really be sure, since I've never felt anything like this for anyone else. I want to protect her, and care for her, and make her happy and give her everything that I am. Is that love?"

"How should I know, I'm only sixteen!" Izzy said, apparently shocked I'd even asked. Then she shrugged. "It sounds good though." She stood there for a moment longer and the tension between us seemed to lessen a little. "I guess you guys can be my dads, here in private. But... when we're in public...? I don't know how that would work and... It's complicated and I'm confused and—"

"How does this sound," I offered, cutting her off. "While were here, and no one else is around, we're all your dads and you don't have to worry. In public, Tyson will be your dad, and we'll be friendly uncles who just like to take care of you like a father would."

She shrugged. "I guess that's okay."

"Works for me," Milo said.

There was a moment of awkward silence before Izzy said, "Can I go now?"

I chuckled, "Yeah, go, I think we're good. And thanks, Izzy. You too, Milo."

"Sure, whatever," Izzy said, but there was just the barest hint of a smile as she left, heading for her room.

"Thanks for taking care of my mom when... those other guys were around," Milo said as he rose. "I'm pretty sure Izzy feels the same way." Then he left.

"That... wasn't as hard as I thought it would be," Tyson said, sounding a little shocked.

"I'm sure there are going to be hard days," I said. "But yeah. Good communication goes a long way."

He nodded. "You've always been wise, Bronn, thanks."

I smiled at his praise.

Now we just needed to figure out how to help Jane feel better.

JANE

I HID IN MY ROOM FOR TWO DAYS STRAIGHT. THE GUYS CAME and went, watching over me in shifts, always someone there.

That... helped.

But I just couldn't face the world. I couldn't face anyone. I'd lost my job and gone psycho on my neighbor. Bronn said he'd talked to the kid and everything had been smoothed over, but I had trouble believing that. I'd seen the look in Erik's eyes — and in Bronn's eyes — when he'd seen me in my hybrid form. Bronn had been scared. I was something that scared a fucking lion shifter!

I couldn't really be proud of having achieved my hybrid form. That was definitely *not* how I'd wanted it to happen. As it was, I never wanted to become that monster again.

The space of hours, then days, didn't make anything that had happened on Monday any better, but it did lessen the pain and frustration and grief a little. Yes, I'd lost my job, but I could find a new one. Yes, my ex was an ass, but the cops had gone away and nothing had come of it. As for what I'd done to poor Erik, I had no idea if that would ever be okay...

Oddly, it was Tyson mentioning Mrs. Khan's message about the Halloween party that got me on the road to recovery.

I always looked forward to the event. Since there weren't many houses on our little street, but there were enough youngsters that might want to trick-or-treat, we'd come up with a novel solution.

For more than a decade, the community had come together on Halloween for a sort of block party. All the houses were open and people came and went, gathering goodies from each. But these weren't just store-bought little candies... oh no. There were cakes and pastries, pies and cookies by the dozens. Not to mention all manner of savory fare as well.

Each house had a spread of treats and shared them with everyone else. The Rosses made hard candy, which they claimed was good for you. Now that I knew they were fae, I actually believed that claim. Did they make them with magic? I'd have to ask.

If it was a weekend, which it would be this year, it was an extra-special event, which lasted all day. If the weather cooperated, things would even move outside and people would provide coffee or warm apple cider or coco. It was a grand party, and it was quickly approaching. Halloween was this coming Sunday and with me having been sulking in my room for two days — finally coming out for a shower Wednesday evening — that left only three days for me to prepare.

But there was something I needed to do first.

I couldn't risk another uncontrolled shift like what had happened with Erik Holt. So, I shooed the guys out of my room and asked them to get Kira. It was time I learned about what I was, time to know more about dire wolves.

I sat on my bed, pillows piled behind me. When Kira arrived, she entered quietly, then perched on the far end of my bed.

"What is it you need, alpha?"

"Tell me about dire wolves. How did this happen to me?" I figured I should say, "Izzy mentioned something about a mutation and trauma?" I was trembling, not sure I wanted to hear this, but forcing myself to do it. I didn't want to lose control like I had with Erik and the first step was to know exactly what I was.

Kira nodded, thoughtful. "First, everything I know is hearsay, legend. My mother passed lore down to me, but as far as she knew, there hadn't been a dire wolf in decades, if not centuries."

"Oh." So, I was *really* rare. Wow... okay.

"The legends tell of wolves, a rare few, over many hundreds of years, who, for whatever reason became dire wolves," Kira said. "It's not something anyone can control or force... but I'm getting ahead of myself. I'll come back to that."

She settled herself, closing her eyes for a moment before nodding to herself and opening her eyes.

"The common thread in all the tales is that of great peril and injury. Usually there is a series of events where a shifter endures great hardships, often wounded and near death. Then, when faced with death once more, they change and become something... more, something stronger. Their trials have reshaped them into the most fearsome of beasts."

"Dire wolves." I shivered.

"Or dire bears or other dire animals, but yes."

I didn't even want to contemplate what a dire bear might be like.

"As I said, it can't be controlled." Kira's brow furrowed, her eyes darkening. "Far too often packs have tried to create dire wolves. They'd subject a shifter to repeated beatings and injury in the hopes of creating a dire wolf. But that sort of forced change never seems to work. The shifter either dies or is enfeebled or goes mad."

Wow, great. Glad I didn't go any of those routes.

"The only time it seems to work is when it's more... natural."

"And for me?" I asked. I could see my own progression, but I was still curious what Kira had to say.

"You were attacked the night of your first shift. My guess is *that*, more than anything else, is what set you on the path. You were so new to being a shifter and came so close to death."

I nodded.

Kira sighed heavily. "And I am sorry, alpha, that I didn't tell you about the risks of being turned at your age. That risk, along with your repeated failed attempts to shift, the pain you endured, as well as the few times things didn't work and you came close to death, all of that added to your trauma. Then, when Brick nearly killed you, that was the last straw and you became what you are."

I swallowed a heavy lump in my throat. "Thank you, Kira. Is there anything else? Anything about living as a dire wolf? Any other dangers?"

Kira gave a breathy laugh. "Danger to you? No. You'll be nearly impossible to kill now."

Yet I heard what she wasn't saying.

"But I'm a danger to others, aren't I?" I asked, my voice small.

"Yes," she replied. "You need to learn to control what you are."

Fuck. That meant more shifting, which was the last thing I wanted.

"Thank you, Kira."

She nodded and rose but stopped at the now-fixed door. "This isn't a burden, alpha. It's a boon, a great one. You should feel inspired and uplifted by this. The rest of the pack does." Then she left.

"Inspired?" I muttered. "Yeah... right."

I sighed and thumped my head back against the headboard, blowing out a long breath.

Well, now I knew.

Next, I needed to learn to control it. And hopefully I could do that, just like I'd learned to shift. Because I was determined to ensure that nothing like what happened with Erik, happened again.

JANE

I SET MY ALARM AND GOT UP EARLY THURSDAY MORNING. I was still upset about being fired and even more upset at myself for wolfing-out on Erik, but I knew what I needed to do to avoid that now. I may not have been one hundred percent, but I needed to get back to my life. I had my kids and my pack to take care of. I'd deal with Halloween, which was in three days, *then* deal with *everything* else.

I'd have the rest of my life to wrestle with the monster inside me.

What I found when I emerged from my room was a surprise. My kids were already up and showered and ready for school. Colt and Bronn were double checking they had everything they needed. It was... heartwarming.

"Lunch?" Bronn asked Milo.

"Yeah, I got everything... *Dad*," he said the last word with the playful sarcasm that came with something new he hadn't fully accepted yet. Still... he'd called Bronn "Dad."

That made me blink and smile.

Colt was talking to Izzy, while Petra braided the girl's hair into a half-up-half-down crown braid, which made her look so mature and beautiful. I drew closer, listening in on what she and Colt were talking about.

"...more practice to make sure you can do it without thinking," Colt said to her. "That grab needs to be just right. If you don't get it, then you're opening yourself up."

"I know, but still, I felt so powerful," Izzy said with a grin. "I had you on the floor and I was just holding your hand!"

Colt laughed. "Yeah, I felt it too. For now, if anyone's seriously bothering you, remember groin-kick or palm-strike to the nose, then run and get help."

It took me a moment to realize they were talking self-defense. That scared me and pleased me all at the same time. I never wanted my little girl to have to use it. But I also knew how many creeps were out there and knowing how to protect yourself was never a bad thing.

"Hey," I said, interrupting everyone.

"Glad to see you up," Petra said, finishing Izzy's braid.

"Mom! You okay now?" Milo asked.

"Yeah, I'm feeling better," I said. "When did you start calling Bronn Dad?"

"A couple days ago. It still doesn't sound right, but he's cool, and so is Tyson and Colt. Oh, and I completed my assignment to talk to the pack, I'm just working on my report now. I should have it ready for this weekend some-time." He smiled, happier than I'd seen him in a while.

"That's great, I'll make sure we get some time to go over it. You still want to be a wolf?" I asked.

He shrugged. "Don't know. I think so... though a lion

or a bear would be cool too. But yeah, it's definitely not everything I thought, so... maybe not, we'll see."

That was progress.

"And how are you feeling, Izzy?" I asked. "Things starting to feel more normal?" She'd been concerned with all the upheaval around her but seemed a bit more settled now.

"Normal... no," she said with a laugh, looking at all of the people crowding our kitchen. "But better, yeah. It's... sort of like having a large family, three dads and a bunch of older sisters and a couple extra mothers."

"Extra mothers?" I asked, curious.

She tilted her head to Kira and Dana. "Yeah, they helped out while you were laid up."

"Oh." Relief edged with sadness rushed through me. Had I been replaced?

Izzy must have seen my hesitance. "Don't worry, Mom. No one could replace you. You're still mother-prime."

"Thanks," I said with a half-grin.

It seemed a lot had changed in the couple days I'd been sulking. Perhaps I should go sulk more often? No, that was definitely not the answer.

"Hey, are you up for helping me bake Halloween treats after school?"

Izzy smiled. "Sure." And I could see a hint of relief on her face. This was something we'd been doing together for years, a hint of our old lives.

We saw the kids off the school, then I got the full report from the pack. Lucas and Winnie were working, liking the new opportunity. Petra and Cassie had completed estimates without me. Mrs. Khan had signed off on hers and they were set to begin work in a week or so. They'd also sent off the estimates for Terry's guest bedroom.

The other potential businesses were also coming along slowly, and Debbie Coles had called while I'd been hiding from the world, wanting to discuss some marketing stuff. I'd need to get back to her on that. Rita and Brutus were keeping a closer eye on the kids at school — as much as they could without getting too close — and there had been no more sightings of Brick and his crew, so perhaps that last one had just been a fluke?

And it seemed my three betas had made some inroads into fatherhood. Bronn told me about his upfront discussion with the kids, which I thought was amazing. I was a bit sorry I hadn't thought of something so simple.

Things didn't seem that bad.

Yeah, I was still jobless, but my savings would last us for a while. I had time to find something new. And I had a pack behind me, ready to help with whatever I needed, which today was cooking and baking, but first, a trip to the grocery store.

Petra came with me. I hadn't thought her one for baking. As I found out, she had other reasons for tagging along.

"Ah... Jane? Alpha?" she asked hesitantly as we drove into town.

"Yeah?" It was clear she had something on her mind and I was curious what it might be.

"Do you think... ah... I... No, never mind, it's silly, a daydream, nothing more."

I had a feeling I might know what she was referring to, but still. "It's okay Petra, you're allowed to have dreams, what is it? You can tell me."

She bit her lip for a long moment, then finally asked, "Do you think humans and shifters could be together? I don't know how a relationship would work without endangering the human and I wouldn't want to do that, but..."

"But you like Terry, next door?" I guessed.

Her large blue eyes widened. "Oh... yeah. Is it that obvious?"

I laughed, "Only to anyone with eyes, Petra. You can't stop looking at each other. I'm happy for both of you. You're good people who deserve to be happy, and I don't see why it can't work between you."

A dark blush stained Petra's tanned cheeks, enhancing her natural beauty. "He's... kind."

I nodded. Given Petra's last man was a lecherous brute who regularly abused her, "kind" seemed like an understatement for the polite and urbane Terry.

"And?" I prompted.

"And we spoke when I was mending your fence. He's very attractive and intelligent and he has two kids, who seem well-raised. He's perfect! I don't know why some woman hasn't snatched him up!" She looked out the window. "And... I don't know what he sees in me."

Ah.

"You're beautiful, Petra."

The woman had a slightly exotic look, probably part Hispanic or Latina, given her beautifully tanned skin. Waves of lustrous dark hair flowed down her back and those large blue eyes made her look like some movie starlet.

"I'm huge," she whispered, one hand absently rubbing her belly. Her voice was even quieter when she mumbled, "And broken, stained, hideous, cursed." Tears traced her cheeks.

I sighed. This was why Petra needed help finding her strength again. I couldn't imagine the horrors Tank had put her through, and she still carried his child, though she seemed to have claimed that for herself. But it seemed she still had scars from her time with that man, even if you couldn't see them on her skin.

Curious, I asked, "What was your life like before?" I'd heard bits and pieces, but perhaps talking about that would bring back some of who she'd been?

She sniffed at her tears and gave a weak smile. "Rough," she said simply. "It wasn't bad, but it wasn't great either."

I nodded and remained silent, hoping she'd go on.

Her smile grew, but it was a sad thing. "My mother was a model. She looked so beautiful in the pictures my father had of her. She died giving birth to me."

Wow, not a blessed start to life.

"My father died when I was seventeen. I was close enough to eighteen that it was like a strange vacation. I went to live with my dad's sister in Croatia for a few months, but she didn't speak much English and my father hadn't taught me Croatian. When I was eighteen, I came back. My dad's life insurance helped to get me settled."

Both her parents were dead? I hoped the story got better from there.

"I thought perhaps I could take after my mother. I tried modelling. But I didn't have an agent, so it was tough to find work. Then, when I did find an agent, he... he was a creep. I got out of that life."

Fuck me. Had there been any light in this girl's life?

"I drifted around for a while after that, doing odd jobs. Then, I got a job as a server at a diner in Summersville. The owners there were good to me, an older couple, Dave and Judy. They had no kids and sort of adopted me, helping me out."

Thank God!

"I started taking business courses at night, hoping to expand my options. Then..." Her voice grew hard. "Tank found me."

So, just when her life was starting to look up a monster stole her away from it all. Fucking hell!

"Do you ever think about going back to that diner to see Dave and Judy?" I asked.

She nodded, distracted. "But... what would I say? I couldn't stay. I'm a monster now. If I cut myself, I could infect someone. That life is behind me. I... I've thought about calling them. I could probably do that. Let them know I'm okay. But I can't go back. If I saw them, it would make it that much harder to leave them again." That same sad smile returned. "And I've got a new home now, with the pack, with you."

I'd been about to refute her comment about being a

monster, but I found I couldn't. I too was a monster now, so what right did I have to say we weren't? She wasn't as deviant a shifter as I was, but still, I understood entirely how she might see herself as monstrous.

"You'll always be welcome here, even if you decide to go off and do other things," I said. "I hope, someday, you find a life you want to live." But that reminded me what had started this conversation: Terry. "And, just so you know, Terry is aware that shifters exist. I told him and he accepted it. He's a good man. I know he'd see past everything you've been through. I'm fairly certain he just sees the beautiful woman you are, inside and out."

Petra nodded slowly. "You think?"

"I do." But there was one other concern. "And if it's sex you're worried about, that's what condoms are for. He'd be safe."

Petra shuddered when I mentioned sex. That didn't surprise me. Her voice was tiny when she said, "Ah... yeah, good to know, but I think I'll just... avoid that for a while."

I nodded, understanding entirely, given what Tank had done to her.

Curious, I asked, "Is there anything you'd like to do? A new look perhaps, for this new beginning in your life?"

She looked over at me. Her cheeks were dry, but her large eyes were still red-rimmed. "I'd been thinking about getting a haircut?"

"Then let's do that!" I said, excited. "Shopping can wait for a bit. I know a good beautician in town, let's get you something fresh and different!"

"You'd do that, for me?"

I couldn't afford any luxuries right now, but this wasn't a luxury. For Petra, I was fairly certain it would be a necessity to help her move on.

"Of course. We're like family now, right?" Then, I put in one last nudge. "And just think about Terry, okay? He's a good guy and I'm certain he likes you. But at the same time, I don't think he'd mind if you needed some time to figure yourself out. There's no need to rush into anything. Just tell him that yourself, if you are interested. Let him know you like him but need time. I'm sure he'd understand and wait for you."

"Yeah?"

"Yeah."

A large smile slowly spread over her face. I guessed she was thinking about Terry. It warmed my heart.

At the hairdresser's, she had them hack off nearly all of her long hair. She decided on a pixie cut, shaved close in the back, but with longer curls in the front, which swept down over her left eye. It was a gorgeous look on her, and she was beaming with liberated joy when we left the beauty shop.

"Thank you, alpha, this is exactly what I wanted!" There was true joy in her voice and a spring in her step.

"And Terry?"

She hesitated, pulling back a little, uncertainty in her eyes. "I..."

"Petra, consider it a strong suggestion from your alpha. When you're ready, talk to Terry. I know he wants to talk to you. See what happens."

She bit her lip then smiled and nodded. "Okay I'll do it... when I'm ready."

I hugged her tightly, trying to give her all the strength and confidence and hope I could in that one gesture. I knew she wouldn't easily overcome the trauma of her previous life, but for her sake, I hoped she could move on eventually.

We did our shopping and returned. Everyone in the pack cooed over Petra's new hairstyle and that stunning smile of hers crept out more and more often. Then she scurried off with Cassie, giggling like girls while Kira and Dana helped me with the baking.

Seeing Petra happy made my day. If she could put her past behind her, then I could certainly put the past few days behind me and move on.

JANE

WHEN IZZY GOT HOME, SHE JOINED IN AND HELPED WITH the baking. I was making pumpkin tarts — essentially mini pumpkin pies — along with apple strudel. We baked all through dinner, the pack making a cold buffet of foods for everyone to nibble as needed. Once we were at the stage where we were just waiting on the oven for the next batch to go in, Izzy left to do her homework and Colt found me.

Massive arms enfolded me from behind and a soft kiss pressed to the top of my head. "How is our alpha doing today?" he asked.

"Better," I admitted.

"You still needed here?" he asked.

"No, Kira and Dana can finish things up?" I phrased it as a question, glancing at the two women, who nodded to me.

"Want to go for a run?"

I turned in his arms, forgetting that he was huge and

that I'd be staring at his chest. I looked up, a bit confused. "A run?" I'd never been one for jogging.

"Blow off some steam, work out any residual negative energy." When that didn't seem to get through to me, he added, "In the woods, shifted."

I blinked. *Shifted?* For a moment I balked, not wanting to go there. But I did need to be shifting more and getting control of my beast. And I'd be with Colt with no one else around, so it should be pretty safe. Also, it might be nice to get out for a moment and just let loose.

"Ah... sure."

He grinned. "Wear something loose, easy to get out of."

A shiver ran through me at the thought of stripping in the woods. Partly because I'd be doing it with Colt, which excited me, but also... "Isn't it a bit chilly to be out naked at night?"

He grinned. "You're a shifter now. When was the last time you felt chilly?"

"I..." It hit me. He was right. Ever since I'd shifted, I hadn't noticed the chilly nights or mornings so much. When I'd first met the pack, I recalled how Tyson and Bronn and Colt had all felt warm — almost hot — all the time. I was willing to bet I did now too. "Oh."

"Come on," he said as he disengaged from his hug to pull me toward the bedroom. "Put on something frumpy and easy to get out of and we'll go for a walk."

I changed into some sweats. Though I took forever to decide whether I should wear underwear or not. I went with not, wearing only a baggy sweater, sweat pants, some slip-on shoes and nothing else. I felt both frumpy and secretly sensual as I left, hand in hand, with Colt.

And he was right, I didn't feel chilly at all, even once we were in the woods and naked.

He'd been in jeans, a T-shirt, and riding boots when we'd set out, and I realized, I hadn't seen him wearing his biker's vest for some time now, which was fine with me. He was sexy-as-sin with that tight white shirt clinging to his muscles. Without it, he was down-right delicious. He hadn't been wearing underwear, either — I didn't think he ever did — and we were both out of our clothes quickly.

We spent a long moment just looking at each other, admiring.

"You're beautiful," he whispered, reverently.

I noted how he hadn't said, *sexy* or *fucking-gorgeous*, nothing that made me feel hot and bothered just *beautiful,* and I blushed.

Colt was too big and too hard to be beautiful. Bronn was beautiful. Colt wasn't even classically handsome. He was a hunk of tantalizing man-meat. He was triple-chocolate cake: undeniably delicious, but bad for you all at the same time.

"You're... impressive." Yes. That was the word. Impressive.

He grinned. "Run?"

And as much as a part of me wanted to throw myself at him, I did want to get out some excess energy first. I nodded and we both shifted. I'd forgotten how big his bear was, but then... I was just as big as a dire wolf.

Then he took off into the forest, fast for all his bulk.

I darted after him, much faster than I'd thought I'd be, easily catching up to him, surprising myself. I'd thought, because of my size, I'd run into trees, but I was also incredibly nimble and light on my massive paws, weaving through the forest like the wind.

There was no moon tonight, but I could see well enough, and beyond that, my other senses told me everything I needed to know about my surroundings. My ears caught every chirping insect, my snout picked up so many scents, even the trees themselves had certain smells, and I figured I could probably navigate by hearing and scent alone, although I didn't try it.

We ran full out for a while. I was far faster than Colt, so I ran literal circles around him as he galloped through the brush. And when we were spent, we rested... sort of.

He shifted, leaning his back against a tree, huffing breaths, and when I shifted, there was virtually no pain. I'd passed my trials along with the danger of shifting at my age. I'd survived so much, and it had made me stronger... although I was still uncomfortable with this new strength.

I leaned against Colt, my breath not quite so ragged. In fact, I was barely winded.

My lips cracked into a smile. That run had been amazing, clearing my mind of worries and doubts, and now energy and a sense of freedom rushed through me. And with an incredibly sexy naked man next to me, I was suddenly wondering why I hadn't been allowing him to be close these last few days.

The complexities of figuring out our relationship didn't matter right now. We were both flushed and vital, and from the heated look in his eyes, he wanted me as badly as I wanted him.

I pressed close and traced the tattoos on his chest and arms, kissing the markings. There was the bear's head on his left pec, with a tank for an eye and a horse racing out of its mouth. On his right shoulder he bore the image of a lion and bear standing behind a wolf. Then he had the stylized pattern down his left arm with facets of a bear mixed in

"Keep doing that and this won't be much of a rest," he said.

I was very aware of that. As aware as I was of his massive cock rousing and pressing against my hip.

"What if I don't want a rest?" I whispered.

"Then I'd give my alpha what she wants," he growled low and throaty.

"What are you waiting for?" I asked stepping back, freeing his cock from being trapped between us. It sprang up before me, tall and thick.

Colt chuckled and picked me up like I was nothing. He held me there with ease, high enough so he could taste my breasts, teasing them with lips, tongue, and teeth.

I wrapped my arm around his head, pulling him close to my bosom, encouraging him. "Yes," I whispered.

"You're so fucking delicious, gorgeous," he breathed between nibbles and kisses.

Meanwhile I was poised just above his cock and I brushed my folds over his tip. Wrapping my legs around him, I pulled myself down just enough to trap his tip between us, rubbing myself hard on his rigid flesh, drawing a low groan of pleasure and want.

"I'm ready," I whispered, wanting to feel his massive cock throbbing inside me.

"No, you're not wet enough," he said between grunts and the press of his lips.

"Then *make* me wet."

"Yes, alpha," he said with a chuckle.

I yelped in surprise as he tore me away from him and tossed me lightly, spinning me around in mid-air, only to catch me again. Then he pressed my back to his chest, one thick arm clamped around me keeping me in place. His cock was now pressed between my butt-cheeks, throbbing and thick, and his other hand, now free, slid down my stomach and through my curls, pressing into my folds.

I leaned my head back against the rolling muscle of his shoulder, eyes closed, submitting myself to his possession and the glorious sensations of his fingers.

"Gorgeous," he breathed, hot on my ear, then began kissing my ear and jaw and neck.

I moaned in the night, unabashedly aroused. I wanted to touch him, so I slid one hand up around his head, into the thick waves of his hair. The other I ran down the rigid muscles of his flank, then behind, finding his rock-hard ass and digging in my nails.

He groaned again and his cock twitched against my ass. His fingers worked on my clit, slow and sure, until I felt more than ready for him. Except when he slid his fingers through my moisture to my entrance, only one could fit inside me.

Guess I was still a bit tight. He curled his finger to stroke lines of fire within me, while his palm ground over my clit. I was hanging, unable to move much, but I opened my legs, giving him more room to work as I squirmed and mewled with ever-increasing pleasure.

He made me feel like the only woman in existence, like I was his and only his. The forest faded away. All I heard and smelled was Colt, near and powerful. I loved how he could make me forget about everything and succumb to the sensations of my body. It was glorious.

I cried out as the brilliant flash of a powerful orgasm surged through me.

And when a second drenched finger joined the first inside me, I came again. "Oh, fucking hell! Yes! I've got to be ready now!" My hips tried to buck against his hand, but his arm was clamped over me, restricting my movement.

"Yes, alpha," he breathed with one last kiss on my neck, then I was thrown into the air and spun around again.

I wrapped my legs around him, pulling myself down onto his thick cock, and grunt-moaned with trembling bliss as his tip filled me.

"More," I whispered. "Take me."

His hands shifted down to my hips as I looped mine behind his head. Our eyes met and I was certain the bonfire of desire within me matched the heat behind his stare.

Our gazes locked and I felt like he was asking me a question with that look: ready?

God, yes. I needed him inside me, and I nodded, biting my lip.

He let out a breathy grunt then his hands forced me down as his hips thrusted up and his cock slid home, sheathed fully inside me.

I cried in pleasure as a small, shivering hint of an orgasm rolled through me.

Colt may not have had Tyson's knot, but he made up for it with pure length and girth. I felt stretched and utterly filled. He was so deep inside me, it felt like he pierced my very soul.

Our lips crashed together, open and needful, and I crushed myself against his hard chest while rocking my hips and moving that monster cock inside me. Colt began to rock his hips as well, thrusting in time with me, drawing a long, loud moan from me that he drank down with a rumbling sigh of contentment.

Another, more powerful orgasm mounted inside me, pushed to the edge. I chased it with determination and abandon. And when it came, it was like a bolt of lightning blasting through me, tensing every muscle. My arms and legs around him clamped tight, and it felt like his cock had grown inside me as I squeezed that monster shaft and flooded around him.

"Fuck, gorgeous! That's so fucking hot!" he said, hot breath on my lips as I gasped and shivered. "Makes me want to make you come even more."

His hands on my hips slid down under my ass and lifted me slowly. I was clamped down on his shaft so hard, I felt every vein on every inch of him, and it only made me come harder. And when only his tip was inside me, I crushed the hell out of it, mewling and whining.

"Oh, yeah!" he hissed as he buried his face in my cleavage again. When his teeth came away clamped around a rock-hard nipple, the bite of pain redoubled my bliss. I wanted him to come so goddamned much, to feel his rush inside me as we reached this amazing peak together, but I had a feeling he wouldn't be so accommodating.

He sucked my other nipple into his mouth, drawing out my bliss even more.

Then his hands fell away and I dropped suddenly. His cock plunged inside me, hard and deep, and somehow, I came again. I roared my ecstasy so loud that everyone for miles must have heard.

I couldn't move. My arms and legs were jelly after all these orgasms.

"You want me to come?" he asked, near-to-breathless before his lips claimed mine again.

"Mmhhmm," I moaned into his mouth, desperately agreeing.

He spun us around, my back now pressed to the rough bark of a tree. I didn't care. The scratches were nothing compared to the fountains of pleasure rushing inside me. His hands on my ass shifted, moving out to my knees, holding my legs open as he leaned back a little. His eyes blazed with molten desire as he consumed me with his gaze. Then he began savagely thrusting into me.

"I want to see you come once more, then you'll have me." He spoke through ragged breaths as he pounded his thick shaft into me.

God! My head lolled back, pressed against the tree behind me, my arms stretched out, still clasped behind his neck as he watched me writhe and squirm. I didn't think it possible to go any higher, to feel any more blissed-out than I already was.

I was wrong. So completely wrong.

Light exploded behind my eyes, blinding me for a moment as his cock slammed into me in the exact right way. My world erupted with rapturous ecstasy, and I tried to scream, but no sound came out, I was too far gone.

Then Colt repeated that life-altering thrust, and this time he kept it there, planted deep. "Fucking Gods! You're so fucking amazing, Jane!"

His cock throbbed as he pumped his release inside me. And with each pulse of his shaft, my unearthly bliss spiked, over and over. Our heartbeats pounded through us, reverberating between us and thundering in the night.

I lost track of everything around me.

When I came to, I lay on top of Colt as he lay on the forest floor. It felt a bit unhygienic to be out here naked in the forest, but also somehow perfect and natural.

Perhaps it had been the run, or just being in nature, but our joining had felt... barbaric. He'd never been this rough with me. And I was surprised how much I'd liked it. Something savage had been unlocked within me.

"Wow," I whispered, my voice hoarse, raw.

"I have to agree," he breathed with a laugh. "Wow sums you up perfectly."

I kissed his chest again, tasting the salty tang of his sweat. We were both covered in perspiration, and tendrils of steam rose off us, but I still wasn't bothered by the cool night.

"We're hot," I said, then chuckled, realizing how that sounded.

"Hell yeah, we are!" he said with a bit of a laugh. Then he stilled a little, his voice growing serious. "Hey, Jane, I just wanted to let you know I'm all in."

"Not anymore, but you certainly were a moment ago!" I joked.

He chuckled but remained serious. "I think you know what I mean. You said before that you've never had a real partner in life. Well, I'm saying I'm here, devoted, dedicated, committed. I've been trying to help out with the kids, even though all I really know is how to fight. I'm teaching them some self-defense, but that's beside the point. I'm saying, I'm here for whatever you need. I may not always be able to anticipate it, but if you tell me, I'll do it. I want to be your partner, not just in bed, but in life."

"Oh..." Wow... "And this isn't just the sex talking?" I had to know. Lots of men got chatty about commitment during sex, though usually it was before to get a girl into bed, not after.

"No. I've been thinking about this for a while. I'm not going anywhere and neither are the others. Whatever you need, whenever you need it... just ask."

I laid my head on his chest and he stroked my hair as I took this all in. Perhaps it was the hazy, post-orgasmic bliss, but I believed him. "Thanks, Colt."

"Talk to the others," he whispered. "They'll tell you the same."

I nodded against his chest. "I'm sorry if I've been a bit withdrawn these past few days."

"No worries. You had a fuck-ton of nasty shit happen to you. You're allowed to feel however you feel."

I was, and I was slowly coming to accept that.

We were silent for a long moment after that as I just rested on him. Our bodies cooled, and as much as I didn't feel the chill of the night, I *was* feeling ever-so-slightly uncomfortable laying naked in the middle of the woods.

"You ready for the run back?" he asked.

I breathed a laugh. "It's a good thing I'll have four legs, because I don't know if I could walk on two." I slowly got up to test my legs. I thought I'd be more tired or fatigued, legs sore or something, but if anything, I felt refreshed, revitalized.

I shifted, and in my wolf form, I felt stronger still, ready for another run.

I chased Colt-as-a-bear back through the woods to where we'd left our clothes, nipping at him and playing around.

I had to admit, as I slipped on my sweats once more, that Colt had delivered on his promise. All the tension and stress of the last few days was gone. I felt vital and alive, and just tired enough that I slept very well that night.

I woke refreshed and ready to face the day on Friday, which told me, I should go for a run more often. Though I couldn't be sure whether it was the run, or the drop-dead amazing sex, which had set me straight. I'd have to experiment with that later. Now *that* was something to look forward to.

JANE

FRIDAY, I HAD A CHAT WITH MY BETAS ABOUT THE Halloween party. It would be a good chance for the pack to meet my neighbors and hopefully make a good impression.

Bronn had the idea of using their carpentry skills to make a special booth for our treats, which would show off what Shining Stone builders could do. I loved that idea and told him to take charge of it.

Tyson said he'd talk to the rest of the pack and make sure everyone was on the same page and on their best behavior. He also mentioned he wanted to apologize to the fae.

"Oh?" I asked. I was curious why he wished to apologize to them specifically.

He sighed. "They knew you before, and it sounds like they're okay with you. But you know what relations were like between fae and shifters. And our pack was in their forest before all of this. You had nothing to do with that.

I'm the ranking member of the old pack. I think I should be the one to speak to them and let them know we're sorry if we desecrated any sacred space of theirs."

He was right. "Just keep that quiet from the other neighbors, okay?"

He nodded. "I will."

"Were you going to do that today?" I asked.

"No," he hedged seeming just a tad uneasy. "I... I thought I'd wait until the party. I'll still keep it quiet, but that way, they can't turn me into a toad or anything if they don't like my apology."

"Turn you into—" Could they do that? "Oh. Okay."

"I'll help where needed today," Tyson finished. Which probably meant he'd be helping Colt, who was going to be working on a new shed, another display piece for Shining Stone.

My old shed was falling apart in the back corner of my yard, and they decided to make a bigger one at the end of my driveway beside the house, a prototype for what they'd make for the Khans.

The day passed quickly for me, between cooking and party preparations. That evening, I took Izzy out costume shopping. Winnie, Petra, and Cassie came with us. They'd never been able to dress up at Halloween before and wanted to give it a try. I had a witch costume I always wore, but given what I now knew about shifters and witches, I thought it time for something new.

It took us a while to find what we wanted, but I ended up in a — slightly more revealing than I might have liked — little red riding hood costume. All the girls thought it was perfect, and the irony wasn't lost on me. I talked Izzy out of a wonder woman costume, which, in my mind, showed far too much bust and legs. Instead, we found her a sexy pirate costume, which covered a lot more of her, but still made her happy.

The three shifter women all went with animal costumes. Cassie and Petra chose conservative, full-body onesies. Cassie got a unicorn, Petra got a bunny. Winnie, being a little younger, decided on a skin-tight, silvery wolf costume, complete with tail and a headband with ears.

When we got home, Izzy rushed off to the basement. Colt had been drilling my kids in self-defense morning and evening, after their homework was done, and I was a bit surprised by my daughter's enthusiasm for it. That was until Cassie mentioned that Jake was also helping and neither he nor Colt wore a shirt while they were training.

Still, I was glad my kids were learning how to take care of themselves, and it was better than them vegging in front of the TV all evening.

Tyson and Bronn wanted to see my costume, so I changed then invited them into my room. The costume was a simple red dress with a skirt to my knees and a sort of white apron-like design on the front. It was cut low, with red on white polka-dotted straps over the shoulders. There was a red-hooded half-cape which tied around my neck as well. Though, for me, what really made the costume was the white knee-high stockings with little red bows on them. When my two betas saw me, their eyes — Tyson's smoldering dark blue and Bronn's mysterious brown depths — grew hungry.

"Wow," Bronn breathed with a wide smile as I gave a twirl.

"Oh, Jane, babe," Tyson breathed. "Does this mean you want me to eat you?"

I considered making a comment about *what a big dick you have*, but just laughed instead.

It was finally sinking in. These men *wanted* me. I'd spent the last ten years convincing myself I wasn't sexy, partly because I was getting older and partly because of everything that had happened with my ex.

And as clear as it was that Tyson and Bronn thought I was sexy, I knew they wanted so much more from me. They wanted *all* of me, my life, my kids, and every awkward moment.

"What if I just wanted to snuggle tonight?" I asked. "Even after teasing you with this?"

"Then we're still the luckiest men in the world," Bronn said.

But my fated pull was burning through me once more, and it had been too long since Tyson and I had been together. I really wanted to be with him *and* Bronn tonight, if that's what they wanted. But first, I needed to clear the air about all the doubts and fears I'd had over the past week. "Can we talk first?"

Tyson closed the door behind him then leaned against it while Bronn sat on the bed.

"First, thank you," I said earnestly even as I paced nervously. "Both of you, all of you, for looking after everything when I was sulking." It was seeing them with my kids and how they'd handled everything in the house over the last few days, which truly told me how they felt. "Second, I'm... sorry."

"For what?" Bronn asked.

"Over this past week, after Brick was dealt with and all the adrenaline and immediacy of fighting for my life was gone, I... I began to doubt all of you. We all came together so quickly and with such urgency that first week, and I just couldn't believe it was true. I figured you'd only been with me because we all felt the urgency of the situation and you were... I don't know... humoring me? I was going to die. You were comforting me, and we *all* got something out of it, but I just figured once all that went away, you'd realize I was just plain old Jane and lose interest in me."

"You're definitely not plain and far from old," Bronn said.

"I'm forty-four!"

"So?" Tyson said instantly. "Yeah, that's older than us, but it's hardly old."

"I dye my hair and have stretchmarks and wrinkles and..." I'd been about to say I had a saggy belly, but I didn't anymore. And for that matter, my stretchmarks were hardly noticeable now and even some of my wrinkles had become fine lines.

I sighed. They were right. And that was why I loved them.

"That's my point," I said, relenting and quiet. "I thought you wouldn't want me, but you still do. I couldn't see myself like you did, but I think I'm starting to. I know I'm your alpha and all, but even so, I thought you might leave me, or at least realize that you only wanted to be betas, and nothing more. And that's what I'm sorry for. For doubting you."

I stopped pacing and took a moment to look at them. Bronn was scarred, inside and out, but still so beautiful, body and soul, and Tyson was dark and dangerous, but also kind and giving.

"It's clear to me now, you're not going anywhere. And you've been making an effort with my kids, going above and beyond my expectations for your first week of fatherhood."

Still, with everything I'd just said, a part of me was uncertain. I remembered what Colt had said last night and I wanted to hear it from these two as well.

"I know this may sound needy, but... I just want to hear it from you."

"That we're all in?" Tyson asked with a sly smile.

"Partners," Bronn added.

I sighed. "You talked to Colt?"

"Yeah," Tyson said with a grin, but then he sobered. "Jane, let me make this clear. I *am* all in, I *am* your partner in life, *for* life. I'm not going anywhere and whatever you need, I'm here for you."

I smiled, my heart swelling at those words.

"Same here," Bronn said. "I've known you'd be my mate from the moment I first scented you. And yeah, I know that sounds odd, but it's true. And in a pride, the male mate provides everything for the female, a safe place, and protection. The female usually provides direction and leadership, but if you want my help with that, then I'm in for that too." He looked at Tyson. "We're all here for you." Then back to me. "Partners, fully, completely."

I let out a long breath. "Thank you."

Only then did I let the simmering heat bubbling in my core blaze a little in my eyes as my gaze travelled between the two men. "Now... what are you waiting for, are you going to get me out of this costume, or what?"

BRONN

I'd meant every word I'd said. I'd be there for Jane however she needed me, and she was making it very clear how she needed me at the moment.

As Tyson and I went to Jane, we shared a knowing look. It was time to show our alpha — our mate, our partner — just how dedicated we could be.

Tyson slipped behind her while I cupped her face in my hands and drew her lips to mine in a tender but firm kiss. I loved how her eyes fluttered shut when our faces drew close, and how her breath hitched as our lips brushed. I loved everything about this woman, mind, body, and soul.

And I would give everything I was to her: mind, body, and soul.

Before she'd come into my life, I'd been tormented for so long that the idea of trusting anyone with something as precious and vulnerable as my deepest feelings was incomprehensible.

When I'd first scented her, I'd known she'd be my

mate, but I'd still been too scared to give her everything. I hadn't been willing to risk losing my heart and soul if she'd died fighting Brick. And when she'd gone into heat, I'd given myself to her physically, but no more.

Even after Brick had been defeated, I'd hesitated, uncertain what Jane as a dire wolf would be like. But her essence hadn't changed. As frightened as I'd been when I'd seen her hybrid form, a part of me had known, she'd never hurt me. As fearsome as her exterior had been, something in her eyes had still been Jane: fierce, but also caring, generous, and kind.

And now I was hers, utterly devoted and completely committed. She'd always give me everything I needed, her heart overflowing with love. So how could I not do the same for her?

Inhaling deeply, I took in her scent: dewy spring grasses and sunned skin. And as she grew more and more aroused, her scent shifted to that of hot, wet grasses after a summer's storm. It was the most wonderous and fulfilling aroma I'd ever known.

My mate.

Jane wrapped her arms around my neck and drew me close, our kiss growing hard and deep. Tyson removed her cape then slid the straps of her dress off her shoulders, kissing where they'd been before burying his face in her hair.

Jane gave a low, soft moan, which echoed into my mouth and filled my senses, sending a shiver of expectant bliss through me. My cock throbbed, achingly hard, but I ignored it. What Tyson and I were about to share with her wasn't about getting off but giving our mate what she needed.

I explored her mouth with my tongue, savoring her flavor as she did the same with me. I carefully slid my hands down from her face and over her shoulders and arms. She let her arms fall away from me so I could push the straps of her dress lower.

When she shrugged her arms out of the straps, the tight dress hardly moved, clinging to her full figure. It was a good thing Tyson and I were in no hurry to undress our mate, our focus solely on making her feel like the goddess she was. Our fingers roamed over skin and cloth in long caresses.

I pushed my hands up over her full breasts, her tight nipples straining against the sheer fabric of the dress. She gasped as I kneaded her and her breath hitched when I slid a hand under the dress to grasp one of her round tits, her skin was searingly hot, her body trembling, breath ragged.

"Fuck," Jane breathed, breaking her lips away from mine. "Will someone get me out of this damned dress!"

Tyson chuckled softly before whispering in her ear from behind, "Yes, alpha." And I heard the zipper being undone.

Jane shivered as he kissed her neck, sliding his hands over her sides, taking the dress with him. Yet, her dark-caramel eyes were locked on me as the dress slowly slid down. When she stepped out of it, Tyson laid it carefully on top of her dresser.

That left her in panties and white stockings, staring at

me with a smoldering gaze. Gods, she was too fucking sexy. I found myself whispering, "You're exquisite."

"And you're overdressed," she whispered back.

Shifters were used to undressing quickly and after stepping back to make room, I was out of my shirt and jeans in record time.

Her eyes locked on mine and she came to me, two slow steps, her hips swaying, the sexiest thing I could imagine. My ragingly hard cock twitched before me as she pressed her body to mine and claimed another deep kiss. When she was done, she slid her body over mine as she turned, pressing her back to my chest.

Looping her arms up and back, around my neck, she hung off me, looking at Tyson. "We're going to give my prime beta a show, aren't we Bronn?"

"Yes, beloved," I whispered in her ear before kissing her neck.

"Ooooh, that's new. Beloved, I like that," she breathed. "Now touch me, Bronn."

How could I refuse that? I pressed my hands to the sides of her hips, then slowly, firmly slid them to the front, over her panties, and pressed her against me. I could feel wetness seeping through the cloth as my fingers brushed by the apex of her legs.

Jane moaned and shifted, biting her lip before whispering, "Stay right there, Tyson. I want to watch you watch me come. I know you're feeling what I'm feeling and we'll come crashing together soon enough, but I want to draw things out, enjoy my time with both of you."

"Of course, beloved," he said softly as he made a show of slowly undressing for her.

Jane leaned her head back on my shoulder, finding my ear with her lips, her hot breath thrilling me as she whispered, "Make me come, my lion, but don't make it too quick." Then, she nipped the shell of my ear and nearly made *me* come.

I groaned my acknowledgement as I slid my hands up her body to encompass her full breasts. Her nipples were stiff and tall, and didn't need any further arousing, but still, every time my fingers brushed over them, she moaned in the most delicious way. And when I carefully pinched and pulled both nipples at once, she gave a throaty groan and shifted against me.

"Yessss," she breathed, shivering.

Tyson stroked his cock, watching her, his gaze locked with hers. His knot was swollen and ready, pre-cum glistening on his tip. His fated pull had to be hammering at him, but he remained still, smiling and patient.

I slid one hand down from her breasts to her white cotton panties, over the cloth, and between her legs. She shifted again with a shuddering hitch of her breath as I felt where she'd soaked through the fabric.

"I'm going to lift you," I warned her, and I slid my hands to her waist and gently lifted her off her feet. Then I walked backwards until my legs hit the bed, and I sat with Jane on my lap, pushing her legs wide, to either side of mine.

"Show your mate how wet you are," I breathed in her ear as I ran my fingers over her panties again.

"Mhm," she moaned, rolling her hips a little.

Tyson's gaze slowly raked down her body, and his nostrils flared as he caught her aroused sent.

That same scent was nearly driving me insane, but still I took my time, teasing her clit over her panties. Her wet spot grew as she moaned and squirmed against me, her pleasure building.

I slid her panties aside to collect her wetness on my finger, then brought it up to her lips. She sucked on my finger, moaning, and that did it for Tyson. He shuddered and his eyes clamped shut as the hand on his cock squeezed hard, restraining himself.

And whether it was some fated connection or just the culmination of her arousal so far, when my hand returned to rub her clit, Jane lost it as well. Her body went stiff as she groaned and shivered. Her hips bucked against my hand, and her release soaked my fingers and more of her panties.

"Fuck, that's hot," I moaned. "You're so fucking hot, so sexy and beautiful and... ohhh!" It was my turn to restrain myself as Jane writhed against me. I pinned her close with my arm, crushing her back against my cock to keep myself from coming.

"Will someone please stick their cock inside me," she begged through her shuddering orgasm.

Tyson was at us in an instant, helping Jane to stand on trembling legs as he knelt, removing her underwear, but keeping the white stockings on. He positioned her at the edge of the bed, laying her back, legs open as he pleasured her with lips and fingers. Jane moaned and mewled, lost to pleasure.

"What do you want?" Tyson asked, breathless. "Bronn first or... my knot."

"Knot!" she begged. "Please!"

"While Bronn takes your ass?" he added.

"Fuck! Oh God, yes!" she cried out.

Tyson laid himself down on the bed and Jane quickly straddled him. She grabbed his cock and positioned it, teasing him over her folds for only a moment before plunging down over him. It amazed me how easily she could swallow up that massive knot.

When they locked together, the two of them shuddered and cried out, and Tyson urged Jane to lay on him, presenting me with her round ass and puckered opening.

I was sure I'd need some lube, but when I tested the tight circle with a finger, it opened readily. Jane gave a shuddering cry as I slid one finger as deep as I could inside her. Her tight tunnel contracted around my finger as she came on Tyson's cock. She was so aroused and accepting that I easily added a second finger.

Jane whined and shivered as I pressed and played, and when I stroked the rigidness of Tyson's knot through her, they both groaned. Jane was more than ready, so I withdrew and pressed the head of my cock against her. Her opening expanded slowly as I took my time pushing my tip inside her.

"Yessss!" she hissed, her voice barely a gasp. "More!"

I grabbed her hips and gave a long thrust inside her, not too quick but still with a little more haste than I intended. Her sheath gripped my cock like an insistent fist, stroking me, and I felt the press of Tyson's knot against my shaft, close inside her.

Jane lifted herself, hands on Tyson's shoulders, and pressed back into me as I began to thrust in earnest.

"Up," she mumbled through her moans, and I slid my

hands up her body, helping her rise until her back was to my chest. She turned her head and, though it was awkward, found my lips for a brief kiss. Then her eyes rolled back, body going tense, and her grip on my cock tightened. Tyson shuddered with her, and I knew the waves of their mutual orgasm would go for some time.

Despite being more than ready, my cock painfully swollen and full, I rode the swells of their passion with them, trembling with the effort to restrain myself so I could join them at the peak of their pleasure.

Then Jane's hands slid up her body and squeezed her tits as her bliss seemed to reach a pinnacle. Her arms continued up behind my neck again as she shivered on Tyson, and rocked as much as she could back into me. She made a sound, which vaguely sounded like the word, "Now!" as she seemed to transcend her body and become a being of pure ecstasy.

Tyson gripped her hips, pressing her down on him as he cried out and groaned, his knot throbbing as he came.

I needed no more incentive. I buried my cock deep inside her and let myself go. My hands slid around to tease her breasts as I pulsed my heat into her. The three of us remained locked like that for some time before our bodies couldn't hold the tension and strain of our bliss, and we collapsed into a heap, panting and sweating and sated. It was awkward, our bodies still entangled but we didn't care.

I covered Jane's shoulders in soft kisses, then simply let myself relax into the wondrous cushion of her hair.

"When I'm with you, I forget all my worries," Jane whispered after a time.

Tyson responded almost instantly with, "When I'm with you, I forget I'm cursed. I believe I can be a good person."

I sighed, agreeing with that. Pleasing Jane somehow redeemed me from the darkness of my life before I'd met her.

"You *are* a good person," Jane said softly. And when she said it, I could almost believe it. I wanted to believe it.

But there was too much darkness in my past. It wasn't just the curse. It was who we'd become — and everything we'd done — because of it.

Tyson and I both made sounds of vague agreement, but it didn't convince Jane. She wriggled free of both of us and knelt on the bed, naked and proud, as she looked down at us intently.

"No, listen to me. You're good people. And I've just realized something that you both need to hear."

JANE

IT WAS MORE THAN A LITTLE EMPOWERING TO HAVE THESE two sexy men lying there, looking up at me with adoring gazes. And they weren't looking at my body, but my eyes. They were seeing *me*, the real me.

And the real me was fed up with their comments about being cursed and evil and all of that. As we'd laid there, after Tyson had said it the first time, I'd finally realized why it bothered me, why it was wrong.

"It may be true that a long time ago, someone was cursed to be a shifter. But can't you see that this isn't a curse? Not anymore?"

The confusion in their eyes told me they didn't, not yet. So, I made it easy.

"Am I evil?"

And instantly they were both talking over each other to extol how pure and wonderful I was.

"See!" I said.

They stopped. Tyson's brow furrowed, confused.

Bronn cocked his head, his gaze shifting as he worked it through. He seemed to be starting to understand.

"I'm a shifter now, too. And if, by your logic, just being a shifter makes you cursed and evil, then I'm evil, right?" I didn't give them time to reply. "No, of course not. But that means *you're* not evil or cursed, just by virtue of being a shifter either!"

Bronn nodded slowly, and I got the feeling he understood my argument but didn't quite believe it yet. Tyson blinked as the realization finally hit him.

"Just being born a shifter, or being turned, doesn't make you evil," I told them. "But I think you've been told that for so long you just believe it. So much so that it became an excuse, a reason to be barbaric and destructive. Am I wrong?"

Tyson sighed. "No."

Bronn chewed it over a moment longer. "The pride was different, we believed we were cursed, but strove to rise above it." He grimaced. "But you're right, it was also used as an excuse to justify some of our more primitive behavior."

"Exactly. You only *think* you're evil because that's what you've been told all your life. And yeah, I'm aware you were forced to do nasty things by Harley, things that have probably stayed with you, but for the moment, let's ignore that and focus on this *curse*."

What occurred to me, during my post-sex bliss, was: "It's not a *curse*, it's a *disease*." From everything I'd gathered, it worked like a bloodborne virus, like HIV or hepatitis. "And it doesn't even hurt you, not really. It's just another way of living. Yeah, we need to be careful, but so does anyone with a bloodborne disease, not just ours. It can be managed and it doesn't need to define who we are, nor dictate how we live our lives. You. Are. Not. Cursed. Period. Agreed?"

Tyson nodded slowly. "You're... right." It seemed like it had been a hard admission for him. "It's just a disease." I waited for him to say the words, but Bronn got there first.

"It's not a curse?"

"Better, but don't make it a question," I said.

He gave a single laugh. "Right. It's not a curse. I'm... not cursed. I'm just a shifter. It's a disease, nothing more." It sounded like he was still trying to convince himself, but it was a start.

They both seemed to understand, even if it might take a while before they truly believed it.

"But..." Bronn said, pain behind his eyes. "What we did..."

I nodded. I had some thoughts around that too.

"Look..." I sighed heavily. "What happened to me and the kid across the street, I know that's nothing like what you were probably forced to do by Harley, but it's something I feel bad about. I lost control, and I became something I didn't want to be. I have to live with that. I can't change what happened, but I don't have to wallow in it either. *That's* what I learned this week. I can't change the past, but I can work toward bettering myself, atoning for what I did, seeking to make the lives of those around me better. And that's exactly what you've been doing these last two weeks with me."

I looked at them intently for a long moment before going on. I wanted to make sure they understood this.

"You may have done bad things, but if you feel bad about them, then you're not really a bad person. You're only truly evil if you do bad things *and like it*. I'm pretty sure that wasn't the case for you, which means..." I paused to make sure they heard this. "You are *good* people who were forced to do *bad* things. And yeah, those things stay with you *because* you're good people. Now it's time to atone for what you did, even if that takes the rest of your lives. But do it *knowing* you are a good person at heart."

I drew a long breath and waited for that to sink in.

Tyson gave a sad, accepting smile. "You're right."

Wow, I'd expected more of an argument. Apparently, my tirade had worked!

Tyson sighed, then said, "It doesn't make the burden of what we did any easier to carry, but it does make my future seem just a little brighter."

"Yeah," Bronn agreed, nodding. Then he turned to me. "And even brighter with *you* in it." He smiled. "And if I ever falter, I know I just have to look at your example to know what's right and good. That's why we need you, Jane."

"You don't need me for that. You know the right thing to do," I whispered as I lay down again, snuggling between them. "You've always known." I found the perfect spot as the two of them curled around me, comforting and warm. "But I'm glad you *want* me."

"We do," Bronn said. "*I* do."

Tyson kissed my back. "I do, and I always will."

Wow, that had sounded a lot like wedding vows. I felt

compelled to add my own. "I want you too, all of you, with me, for the rest of my life."

"Good to hear," Colt said as he crept into the room. "The kids are just having a shower, then they're headed to bed. I've asked Kira and Dana to help them with anything." He stripped off his clothes and joined us on the bed.

"We were just vowing our undying devotion to Jane," Bronn said as if it were nothing.

"Yeah, I heard from the hall," Colt said, close behind Bronn. He reached over to rub my shoulder then cup my cheek affectionately. "I do," he whispered reverently.

And there it was. A union, sealed in love. Even if the rest of the world never knew about it, *we* knew, and that was all that mattered.

JANE

I TOOK A BREAK FROM COOKING AND PREPARATIONS ON Saturday and wandered outside. It promised to be a mild weekend, warm and sunny for this late in October, and several of my neighbors were setting up tables or shelters in their yards. But we were the only ones building something from scratch.

From the bits of it I could see so far, it looked like there would be a three-sided table, like a hexagon cut in half. Over the open end would be an archway with a sign, which was being designed and painted by Cassie. Bronn was helping my son, Milo, to sand down and assemble the various pieces, and Niko was there too, using power tools to cut the wood.

I watched for a long moment as Milo nodded, wide-eyed and curious, at what Bronn was saying.

"Now you see these grooves here," Bronn said. "That's called a dovetail joint. Niko's cut the wood so it will just slip together... like this, see?"

"And that will hold all on its own?" Milo asked.

"We'll put some glue in to make sure, but yeah, it should. We'll make the sign and stand using a cross-lap joint, but we won't use glue on that one so we can take it apart later. We could make this whole table without using any nails or screws, but we're not going to worry about that for some of the lesser joints."

I smiled as Bronn walked my son through the process.

Waiting until they seemed to be at a stopping point, I called to my son, "Milo, got a sec?"

He looked up and nodded. Bronn smiled over at me as Milo left and joined me.

"What's up, Mom?"

"Ready to talk about your wolf-report?"

He blinked. "Oh... yeah, right." He shrugged. "I've decided I don't really want to be a wolf right now."

"Oh?" I said, curious. "Why not?"

Milo shrugged again. "I guess I don't really have any good reason to?" he said, though it sounded more like a question. "I wanted to be a wolf to be strong, but... it's not a solution. It's not even that much of a short-cut apparently. I'd still be me, just a wolf. I'd heal faster, and I'd be a bit stronger, but really, wolf or not, I just need to work out to be stronger. So, for now, I'll wait and do my best to get stronger on my own. Tyson is helping me work out a bit, and Colt's self-defense training is hard. I don't think I'll be a shrimp for long."

"I don't think you're a shrimp at all," I said crouching — not that far down — to look him in the eye.

He rolled his eyes. "That's cause you're my mom. I'm scrawny, but I'm okay with it, because hopefully I won't be for long." He smiled. "I just need to work at it, no shortcuts." He shrugged again. "And if some day, I decide I want to be a wolf, then I *can* be, but since I can't go back from that, I think I'll just stay human for now."

I reached out to give him a reassuring shoulder-squeeze. "That's very adult of you, Milo. I'm proud of you."

He beamed. "Thanks, Mom. Can I go back to helping Bronn now?"

"Yup, go." I released him and he ran back to help with the booth.

A moment later, Danny from next door came running over to join Milo and Bronn. I looked over to see Terry following along a bit slower, and I stood to greet him.

"Hey," Terry said as he reached me. "You've got a lot of people helping out this year."

I nodded, still smiling. "The hope is that they'll help everyone here, if people will allow it."

"But..." He lowered his voice. "...they're all werewolves?"

"Yup." I shrugged. "I figure it will make telling the community easier if the community already accepts them as helpful neighbors first, though."

Terry nodded. "And they're... ah... all werewolves?"

It took me a moment to figure out why he was repeating himself that way. Then it sank in.

"No, some are werebears," I whispered. "Bronn, over there, is a werelion. Oh, and they prefer to be called shifters, not were-creatures. As for what I *think* you're asking... Petra is a bear shifter."

His eyes went wide. "A bear? Really?"

I watched him carefully. "Does that change how you feel about her?"

"I..." He blinked and blushed. "Ah..." He smiled and let out a laugh. "I honestly don't know. I mean, it's not like she walks around as a bear or becomes one when she gets angry, right?"

"Well... there is the slight possibility that extreme emotion, usually anger, might bring out her bear." I had to be honest. "But I don't think you plan on making her that angry, do you?"

"Ah... no. I certainly hope not."

"You want to talk to her?" I asked. "She's inside."

His blush deepened a little. "Ah, yeah... sure, if *she* wants to." He laughed, losing some of his tension. "I must seem like some love-struck fool to you."

"It's cute," I teased him. "And I'm pretty sure she wants to talk to you." I couldn't stop grinning. "But Terry, she may want to take it slow, like *snail* slow. I think I mentioned the guy she was with before was a brute, well... yeah. Trust me, it wasn't good for her at all. She's got some things to work out and may need some time."

He nodded, solemn. "You'd mentioned that before. Yeah, I understand." Then a hint of a smile returned. "I've waited a long time for the right woman to come along." He'd been interested in me for a while, but I'd never quite felt the same. "I'd be willing to wait a little longer for her."

I nodded and invited him in. "Petra!" I called.

"Yes alpha!" I heard the distant reply. I really needed to get them to stop calling me that so easily. It might come out in public.

Petra came up the stairs from the basement, then stopped when she saw Terry, and her blue eyes went wide.

"He's just here to talk, if you'd like," I said. I pointed Terry to the couches of my sitting area while I went to Petra. "I told him you may need time and may want to take it slow. I think he just wants to get to know you. So... talk... if you're comfortable with that."

She gave a shy smile and nodded, then went over to sit with him. She chose a spot not on the same couch, but still close to him, in another chair.

I wasn't needed in the kitchen for another few minutes, waiting on things in the oven, so I went back outside to watch Bronn with Milo and Danny. The boys were eating up everything Bronn had to say, listening intently, and I couldn't stop smiling. Slowly but surely, this strange new life of mine was starting to feel settled and comfortable.

When Kira called me back in, Terry and Petra were gone.

"The two lovebirds went out back to walk around the yard and talk in private," Kira said, seeing my confused look.

I nodded.

Dana added, "We've got things under control here, if you wanted to rest or tend to other matters."

The two of them really seemed to enjoy helping me with the cooking for the party, and I did have one thing I needed to attend to.

"Thanks, ladies." I smiled. I could get used to this extra help around the house.

I gathered a few things from my room, including my laptop, slipping them into a satchel, then texted Debbie Coles:

ME: *You have time to go over those ideas you'd mentioned?*
Debbie: *Now? Yeah, that works, come on over.*
Me: *On my way.*

I HEADED ACROSS THE STREET AND DEBBIE MET ME AT THE door. She had a moment of hesitation, but then she sighed and let me in.

That was progress.

I smiled, trying to be as passive and friendly as I could be, determined not to lose that little step forward.

"In here," Debbie said, leading me to the small office just inside the house, to the right.

I entered slowly, looking around. One wall was covered in shelving filled with books and curiosities, a beautiful collage of Debbie's experiences and education: everything from herbology to web design.

The far side of the room had been set up as an art studio. I knew Debbie painted, but I'd only ever seen a few of her pieces. She was generally quite reserved about showing them off, yet there had to be several dozen canvases stacked against the wall.

I could only see bits and pieces, but what I saw looked lovely. And the work in progress on the easel was stunningly beautiful. It looked to be a study of age: half

Debbie's own face, half her daughter's. The transition from one to the other was seamless, giving this slightly unsettling duality of energy versus experience.

"Over here," Debbie said, clearing her throat. "Please... don't look at that."

I turned to her. She'd gone to a desk beside the door and was pointing to another chair beside hers. She jiggled the mouse to wake up her computer.

"Why?" I asked, trying not to pry. "It's stunning."

She blinked at me. "You... really think so?" She didn't believe me, skepticism clear on her face.

"I do. You're an amazing artist."

She grunted. "Ah, thanks." It was clear she didn't believe me.

She pointed to the chair again, and I sat as her large monitor came to life. She toggled around quickly, bringing up the marketing material she'd outlined.

"The dog training business doesn't have a name, right?" she asked.

"No, not yet," I confirmed.

She clicked a few things and a logo appeared on the screen. "How about Ruff Love?"

I contained my guffaw, because the name was perfect, even if it reminded me a bit too much of my own bedroom habits. The logo had the name arched above the image of a dog's face, only it was split in half, one side snarling the other sedate and happy.

"That's perfect!" I said, amazed.

Debbie nodded. "I'll mock-up some sales tools: fliers and brochures and things with the information you sent me. But if you want a website, I'll probably need a bit more about the business. I'll email you with what would be needed."

"That would be great, thanks."

Debbie clicked around and that logo vanished. "And the construction business was Shining Stone, you said? An odd name, but easy to work with for images." She loaded several images for possible logos. "I wasn't sure which direction you wanted, so I tried a few different things."

There was one with a sculptor carving into a chunk of rock, another with a stone surrounded by an aura of light. The last one, and the one I liked best, was a stone archway, with the capstone at the top shining fourth and the name of the company inside the arch.

"Send those to me and I'll discuss them with Petra and Cassie, but I like the archway one."

Debbie smiled a bit. "Yeah, I think that's the best." She clicked around again, bringing up several mock-up brochures and things, even a sample webpage. "Given they're just starting up, and their actual contracting experience is limited, I thought to focus on the people who make up the company, make it a personal connection sort of thing. Talk about how they're reforming themselves, and their story and get the sympathetic vote. Then, once they've done a few things and have images and such, they can build a portfolio page."

"I like it, I'll talk to them about sending you more info on each partner."

Debbie nodded. "Now... about the cost."

I sighed. News on our little street spread fast. She knew I was out of work. We discussed some possible options for packages and pricing. I said I'd think about it, and she emailed me all the details. That was it.

I rose. "Thank you for all your hard work on this. I... and the pack... really appreciate it."

She grimaced and nodded. "I can't believe I'm helping a wolf pack, but—" She sighed. "You don't seem to be *that* bad." She quickly added a qualifier. "So far!"

I laughed. "Thanks, that means a lot coming from you." I turned, but not toward the door, but back to that painting. "Have you ever thought of selling your work? I think you could do really well. That's a beautiful piece."

"You want it?" Debbie asked, sounding a bit sarcastic.

"I couldn't afford it," I whispered.

She was silent for a moment and when I looked back at her, she was just blinking at me with a stunned look. "How much do you think it's worth?"

I shrugged. "Art is subjective and from what I've seen, usually it's the artist's name that dictates the price. But just on your skill alone, I'd still say that piece is worth thousands."

Her eyes went wide. "Really?"

I nodded. "Put it up on-line when it's done, see what interest you get."

"Maybe I will," she said, sounding thoughtful. "Thanks, Jane."

She saw me out, seeming distracted as she closed the door behind me.

I smiled as I returned home. Things might just work out with Debbie after all.

TYSON

Izzy and I spent the afternoon stopping by farmers' stands to find the perfect pumpkins for Jane's house. We didn't have a large budget, but we managed to find three large pumpkins and a handful of mini pumpkins and gourds.

We were on our way home, in Jane's car, when Izzy spoke up. She'd been friendly enough that afternoon, but her voice was just a little serious when she asked, "So... what do I call you?"

I tried not to tense up. This was it, *the talk*... about being a father, or a stepfather at least.

"I don't think I'm ready for 'Dad' yet," she said. "And 'Father' is way too formal. I wouldn't even call my own dad that unless I was trying to patronize him. And 'Daddy' is just *wrong*. I've heard the others call you beta, but... I think we should work on not saying that in public."

I relaxed a little as she spoke, settling into this conversation, glad she'd gone over those options.

"You've been calling me Tyson all afternoon. That works," I said.

She nodded, then tested it out. "Tyson... Colt... Bronn." She shrugged. "Yeah, I guess that works." A heavy sigh. "From no dads to three dads." After a moment she added. "And three moms, sort of, and a whole lot of new sisters and brothers and..." She blew out a breath, seeming just a bit overwhelmed.

"That's essentially what a pack is," I said slowly. "A family, of sorts." Feeling free enough to say so, I added, "Though we were a fucking dysfunctional family until we met your mother."

Izzy gave a snort of laughter.

I smiled.

After a moment she asked, "How does a pack work? Like, I know my mom's the alpha, but if it's a family, how does that work with the alphas and betas and things?"

"Well," I said, feeling confident since this was territory I was familiar with. "The alpha and the betas are sort of like the mother and father, the heads of the family. Though historically, female alphas or betas were pretty rare. Usually, an alpha rules by strength and fear and the betas are their enforcers. Everyone else is sort of like kids, but with a strange internal rank system that can vary from pack to pack. A senior female who is close to the alpha or a beta might be more like a mother. And older members tend to have more power than younger or newer members and can be a bit... ah... brutal about it. The one way a pack *isn't* like a family is that everything is harsh. Everything is a fight."

"I know some families like that," Izzy said softly.

I nodded at that. "Your mother has created a different sort of pack. She's allowing people to be whatever they want, and — more importantly — express themselves however they want. Strong women, like my mom and Dana Juarez would have had to be very careful in a normal pack or risk offending the alpha. But your mother encourages them to have their own opinion and doesn't chastise them for disagreeing with her. That's allowed them to really flourish, I think, and like you said, they're more like mothers to the pack now. Your mother is sort of like... the *number one* mother, and we betas... well, we're learning to be fathers. And someone like Niko, who doesn't really want a leadership role, he's..."

"Like a fun uncle," Izzy finished.

"Yeah, exactly."

"What about Cassie and Petra?" she asked, head tilted in thought. "They're older and could be like mothers. Cassie *is* a mother to Jake, but she still feels more like a sister for some reason."

"Yeah, they're like Niko, less dominant."

"Oh! So, like aunts, not sisters? Yeah! That makes sense." She then muttered something that a normal person probably wouldn't have heard, but I did. "Which means... I want to date my cousin?"

"Interested in Jake, are you?" I asked with a laugh.

"Ah... what? You heard that? Fuck." She huffed. "Is that... okay? If we're like a family, is it gross to date someone who's like your brother or cousin?"

"No," I said easily. "Yeah, we're structured like a family, but blood is still blood. If they're not related to you by blood, they're fair game. I'm pretty certain Winnie and Lucas are dating."

"Oh, they are," she said with a knowing nod. "I think they stop on their way back from work to... ah... make out before they get home."

That wouldn't surprise me. "And you like Jake?" I confirmed.

"He's... cute, and kind and... yeah."

"And your mother has talked to you about sex, condoms? I'm guessing you don't want to become a wolf right away, do you?"

"Tyson! Eww! Yes, we've had the talk, and yes, I know *all* the details. And no, Jake and I aren't doing *that* yet." She sighed. "And I don't know about being a wolf." She sounded confused. "Milo really wanted that, but I didn't, not at first. But then... I'm around the pack all the time and my mom's a wolf now... so it sort of feels strange *not* to be a wolf."

"Then feel strange," I said firmly. "What you shouldn't feel is compelled. You definitely *do not* have to be a wolf." I sighed. "I've recently been coming to terms with what it means to be a wolf, and I no longer think it's inherently evil, thanks to your mother, but still, it's not a choice to be taken lightly. It will change your life. As a human, you have a lot more opportunities out in the world. We wolves can't let anyone find out about us... at least not anyone we don't trust. So... consider that before you do anything."

She nodded. "I hadn't really thought of that. Thanks, Tyson."

And there it was, our first real father-daughter

conversation and neither of us had come away emotionally scarred.

I considered that a win.

We got back and unloaded our trove of pumpkins into the house.

That night, the pack had a big dinner together. Our meals were becoming a little less extravagant, not as much steak, since we were trying to conserve money, but what we ate didn't matter as much as who we ate with. There were laughs and stories of the day, and after dinner, I sat with Jane on my lap, her arms around my neck, just casual and close as the evening wore on.

It was comfortable. It felt *right*. My fated pull had been sated the night before and just being close to her was enough. We could enjoy each other's company without distractions, and I was finding I truly did enjoy just being with this woman more and more every day.

The pack was my family and Jane was my mate. And this new life of peace and freedom was far better than my wildest dreams for our pack.

And all because of Jane.

"Okay," Jane said, hopping off my lap. "It's time for the pumpkin carving competition, who's in?"

COLT

I WAS PRETTY GOOD WITH A KNIFE... BUT MY ARTISTIC SKILL was lacking. My jack-o-lantern was scary-as-fuck, but only because no face should look like that. Milo's was good, but Izzy's was amazing. She'd carved a headless horseman — riding a motorcycle instead of a horse, which was cool — carrying a flaming pumpkin head. And she even used shading and light to add depth, somehow peeling away layers of the pumpkin on the outside and varying the depth of the cut on the inside. That girl had some real artistic talent, and everyone unanimously picked hers to win the contest.

After that, we carefully carved or painted the smaller pumpkins. Jane roasted up the seeds with some spices, which was delicious, and there was cider or hot chocolate for all. It was a cozy evening, something I'd never experienced before... and I loved it.

When we went to bed with Jane curled up between the three of us, she breathed a contented sigh and whispered, "Thank you. That was a wonderful evening." She

snuggled back into my chest a bit more, Tyson in front of
her, and Bronn as a lion at the foot of the bed. "Today was
a good day." And those words meant everything to us
betas who lived to serve our alpha. Finally, we'd managed
to give her a fulfilling day.

The next day we were all up early with the final
preparations for the Halloween party. We set out a wide
variety of treats and delicacies on our newly made
display table. It was roughly "C" shaped, three sided with
rounded corners, all sanded to smooth perfection. The
front was covered and there were shelves below the
counter for storage. Two four-by-four wooden pillars held
a plank in place as a sign over the open back of the table.
Petra, Cassie, and Izzy had painted the sign which read:
Myers Magnificent Treats in fun, bold letters. In smaller
letters, on the sides, was: *Shining Stone Construction* and
Ruff Love Dog Training.

Not everyone in the pack wore a costume. The
women had the ones they'd purchased. Milo had a Thor
costume and had convinced me to wear only shorts and
be painted all green as the Incredible Hulk. Jane, in her
Little Red Riding Hood costume looked flirty and fun,
and I had trouble keeping my eyes off her. And whenever
our gazes met, she'd smile brightly and shake her head a
little. She'd been quite surprised that I'd agreed to let
Milo paint me green. But then... I loved how her gaze
grew just a little hungry when she saw me.

It hadn't been his idea, but Tyson was wearing a wolf
mask as his costume, that was it, wearing normal clothes
instead of anything else. It had been Winnie's idea, and
she'd bought the mask when she'd been out with Jane

but hadn't told Jane. Winnie had thought it would be perfect if Tyson was *the big bad wolf* to Jane's Red Riding Hood.

Bronn, like several others in the pack, had opted for no costume, helping out mostly behind the scenes.

All the neighbors were out, although it was clear who really liked and got involved in this event and who did it only because it was a community thing and they felt they had to.

The Longs and the Khans on either side of the open end of the street had lavish spreads, as much or more — which was hard to believe — than we did. The fae, Iris and Fern, also had a massive display of candies and treats and fawned over any kid who came by.

Terry Cooper was apparently a domestic god of a man, with a spread of rich foods, both sweet and savory. He also had a large bowl of fruit for those who were more health conscious. The Coleses and Herreras were moderately invested with smaller spreads of less decadent delights. The Herreras had a large pavilion tent, which they were struggling to put up over their table, making me wonder if Elena Herrera, who was quite pregnant, didn't want to be out in this unusually warm October sun for too long?

Lastly, there were the Pearsons, the Jacobses, and the Holts. They all had small tables of mostly store-bought goods. The Holts' had been set up by Erik's mother — a small TV table, that was it — before she'd left for work, and it was manned by Erik, who couldn't stop staring at Jane. So far, he hadn't said anything about her being a wolf or monster. At least, not that we knew of.

I smiled as I looked back at our display, not only the bounty of food, but that gorgeous counter and sign. And it seemed others had noticed too, drawn to our little stall. I sighed, and for a moment, I felt completely at peace. It wasn't something I'd felt often in my life, but now that the old pack was gone and Jane was in charge and things were starting to settle, I was finally allowing myself to relax into this new life.

My job, for the moment, was to mind Milo, since our costumes sort of went together anyway. The kid was impatiently waiting for his friends to be done helping their families set up so they could go around together, but he was also distracted by something else. When I looked to where he was staring... I thought I understood.

Debbie Coles, the witch across the street, hadn't done much for her costume, just thrown on a hat and a cape as a stereotypical witch, which I found just a little ironic. Her daughter, Kathy, however, had a rather elaborate costume as Scarlett Witch. Milo couldn't seem to take his eyes of her as she helped her mother set up.

I knelt next to the little man. "You like her?" I whispered.

He pulled his gaze away from the young woman, blushing. "Who?" He feigned ignorance.

"Yeah, sure, I didn't see a thing," I said, about to stand again when Milo grabbed my hand.

"Wait."

I raised a brow in question.

"Okay, so... if I did like *someone*, what would I say?"

I chuckled. "Today makes it easy. Just go over there and tell her you like her costume."

"I really do, I can't believe she chose a superhero like I did. I wonder if she likes the Avengers."

"It even sounds like you have a good follow-up question." I patted the boy on his shoulder.

"Yeah, but... then what?"

"You could ask her if she made the costume or bought it, and if she made it, then tell her how good she did. Then... see what happens. Talk and be honest. Be yourself."

Milo sighed, looking at his costume's fake muscles. "My puny self."

Yet, I'd seen how hard the kid had been working. Every day he got up early and ran out into the forest to lift logs, then he trained with me a bit before school. Sometimes we'd train in the evenings too. It had only been a few days, but the kid was starting to get a bit of muscle on him. And I knew he had to be sore every day, but he'd never complained once.

"Look, Milo, if she doesn't like you for you, you don't want to be with her. If she's just looking for muscles, that's superficial."

"Yeah... I guess." He didn't sound convinced.

I tried again. "Let me put it this way. I know you've been working hard. If you keep that up, then by the time you're sixteen you're going to be ripped. Now... do you want a girl who just wants you for your muscles and will leave you for a guy who happens to be bigger? Or do you want a girl who was with you *before* you got ripped, who likes you for you and just really appreciates the work you've put in to get fit?"

He nodded. "Yeah, I guess you're right." He scoffed

though. "It just doesn't *sound* right coming from someone as big as you."

I laughed. "Milo, I've only loved two women in my life, and both of them didn't love me for my size, they loved me for who I was on the inside, even if that wasn't something I liked to show people. Trust me, love is about much more than how you look. It's about how you feel when you're with someone and how you make them feel."

He nodded. "Yeah, yeah, I got it."

I didn't think he did, not yet... but hopefully it wouldn't be too long until he did. "So, are you going to go talk to her?"

"Will you come with me?"

I had to keep an eye on him anyway so... "Sure."

With that, he squared his shoulders and marched across the street, like some soldier going to war.

"Hey there... ah... Kathy," Milo said waving as we got close. The young woman looked over at him and gave a curious smile as Milo pushed on. "I like your costume. It looks really good! Do you like Marvel stuff?"

She shrugged but smiled. "Never read the comics, but I like the movies and shows." She sounded excited. "That's a great Thor costume, but..." She looked up at me. "The hulk really should have dark hair."

I laughed.

"I couldn't get him to dye it," Milo said, sounding disappointed. I was okay with some skin paint, but hair-dye was where I drew the line. "Did you... ah... make your costume?" Milo asked.

"Yeah, it took forever!" And the young woman began

going into detail about her process. I didn't think Milo cared much about that, but he listened intently.

"Hey Milo!" Another boy came running up. This one had dark skin and was wearing a spider-man costume that was mostly black, with a coat and a hood. It looked well made.

"Oh hey, Cal." Milo said. Ah... so this was Calvin Long, the youngest son of Bree, Jane's friend at the open end of the street.

Calvin looked at Kathy and asked, "You going to come around with us?"

"Can I, Mom?" The young woman asked.

Debbie nodded. "Yes, but don't eat too much all at once."

"I think we're going over to Danny's place, so I'll get some fruit," Kathy said to appease her mother.

"And I'll be keeping an eye on all of 'em," I said.

"I don't know if that makes me feel better or worse," Debbie muttered.

The three kids ran off across the street to the Coopers' place. I followed, lagging behind a little to let them have their freedom.

Terry Cooper nodded to me from a distance as the kids arrived and joined up with his son Danny, starting in on the fruit. Petra, in her bunny costume, was on her way over to Terry's booth as well.

"Hey Terry, can you give us a hand with this?" Hector Herrera called from next door. He was struggling to put up that large pavilion-tent. I looked back at Terry, who gave me a *I've got to stay here* look. So, I shrugged. Time to be neighborly. I figured the kids were safe with Terry for the moment. I called to Milo, "Just let me know if you're going anywhere." He nodded. Then I turned to Hector. "I can help with that."

"I... bet you can," the small Hispanic man said, blinking at me. "Here, hold this post while I secure the rope line."

I did as asked, keeping an eye on the kids, and otherwise enjoying myself on this beautiful October day.

Then I heard the distant sounds of engines approaching. I was instantly on edge. Everyone in the community was here, so whoever this was, they were an outsider. And for some reason, that got my hackles up.

TYSON

My heart pounded and my throat turned dry. If it was any hotter out here, I'd have been in a full-on sweat. Nervous was too light a word for how I felt as I approached the Rosses' house, so I could apologize to the fae.

They had several tables set up, laden with all manner of treats, and the two women flitted about making everything look perfect.

The smaller of the two, with bubble-gum pink hair, looked up as I arrived. Her expression instantly turned sour. "Oh... what do you want, *wolf*?"

"Be kind, Fern!" the other said with a swat to her partner's shoulder. "They're helping Jane." She scrutinized me as she said, "They can't be *that* bad...?" As if she was daring me to prove otherwise.

"Jane I can accept," Fern said. "But the others? Well, that pregnant one doesn't seem that bad, and the other young woman who's helping her, and..."

"I've come to apologize," I said over top of the two women.

"Oh?" Iris said hopefully.

Fern glared at me suspiciously, though. "For what? What did you do?"

"Nothing... recently," I said. Okay, here goes. I drew in a long breath. "But... back before we met Jane, our pack ran in your woods. We shifted and hunted every night. I'm assuming these woods are under your protection and care. I— *We* had no clue there were fae around." I grimaced. "Even if we had, we probably wouldn't have done anything differently, but I know *now*, and as the ranking member of the pack left from those days, I wanted to apologize for anything we may have done, any plants or animals we may have harmed. I know you care deeply for nature, and I'm hoping we can all live peacefully now. But I wanted to apologize for the past before we tried to move into the future." There, I'd said it.

Fern was still eyeing me with those violet, pink-flecked eyes. "We were *very aware* of your pack tromping around the forest," she scolded.

"Yes, but you didn't harm much," Iris said with a shrug. "The damage is easily mended and the forest will be well again in a year or two."

All three of us kept an eye out for anyone who might approach and overhear us. This wasn't conversation for humans to hear. Yet the only one's nearby were the Pearson's on the other side of the park, and they weren't close enough to hear anything. No one else was wandering around yet, so we were safe.

"If there is anything I or my pack can do to help the forest recover, please let me or Jane know, okay?"

Fern made a sound. "Like we'd ask you."

Iris gave Fern a look. "We'll... consider it, thank you. Was there anything else?"

There was. "Actually, yes. I don't know if Jane mentioned it, but we're looking to help her out any way we can, including financially. One of the ideas we had was to do survival camps in the woods, teaching people — small groups only — how to live off the land and do ethical hunting, using all parts of whatever they caught. But we would never consider doing it if we didn't have your permission." Seeing two skeptical faces, I hurried on. "We'd make sure to use the same site every time, so we're not abusing different parts of the forest, and we'd clean up after ourselves, using as little of the natural resources as possible. We'd also make sure we weren't hunting any one animal too much to keep the ecosystem balanced."

"Absolutely not!" Fern said flatly.

"Perhaps..." I could tell Iris was trying to give me the benefit of the doubt, yet it was clearly pushing the limits of her kindness. "Please give us a full write up of your proposal. Then, if you agree to abide by any adjustments we make to those plans, *maybe* we'd consider it... right Fern?"

Fern glowered. "Maybe," she said with spite.

That... wasn't as bad as I'd thought. "I can live with that, thank you. I'll draw up some plans and send them over. Thank you, ladies." I turned to go.

"Wait!" Iris called. I turned back, curious what other

conditions they might have. "Aren't you going to try some?" She waved her hand over the many trays of sweets and goodies."

"You wouldn't mind sharing with a wolf?" I asked with a laugh.

"I mind," Fern muttered.

"Not at all," Iris said with a smile.

"Then... I might just try some. What do you have?" I asked, then I listened intently as Iris went over the various goodies. Sharing food with fae was *never* a good idea, but I wanted to show them I trusted them, and this seemed like a good place to start.

As Iris spoke, I heard the approach of vehicles in the distance and a part of me tensed. It didn't sound like motorcycle engines, which was good, but still...

A feeling in my gut warned me something was wrong.

JANE

I left Cassie in charge of the booth, deciding it was time to talk to Erik Holt.

He'd been staring at me all morning. And as much as I was fairly certain he hadn't told anyone what had happened, it was also clear he wasn't comfortable with me being so close.

He tensed as I made my way across the street, but I smiled and waved, and once I was close enough, I whispered. "I just want to talk. I'm sorry about what happened."

His expression seemed to leap around, jarred with emotions: suspicion and fear mixed with uncertainty and confusion. Then he seemed to settle on terror, shying away from me.

"So... that was... real?" he breathed.

Ah. So he'd thought it some nightmare perhaps? Had I just made everything worse?

I took a long slow breath in and out. "Erik, I'm not..." *a monster?* Except I *was* a monster, or at least, I could be.

"I'm..." Fuck, why was this so hard? I'd just wanted to apologize and make peace. "What will make this better?" I asked.

His eyes darted around. No one else was nearby. The Longs were still setting up their stuff on their lawn. "What... *are* you? What *was* that?" he hissed, keeping quiet.

Maybe it was time for the truth. Erik deserved better than uncertain nightmares... although I didn't really want to have this conversation with so many people out and about.

Fuck it. Here goes.

I knelt next to Erik. "Do you believe in the supernatural?" I asked.

He shook his head vehemently.

"Well... you do now!" I said as a bit of a joke. "Look, I know this is a shock. I only found out a couple of weeks ago, but apparently magic and other things are real. I'm... a werewolf. A wolf shifter to be exact, only it turns out I'm special — not that I want to be — and I look even scarier when I shift." His eyes were wide with confused terror. I hurried on. "I didn't mean for that to happen. Our forms can... slip sometimes when we're really upset. I'd had a very bad day and I had a moment of weakness. I'm *so sorry* Erik. I'm no threat to you. I'm not going to hurt you. We only want to keep to ourselves and keep each other safe and—"

"Were...wolf?" he stuttered out.

Oh... he was stuck back there.

Yeah, I didn't blame him for that.

"Yes," I said. This time I waited to see if he had more questions.

He stammered for a while, his brain clearly not wanting to make sense of this. "I... You..." he tried, but nothing came out after that.

I sighed, understanding. I'd had to see Tyson as a wolf before I'd believed any of this. And Erik had seen me, but... if he still thought that a dream then... who knew what he was thinking right now.

As Erik tried to sort this out, my ears caught the distant sound of a vehicle. *Odd.* The next moment, I was surprised to realize I could hear two distinct engines, not just one.

Very odd.

One car heading this way might just be a courier dropping something off ... though it was Sunday and that wasn't likely. But more than one...?

It might be a convoy of lost campers. It wouldn't be the first time that had happened. I tried to tune it out and focus on Erik.

"What matters is that I'm sorry and that I'm no danger to you, okay?" I whispered.

Those two car engines drew closer, definitely heading this way, but then I heard the crunch of tires on gravel. They had pulled over. From what I could tell, they weren't far away.

The engines stopped.

I heard doors opening and closing. They were probably just taking a break and checking their phones for directions. But then I caught a strange scent on the air.

I sniffed, distracted by this odd odor. I'd smelled it

before somewhere, as unfamiliar as it was. It tickled at my mind, bothering me to no end. *What is that scent?*

It came to me in a rush, memories flashing in my mind. I'd been afraid, feeling threatened by the bikers on my street. I'd gone to a gun shop and *that's* what this smelled like...

Gun oil.

Gun oil!

I shot to my feet and spun around in time to see a man with a machine gun come into view at the end of the street followed by a lot more, at least twenty!

Mrs. Khan screamed, followed by more cries of alarm, until a rapid-fire burst of bullets silenced everyone.

"Nobody move!" one of the men shouted.

We all froze.

The gunmen, whoever they were, kept moving. Two ran over to grab Mr. and Mrs. Khan, threatening them with their weapons. Another jogged to Bree and Parker Long. Bree threw her arms up in surrender, but Parker must have taken a little too long, and he was a big young man, imposing. A loud shot rang out and Parker screamed in pain, shot in the leg.

"Let that be a lesson!" the first man called out. "We don't want to hurt you but resist us or try to run and we won't hesitate to shoot. Got it?"

And as I stood there, frozen, I realized I'd missed any chance I'd had to act. Maybe, if I'd reacted as soon as I'd identified that odor or seen the men, I might have been able to do something, but now, with people at gunpoint, anything I did would only result in them getting hurt or worse.

"What do they want?" Erik said from behind me. He still sounded terrified, but I didn't think it was because of me anymore.

"I don't know," I whispered, also curious why armed men had interrupted our quiet Halloween celebration.

"We're only here for four of you: Jane, Tyson, Colt, and Bronn. If those four surrender, we'll leave the rest of you alone!"

Fuck.

A cold ball of dread formed in my stomach.

Given that very specific list, I now had a good idea who had sent these thugs: Brick. He couldn't win against me in a fair fight, so he'd started a fucking war!

BRONN

BRICK WAS BEHIND THIS. HE'D HIRED SOME GOONS TO DO his dirty work for him, and he knew just how to thwart us. By taking civilians hostage, he limited our options and ensured we couldn't shift, at least, not if we didn't want to be discovered. We had to surrender... or at least appear to.

I had to think quick, but I knew these gunmen wouldn't let us stall for long. Already more of them were filtering down the street.

I locked eyes with Jane, across the street, and she nodded to me, face grim. She'd surrender.

"I'm Jane!"

Both Jane and I were stunned at the proclamation... which had come from Dana Juarez.

I was baffled for a moment, but then realized what she was doing. These gunmen probably didn't know Jane by sight. I doubted Brick had a picture of her. If anything, they had a rough description and Dana would fit that description. Her skin tone was a bit darker than Jane's, but other than that, they were roughly the same height and build with dark hair and brown eyes.

"I'm Tyson!" Tyson called from the far end of the street.

And I wasn't going to let anyone take my place, so I quickly proclaimed, "I'm Bronn."

"I'm Colt," Colt said.

He whispered a few quick words with Petra, who was with Terry and the kids, even though Petra didn't need anyone to tell her to protect them. Then Colt and Tyson began moving up toward me and Dana.

I glanced down to the space beneath our booth's counter. After that first scream, Jake had grabbed Izzy and ducked under the booth with her. The booth wouldn't protect them if shooting broke out, but Jake had his back to the gunmen, shielding Izzy.

"Stay," I hissed at him.

He nodded. He'd protect Jane's daughter.

The others in the pack milled about, moving slowly so as not to draw attention, but making sure they were between the gunmen and Izzy as well.

I walked slowly, Dana beside me, allowing Tyson and Colt to catch up. The gunmen didn't seem to mind the four of us taking our time or gathering as a group.

Yet, our slow pace meant that some of the armed men made it to the Holts' house and two of them took Jane and Erik hostage.

Jane gave the group of us a long stare, unable to do much more. But I thought I understood the thought behind that look. *Do what you have to. Free the others. I've got these two.*

After that, the four of us hurried toward the gunmen, so they wouldn't be able to take any more hostages.

"Plan?" Colt breathed, voice hushed. We'd hear him, but anyone else wouldn't.

"Get close, shift, free the hostages, take out the gunmen. It's not great, but it's all we got," Tyson whispered, and he was right.

The big question was, had Brick told these gunmen about shifters?

He couldn't have turned them. The next full moon wasn't for another two weeks. But he could have told them about us. If he had, they might be expecting us to shift.

Except telling humans was never easy and few people believed us. I had to hope Brick hadn't told them. That meant, when we shifted, they'd probably freak out and we might have a moment to overpower them.

"Dana," Tyson hissed. "You get the Khans. Bronn, you have the Longs. Colt and I will get as many of the rest as we can."

"Stop there!" the lead man said when we were still a dozen feet away. Then he gave a cocky smile and shook his head. "I didn't think it would be that easy, but fuck, here you are." He raised his weapon. "Kill 'em, boys!"

We reacted instantly, clothes shredding as our hybrid forms burst forth.

The reaction of the gunmen made it clear they hadn't known about shifters. The men screamed, obviously terrified. Some dropped their weapons, some fired, all were wide-eyed and panicked.

Dana leaped one way, I went the other. Luckily, the

two guarding Breanna and Parker Long aimed their guns at me — not the hostages — and fired. Bullets hurt us in our hybrid form, but it was more like a nasty bug-bite. It would sting and swell and there might be a little blood, but not much. If they were using armor-piercing rounds, that was a different story, but these two weren't. The bullets bounced off me, stinging like hell, but not stopping me.

The downside of this plan was that we'd been forced to come out to the neighbors, and not in a friendly way. Breanna and Parker were also terrified and screaming as I landed beside the first gunman. One swipe of my claws removed his forearm. I didn't want to kill anyone if I didn't have to. That one fell, screaming louder as two more shots from the other pinged off me. I was at the second man in an instant and he too lost his arm.

"Go! Get inside, hide!" I shouted at Breanna and Parker.

I was scary-as-fuck at the moment, so they listened to me. Breanna helped her hobbling son quickly get to their house.

I spun to see how the others were doing. Everything was chaos. The gunmen were screaming as Tyson and Colt moved through them. The rest of the pack had shifted too, hurrying to help.

But when I turned to check on Jane, something else caught my eye. Down, at the far end of the street, three wolves and a bear were sprinting out of the forest.

I cursed as I realized this whole thing had been a distraction.

JANE

I'D HOPED I'D NEVER NEED TO USE MY HYBRID AGAIN, BUT IF anything warranted it, this was it. So, when the others had attacked, I'd shifted, tearing out of my costume. It had been far easier than I'd expected. I'd already been harboring a seething resentment and hatred for these gunmen. They'd shattered the peace of what should have been a fun day. I'd simply given in to that rage and let my beast out.

I had no clue how strong my hybrid was, so I tried to restrain myself when I spun on my attacker with a back-handed strike. The bone-armor on the back of my massive hand struck his skull and sent him flying into Erik's hot-rod car. When I reached for the other man, my claws sank into his shoulder, chest, and back far too easily. I only meant to yank him away from Erik, instead I sent him flying into the Holts' garage door, leaving a dent in the metal.

Fuck! I hope he's not dead. As much as these men needed to be stopped, I didn't want to kill anyone.

"Run, get inside!" I said to Erik as I shielded him from any random gunfire. Already wide-eyed and panicked, he nodded and bolted for his front door.

And from the corner of my eye, I saw the four animal shapes running out of the forest toward the Pearsons' home.

Oh, hell no!

I launched myself down the street with as much force as I could, surprised to find myself flying over asphalt and lawns. I saw Jake helping Izzy get to my house. He wasn't a hybrid or even a wolf, just shielding her body with his. Brave boy. I also caught sight of Petra — as a bear-hybrid — protecting Terry and the kids as they fled into his house.

Good.

I landed on the Herreras' lawn, having made it almost all the way to Brick and his cronies. They were just about to reach the Pearsons' house. Luckily, James and Carry Pearson had already been fleeing for their front door.

They managed to get inside and close the door, which was good because the Herreras were still exposed. Hector was trying to help his very pregnant wife Elena up from where they'd both been huddled behind their food-stand, but it was clear they were both shocked and terrified.

"Get her inside as quick as you can. I'll protect you!" I shouted at them, trying to make my words clear, but that was very hard with this wolfen mouth.

Then a massive wall of thorny brambles rose up between me and the Herreras. A second one sprouted up, blocking the door to the Pearsons' house. That stunned me for a moment, until I saw Iris and Fern, just outside their house, holding hands between them with their other arms outstretched. So... *that's* what fae could do?

I nodded to them and they darted inside as I headed for Brick and the others.

The four shifters spread out, shifting to hybrids. Tank's bear-hybrid stood head and shoulders above the others... but I still looked *down* at him, a full head taller. And it was clear the group had no clue what to make of me. They'd seen my dire wolf form when I'd fought Brick, but not my hybrid, which was an order of magnitude scarier, what with all the exposed bone-armor and the bone-spikes jutting out from more places than I cared to count.

"Fucking hell!" I heard Ginny say through her fanged mouth.

"We can take her!" Brick snarled.

Tank just roared a bear's bellow at me, exposing yellowed teeth.

I roared back, louder, and sounding like nothing I'd ever heard before. All four of them flinched back.

Hell, I'd even scared myself!

"Let's *end* this," I growled.

As much as I hated it, this would be a fight to the death. These villains had left me no choice. I'd told them to go away, and they hadn't. Which meant they wouldn't. They wanted what I had, and it was clear they weren't going to stop trying to get it. Not unless I stopped them. The thought sickened me.

The question was... could one dire wolf beat three wolves and a bear?

We were about to find out.

Yet before we began, another roar sounded nearby, one that was neither wolf nor bear, but a lion.

Tank chuckled. "I've got the pussy. This'll be fun!" He broke off to meet Bronn, who charged toward us.

Be careful my beautiful beta, I prayed, then set myself for a fight.

The three wolves had me surrounded. I had to spin this way and that to try to keep them all in sight. Yet, they knew time was on my side. The longer they delayed, the greater the chance one of my other betas — or another member of the pack — would come to my aid.

Brick glanced at Ginny, nodding, I spun in that direction. She snapped her jaws at me, but it had been a feint. Brick and Sonny rushed in. I swung a hand back at Brick, but he ducked under it and came in low, tackling my hips and legs as Sonny leaped onto my back.

I staggered, but it was a testament to how much bigger and stronger I was that I didn't fall. And I didn't think they liked what they found when they tried to bite me. Sonny's jaws clamped onto my shoulder, but he was only gnawing on the exposed bone, his teeth unable to get much purchase. It stung, but more like a housecat biting me, not a full-grown wolf-man.

I reached back and grabbed his shoulder, tearing him off me and tossing him to the ground. He landed with a thud, stunned.

Brick had gone for my leg, but his jaws only scraped off my bone armor. I swiped at him, but he ducked in close to me and raked his claws over my stomach. He managed to find a break in my armor, scratching deep, but he didn't have time to take advantage of the injury. He danced away as I struck at him again.

The wound on my abdomen stung, bleeding a little, but it wouldn't slow me down.

Ginny darted in, biting my ankle, trying to trip me. She shook her head and twisted her body to no avail. I was too big, too solid. I kicked her away. She yelped as she landed and rolled.

Round one had gone to me. My armor was too thick for their claws and fangs. I had a few weak spots, but mostly... I was a bad-ass bitch.

Time to put this form through its paces.

I went on the offensive, lunging at Brick. He threw himself out of the way. I still managed to catch him with a back-handed strike, which sent him tumbling. My arms were longer than both of us had expected.

I spun toward Sonny, who'd just gotten up from where I'd thrown him. I didn't think I'd grabbed his shoulder that hard, but he was bleeding from where my claws had marked him. Raw terror flashed in his eyes as I swatted at him. He dove away, but one of my claws scored a long line up his back.

Something hit my back, making me stumble a couple steps. I threw myself backward to the ground, landing with all my weight on whoever had tried to ambush me. When I rolled away, I saw Ginny, half-crushed and bleeding from multiple gashes across her torso. I guessed I had some spikes or ridges on my back, which had torn into her.

She was whining, twitching, clearly in a bad way, dying. I should let her suffer, but even in this form I apparently still had a modicum of mercy. At this point, I could at least give her a quick death.

I turned toward Brick and Sonny, making sure they saw this, as I said, "You had your chance to run, to live, to get away from all of this, but you chose death instead." I swiped my claws across Ginny's torso, shoulder to hip, tearing through flesh and bone with equal ease. Blood and organs spilled out. She went still.

Brick and Sonny gaped, horrified.

A part of me shuddered with revulsion, disgusted at what I'd done. Yet my sickness was subsumed by rage at what these villains had made me do.

Sonny turned to run, but I leaped with lightning speed, passing over him and spinning in the air to land in front of him. He hadn't expected that. Nor did he expect my claws across his throat, tearing away almost all of his neck. He fell to the side, dead.

Brick knew he couldn't escape, so he leaped for my throat. His jaws clamped around my neck, claws raking over my chest in a savage, last-ditch effort. He found a few soft spots, opening my flesh, but the vital areas were covered in too much bone. His teeth sawed over my throat, and he even managed to tear away one plate of protective bone — which hurt like hell — but by then I had him. Grabbing the back of his neck, I pulled him off me.

I didn't know what he saw in my eyes, but he wet himself as he thrashed and struggled in vain to get out of my grip.

I squeezed the hand around his neck, sinking my

claws into his throat. Blood poured out as he gasped and flailed until he went limp. Then I tossed him away.

My revulsion rose, almost overwhelming my rage... but I wasn't done.

Tank still fought Bronn. Only, when I looked around, I couldn't see them. That large bramble wall was still jutting out in front of the Herrera's house, perhaps they'd fought their way behind that?

I ran around the wall to find a scene of utter butchery and bloodshed. Tank was dead, ripped to pieces, a bloody mess, not even recognizable as man or bear or whatever. Bronn didn't look much better. He'd lost his hybrid form, a man again, naked and bloody, struggling to breathe. Petra — as a woman, not a bear — held Bronn's head in her lap. She too was covered in blood.

Seeing no threat — even the fighting with the gunmen up at the mouth of the street seemed to be done — I let my hybrid go and shrunk back to myself.

Instantly, my stomach rebelled. I'd seen — and been a part of — too much bloody violence today and the smell of gore around me made me want to vomit. By some miracle, I managed to keep myself from being sick as I ran to Bronn.

"What happened?" I asked Petra.

"I... he..." Petra seemed traumatized, stammering. And it was only then that I realized what was wrong with this picture. She had far too much blood on her. She'd been a part of this fight too. "I couldn't... he... I..." She was in shock or something. A moment later the façade broke and she began sobbing.

I huddled in close, one arm around Petra, a hand on Bronn's cheek.

"I'm here," I said softly to both of them. "Just... hold on." But I didn't know what to hold on for. As shifters, we could heal most wounds, but Bronn's injuries looked like they'd kill him before his shifter healing would do anything. We could try to bandage him, but something told me that by the time I left and returned with enough bandages, it would be too late. Nothing short of a miracle would save him.

"Get out of my way, I can help!" The woman's voice was surly, as if she didn't *want* to help. I looked up to see Debbie Coles standing over us with an armload of jars. She knelt, setting everything down. "Get back!" she hissed. "I can heal him, but you're both in the way!"

Heal him?

It took my brain a moment to understand.

Heal him... with... magic... because... she's a witch!

"Oh, thank you! Yes, please." I helped get Petra away from Bronn. She couldn't seem to move. And once we were clear, I bundled her in my arms, smearing myself in the blood that covered her. She clung to me, weeping on my shoulder.

"It's over now," I whispered to her. It was just a platitude, but then I realized, it really *was* over. After far too much violence and bloodshed, the looming threat of Brick and his gang was finally gone.

I found myself overcome with emotion — relief and horror, revulsion and triumph — and wept with Petra.

JANE

WE'D BEEN INCREDIBLY LUCKY. NONE OF OUR OWN HAD died. There were injuries abounding and many of the pack — and some of my neighbors — would be laid up for a while, but we had all survived. Even the attackers had mostly survived, only three gunmen — and Brick's four shifters — had died.

But that was also a problem.

"We have to call the police!" Marnie Jacobs yelled at Tyson as I arrived at the end of the street.

After Debbie had healed Bronn, Terry and Hector Herrera had taken him to Terry's house to rest. Terry had returned with some of his clothes for me and Petra. They didn't fit us, but we were covered at least. I hoped he never wanted them back, because they were probably stained with blood now. Terry had taken Petra inside and he still had the neighborhood kids at his place as well. I'd quickly stopped in at my house to get some shoes, but otherwise I'd come straight here.

I needed to get this situation sorted out.

"And tell them what?" Tyson asked Marnie. His voice was mostly calm but edged with more than a little exasperation. "I'm assuming you saw what happened? We're werewolves, how are you going to explain that to the cops?"

"I..." Marnie stammered, her eyes a bit wild. It was clear she had seen what had happened, but her mind hadn't fully come to terms with it yet. "I... I don't... know? But... we can't just leave these people here."

"And we can't let them go!" This from Mr. Khan. He looked shaken, and also a bit wild-eyed after the events of the morning. "They attacked us, they need to be..."

"Punished?" Colt offered. The big man looked rough, covered in grape to plum sized welts. He looked at the villains in question, who were tied up with an assortment of household items. Several of them had lost hands, which had been crudely bandaged. Others had nasty slashes and scrapes. They looked... like they'd been mauled by wolves.

"Something tells me they've been punished enough," Colt said. "Especially since none of our own were killed, only hurt."

"But they need a hospital or something, don't they?" This from Mrs. Khan. She sounded conflicted. I understood that sentiment. She was trying to be kind... to people who'd held her hostage.

"They really do," Nico Juarez said. He was tending to them. "Some of these men may die if they don't get some additional help soon."

I wondered if Debbie might heal them. I checked over my shoulder to find her not far away, approaching us.

"Could you...?" I asked.

"No," she said bluntly. "I can't. And nobody can know I helped you. I only did that because you and your *men* saved us all. But I can't help anyone else. These guys already know about... *you*. They can't know about me and my daughter." She kept her voice low, just for me.

I nodded. I understood. But that meant these men really did need a hospital.

Fuck it. "Someone call nine-one-one," I said.

"But—" Tyson tried.

"Call them now!" I insisted, staring the man down. I was not in the mood for another fight of any kind, and I think he sensed that. He nodded.

"I'll do it," Melody Khan said, pulling out her cell. "What should I say?"

"As little as possible," I advised her. "Say... wild wolves attacked, people are hurt. That's good enough."

"No one's going to believe—" Dana Juarez tried.

"Yes, they will!" I insisted. "Because that's the only thing that make sense!" I strode over to the captured gunmen. "I'm at my wits' end, so I'm only going to say this once. Do any of you want to go to jail?"

Heads shook all around.

"Then as long as you cooperate, it's your lucky-fuck-ing-day. Here's the story. You're a group of hunters. I don't know why you were hunting with machine-guns, but you'll come up with something to explain that. You spotted a pack of wolves about to attack our street party and you began shooting. But some of the shots missed and hit some of us. And none of us are going to press charges for any of this as long as you keep to that story.

Where are the wolves now? They ran off. You hit a few, but you didn't kill any of them."

"No one's going to believe that. And it's only going to get animal control out here," Tyson hissed.

"They'll believe it because it's the only thing that explains all of this." I waved my arm at everything around me. "And animal control can come, but they're not going to find anything, are they? They'll give up after a while."

None of this was perfect, but it was the best we could hope for. I turned back to the gunmen. "You good with that story? If not, we can just kill you now."

"Jane, no!" Mrs. Khan shouted, covering her phone. She lifted it again. "What? Oh nothing, yes, I'll stay on the line."

I didn't flinch. "You don't go to jail. We don't get exposed. That's the deal," I said. "Take it or leave it." Then I knelt close to them. "And trust me, if you try to tell anyone what actually happened here, no one is going to believe you. They'll think you're insane. And on the off chance they *do* believe you, *we'll know* it was *you* who spilled our secret and we'll hunt *all of you* down." I made a show of sniffing the air. "We have your scent. We can find you *anywhere*." I took a long moment to make eye contact with each of them. "So, keep each other quiet, because if even one of you spills our secret, you'll all suffer for it. Got it?"

They all nodded, clearly terrified of me. I didn't know how much of me-as-a-beast they might have seen, but perhaps it didn't matter. I was an angry woman in their face after they'd faced a pack of werewolves so perhaps anything would have seemed scary.

I rose. "There, it's done."

"I still think this is a bad idea," Dana Juarez said. When I looked over at her, she was shaking her head, a grimace on her face. "But I don't have a better one that doesn't include killing these bastards." It was clear she thought *that* was the best option.

"No more killing," I said, my voice finally losing some of its strength. "We're all done with killing, *forever,* got it?" Mostly, I was hoping that would apply to me. I'd killed four people now and that was four too many.

Tyson drew me aside. "We can't let anyone get their hands on the bodies of Brick and the others. DNA and blood tests..." He let that hang.

He was right. "Go talk to Iris and Fern quickly, see if they can do something about the bodies. They'll make good fertilizer, I'm sure." Tyson nodded and ran to do as I'd asked.

I would have returned to the others but being reminded of the bloody carcasses — those I'd killed — got me feeling rather ill. "I... need to..."

I strode away swiftly, heading for my back yard. I didn't know why I couldn't let anyone see this, but I couldn't. Colt followed me and was the only one who saw me throw up once I was out of sight. And once it started, it wouldn't stop. I kept retching until I was exhausted and weeping and weary.

It was around then... that the police finally arrived.

JANE

Luckily, Kira had been on the ball and made sure my pack — and the community — had our stories straight.

Rita found me as I finished my vigil of sickness and made sure I knew all the details they had worked out. She also told me the fae had done as Tyson had asked and dealt with the four shifter bodies. They'd also taken away their strange walls of brambles, which was good because I'd completely forgotten about those.

I went inside to clean up and change into my own clothes, then went to face the music.

And so, after that horrific morning, came a long and trying afternoon as police crawled over our neighborhood. The "hunters" were taken away in various ambulances or whatever would carry them. Some crime scene people poured over the three dead men.

Then came the questions.

With this many dead, the lead investigator from Charles Town, a cold and analytical man known as Lieutenant Newman, came out. One of his detectives, a keen-eyed woman named Price, came with him. They poked around all afternoon, asking all the questions we didn't want them to ask. They seemed stuck on the fact that no wolves had been killed.

I didn't have to feign exhaustion when my time came to speak with them. It quickly became clear they didn't suspect *me* of anything. What could a single, small woman do? They questioned Tyson and Colt for some time, though. Bronn was still out cold. They'd have to return to question him. It was all informal, done at our house, but still, it felt like they knew this was all a hoax.

And when the police had finally left and the bodies were removed, as much as I wanted to just fall into bed, I knew my day was far from over. I had some explaining to do to my neighbors.

No one house would fit all of us, but it was a warm enough evening to gather outdoors. Chairs were brought. My large booth hadn't been taken down yet, and people gathered around that, leaning or sitting on it. All the various treats were brought to help feed the crowd. Everyone was there except for Parker Long, who'd been taken to the hospital, and Bree, who'd gone with him. Terry was still looking after the brood of young teens including Bree's son Calvin. Several others had been to the hospital and returned already, patched up from less serious wounds.

I stood on my front step, bone weary, but with Tyson and Colt nearby for support.

Before I began, Mrs. Khan spoke up. "I just want to say a heartfelt thank you to Jane and her... companions, who saved us all today, no matter what they might be."

Her voice quavered just a little at the end there, belying her nonchalance.

"Yeah, exactly. I stand with Jane," Terry Cooper said. "Things would have been a lot worse without her and her pack around."

"None of this would have happened, if she and her pack *hadn't* been around," Debbie Coles bit off. Still, I could see a bit of sympathy in her eyes.

"Pack?" Hector Herrera said, confused.

"Of werewolves," Erik Holt said. "I would have thought that was obvious."

This was getting out of hand quickly.

"Yes!" I called, stopping the murmurs which had started. "Please let me explain everything." *Even if you probably won't believe it.*

The crowd hushed.

Here goes!

"I'm assuming you all know what happened on the morning of the fourteenth, but just in case you don't, here's the full story." I told them about Milo running out and my confrontation with Harley. I stumbled over some parts, not wanting to relive that horrid day but strong hands on my shoulders — Colt and Tyson — bolstered me and helped me through it.

"What I didn't know at the time, was that these folks were more than just a group of bikers, but a pack of shifters. That's the real name for what they are, not were-wolves. And as I'm sure you've noticed, they're not all wolves anyway."

I could see questions forming from the confused expressions on some faces, so I pushed on quickly. "I'd killed their alpha — their leader — which meant I became their leader, and so... I took them in, hoping to help them find a more peaceful way to live."

It took longer than I expected to retell the story of what followed, members of the pack reminding me of details. Of course, I didn't go into detail on my relationship with Tyson, Colt, and Bronn, as much as I'm sure several people were wondering. I focused on how nasty Brick and his crew had been, how I'd given them the chance to simply go away. I'd tried to be civil, and in the end, that's what had led to today's attack.

I found the words harder to say as I got to the end. "I... I suppose I should have killed Brick and the others when I had the chance. But... I'm not a killer. I didn't want... I..."

I felt like I was going to be sick again, even though I hadn't eaten since my first round of vomiting. "They forced my hand today, but I still didn't want to do what I did. It was horrible. I..."

"You did what you had to, to save us all," Terry said, finishing for me.

Stunned silence hung over the crowd. I didn't know if they sensed the impossible situation I'd been in, or if they were still confused and overwhelmed at the existence of supernatural beasts.

Terry turned to James Pearson. "You were attacked by the bikers, yes?"

"Exactly!" the man said, indignant.

Terry quickly countered with, "Was it by any of those who are with Jane now?"

"Well... no, but—" James faltered.

"That's right. The ones who assaulted you are gone. Jane did that for you. If she hadn't, those men would still be terrorizing our street unopposed. Is that what you want?"

"Of course not, but—"

"But what?" Terry was firm, unrelenting. "Do you honestly think things would be better if Jane had done nothing?"

"I... I don't know." Then, it seemed James found some reserve of resentment and pushed on. "I just feel like there could have been some other way to do this which didn't affect our lives as much."

Our lives? No, he meant *his* life. The man was selfish. I could see that now. He didn't care what happened to others, as long as he was left alone. He had some imagined situation in his head where the bikers had just gone away.

"You were assaulted once," Terry bit out. "Jane did something horrible that helped all of us, then had to put up with those vile men in her house until she kicked them out. And today, she got rid of them for good. So, tell me James, whose life was affected more, yours or hers!" Terry was practically shouting.

James Pearson knew he was beat. I could see it in his eyes. Yet, he wasn't going to give up. He doubled down on his anger. "Frankly, I'm fed up with this entire community! Who knows what other enemies these *creatures* might have? I don't think it's safe for any of us anymore. I, for one, will be moving out as soon as I can!"

Good riddance to the ungrateful bastard.

And apparently, I wasn't alone in thinking that. "Feel

free, James." Melody Khan's voice was civil with an undertone of jagged ice. "In fact, we'll buy your house off you for a reasonable price, to help you on your way all the quicker. If you're that blind to what Jane's done for all of us, then by all means, *leave*."

"We'll be leaving too!" This from Will Jacobs. The Jacobses had always been a bit insular, barely participating in community events. Will spoke so infrequently, I'd forgotten what his voice sounded like.

"Then I'll extend the same offer to you," Melody said. "Anyone else?"

I expected Debbie Coles to be next, or perhaps the Herreras, but there was silence.

I blinked.

Oh... wow.

I had to ask. "Debbie? You're staying?"

Conflict played over her mousy features. "I can't say I like *shifters*." She put a lot of displeasure behind that word, but then she sighed heavily. "But it's clear your intentions are to protect this community, not harm it." Her gaze slid to Fern and Iris. "And, I have friends here who... understand me." She glanced back to me, lips tight. Then, looked back and forth from me to her daughter few times before adding, "Maybe... a few new friends, too?"

I smiled, surprised. "Of course."

Hector Herrera spoke next. "I ah... I still don't really know what you are, but... maybe I don't need to. I know that you didn't hurt us and tried to protect me and my wife. And..." He gave an odd, uncertain laugh. "I guess I'd rather have monsters on my side than the other way around, if I have to choose."

I didn't like being called a monster, but it sounded like he was starting to accept us, and that meant a lot.

I turned to Erik Holt with a questioning look. His mother was with him, having come home from work when she'd been notified of the attack. She looked wide-eyed, stunned, confused and horrified.

Erik shrugged. "I'm pretty sure you're not a monster," he said. "Whatever you look like doesn't matter. It's what you do, right?" He glanced at his mom. "I'll make sure my parents understand."

My eyes burned with tears. That was quite the turn-around for the kid.

"If you need help fixing up your car, let me know," Lucas Juarez said to Erik. "It's a beauty."

Erik nodded to Lucas with a bit of a smile.

There were more questions after that, a lot more, but they were less about what we were and more about what had happened and how we were all going to deal with it. Nothing concrete was decided, and we were all tired. So, we planned to talk again tomorrow and the crowd dispersed.

Even then, I didn't go to bed. Both Terry and Mrs. Khan came to me after the meeting wanting to talk. I didn't know what they wanted or why it couldn't wait. I just hoped it wasn't more bad news.

TYSON

WE INVITED TERRY AND MELODY KHAN INSIDE. IT WAS late and the night air was chilly... for humans at least.

Milo took Terry's two kids and Calvin Long — who'd stay with us tonight — back to his room to get them out of the way, bright kid, while Jane sat on a couch, looking haggard and exhausted.

"Yes?" she asked.

Our two guests remained standing, perhaps not intending to stay for long. Melody and Terry looked at each other.

"Can I go first?" Terry asked.

Melody nodded.

The man smiled and looked at Jane, then around at all of us, lingering on Petra. It was clear he liked her.

His gaze returned to Jane. "This was the first I'd heard that you'd lost your job. I'm so sorry, that's got to be hard, especially with so many to take care of. So, I just wanted to say, if you need anything, I'm more than happy to help."

"Terry, no, you can't—" Jane tried to protest, but he spoke over her.

"Nonsense. You're a neighbor and a friend. And it's very possible you saved my life today, and that of my kids. You know I've done well for myself, and when my dad passed, he left me a *sizable* inheritance. I have more than enough for several lifetimes. Please... let me help you. I'm not saying I want to support you fully, or that you aren't capable of taking care of this now-very-extended family, or that you won't get another job if you want to. I'm only saying I *can* help, *if* you need it."

And we probably would. Jane was more than willing to bankrupt herself to take care of us. I hoped she'd accept a little help, at least until she was back on her feet again.

Jane sighed, running a hand over her face, then she gave a breath of a laugh and smiled wearily. "Thank you, Terry. I may take you up on that. We can talk more later, okay?"

"Okay." Terry smiled. "Kids!" he called. "We're going home now!" He gathered his two children and, with a smile and a nod to all of us — and slightly larger smile for Petra — he left.

Melody Khan laughed. "I don't know why you didn't marry that man when you had the chance," she said. Then she looked at the rest of us, stopping on me and Colt. "But then, I guess you did okay in the end, didn't you?"

So, she knew about our relationship? Interesting.

Mrs. Khan didn't wait for Jane to answer her probably rhetorical question. Drawing a breath, she launched into what she had to say. "I'm here for a similar reason to Terry. I want to help, but in a very specific way." Jane raised her brows and seemed like she might try another protest, but Melody pushed on. "I know you don't want any charity, and this isn't... really. Consider it more an opportunity, if you will." She seemed excited. "There are far too many of you in this house, and I thought with the Pearsons and the Jacobses moving out, perhaps some of your... ah... pack could take the vacant houses?"

I was stunned.

Jane gave a few wide-eyed blinks. She looked how I felt. "We could never afford that!"

"You could, if we didn't bother with banks, and we gave you an extended timeline to pay us back. Like I said, it's not a gift, it's a loan." She bobbled her head for a moment. "Okay, so I may knock a few thousand off the price as a sort of thank you, for saving my life. But otherwise, it's just a loan. And you all seem very industrious. I'm sure you'll have no trouble paying it back."

"Melody," Jane began, but couldn't seem to find words after that.

I stepped in. "That's a *very* generous offer, and we're *incredibly* honored that you'd think of us. Why don't we talk about it and get back to you?"

"Yes, of course." She nodded. "I just... I can't say I understand everything that happened, but I know *you* Jane, and I know what I saw today. Okay, I don't *understand* what I saw today, but I know that whatever you all are, you saved me and my husband and we're very grateful. So, think about it, okay?"

Jane nodded, rising to see Mrs. Khan out. And when

Melody was gone, Jane closed the door and leaned on it heavily. "Did that just happen?"

I went to her, pulling her into my arms, supporting her seemingly fragile and near-to-limp, weightless body. "It did. Sleep on it." I kissed the top of her head. "It turns out, you've got a couple saints as neighbors."

"Yeah," she said with a laugh. Then she collapsed into me a bit more. "Now... bed, okay?"

"Okay." I swept her into my arms as the pack dispersed. Several went to take care of the booth outside, others to get Bronn from Terry's house, but most were headed to bed. Colt organized things, which meant I had Jane all to myself as I laid her in bed. I removed her clothes carefully. She helped a little but was already half asleep.

"Did you want a nightgown?" I offered.

She shook her head.

I stripped and slipped in beside her, then pulled the sheets up over us.

"Sleep well, my love," I whispered, holding her gently in my arms.

She was out cold, drooling on my chest, in less than a minute.

That gave me time to assimilate the events of the day. I lay there, replaying the fight in my head and not seeing any way to have done things differently.

A growing angst gnawed at my soul.

I should have been there for Jane. I should have been the one to kill Brick and the others, not her. Not because I had to protect her, but because killing had already stained my soul. It pained me to see how troubled she was at what she'd done. That should have been my pain to bear, not hers. No one should have to go through that.

And the fact that everyone she'd killed had been a horrid fiend of a person didn't matter. Killing was killing. And killing a horrible person meant you were always questioning, was it right? Was it necessary? Did I have to? Is the world better? And that led to a strange ambiguity of thought which could torture a person.

There was nothing I could do about it now, though, and running it over in my head was only torturing me. I'd be there for her, help her in any way she needed. If she needed time to recover, I'd step up in the coming days. It was the prime beta's duty to lead in the alpha's absence, and I would.

That helped to settle my soul.

I found sleep eventually, but morning arrived all too soon.

Jane slept, still drooling on me — Gods that was adorable — but I could hear the house starting to stir. It was Monday, a school day. I'd make sure the kids were okay and got to school — although they may need a day or two off, after the trauma of yesterday as well.

As I left Jane's room, I caught Jake sneaking out of Izzy's.

He caught my warning look and held up his hands in surrender. "Nothing happened, you can ask Izzy. She just wanted someone to stay with her last night!"

"*Nothing* happened?" I confirmed. I sniffed the air. Izzy's sent was all over the boy, though it didn't smell too much of arousal.

He blushed. "Ah...we may have kissed a little, and I

held her close, but that's it!"

I nodded, trusting the boy. "If you say so." Then I considered things. "Look, Jake. Izzy's mother and I may have our hands full over the next few days. If Izzy feel's comfortable with you, then you can stay with her... as long as nothing happens, understood?"

"What if *she wants* something to happen?" he asked, just a bit too eagerly.

"Then you'll say no. You'll explain that she's going through a trying time and she may not be thinking clearly. Tell her you'll be there for her in every other way." I lowered my voice so only he'd hear. "I don't care if she begs for it. If you get your dick wet, even with a condom, I'll cut it off, you hear me, boy?" He nodded, wide-eyed. "Respect that girl and someday you'll be with her. I don't care what you have to say, but you wait. Got me?"

He nodded. "Yes, sir."

"Good."

He scrambled away, which meant he didn't see my smile. I was fairly certain that boy had it bad for Izzy. I hoped she felt the same. We all needed someone to comfort us right now.

That thought made me peek in on Milo.

He slept peacefully, arms around Brutus-as-a-wolf. Milo had his face buried in Brutus' fur and it was adorable. Who knew my brother could be so patient and caring? Calvin Long slept on the floor, out cold.

Colt found me. "Bronn's awake and he's got something to say." Colt's tone didn't make it sound like it was a good *something* either.

Fuck. What now?

BRONN

TYSON DIDN'T LOOK HAPPY WHEN HE ARRIVED IN THE downstairs guest room where I'd been put to rest and recover. Colt closed the door and leaned on it. He already knew what I was about to say.

Tyson sat on the side of the bed. "How're you doing?"

"Good enough, seeing as I should probably be dead. Is it true the witch healed me?" Tyson nodded, seeming as surprised as I was about that. "Fuck. I owe her big time."

"You do. I'm sure you can figure out some way to repay her. Is that what you wanted to tell me?" He looked confused.

I shook my head on the pillow, barely able to lift it. Even after whatever the witch — no, her name was Debbie — had done, I was still incredibly sore and weak. I'd be laid up for a few more days, even with my advanced healing. She'd made sure I wouldn't die, but I wasn't sure how much beyond that her healing had gone.

It was taxing enough just to be talking now, but Tyson needed to hear this.

"I didn't kill Tank."

His brow furrowed. "You probably just don't remember killing him with everything that happened to you."

I shook my head. "Oh, I saw him die, sure enough, but it wasn't me who killed him. It was Petra."

Tyson blinked. "Jane said she was there, but..."

"She saved my ass," I said, grateful beyond measure. "But... Gods... it was like she was possessed or something."

Tyson sighed. "Just tell me straight, from the beginning."

I gave a weak nod. "I was so stoked to fight Tank." I gave a single laugh. "And terrified. I didn't know if I could take him one-on-one, but I was determined to try. After everything he'd done to me, I wanted to take him down so bad. I knew he was stronger, but I hoped I was quicker... and I was."

I swallowed, my throat dry. Tyson found a cup of water on the bedside table and helped me drink before I went on.

"I gave as good as I got, tearing into him and avoiding the worst of his blows. But as the fight wore on, we both got worn down, tired and wounded. I got sloppy, too slow, but he was still strong enough to lay me out with a blow. I thought that was it. He laughed and came to finish the job." I remembered that part far too well, as well as what came next.

"I thought I was a goner for sure, but... that's when

Petra came out of nowhere. She hit him so hard she knocked him down. He was wounded, and she was... fucking savage. He never had a chance. She didn't just kill him, she fucking destroyed him." Tyson nodded, his expression grim. I guessed he'd seen the body. "And she kept tearing at him long after he was dead. Eventually, she stopped, shifted back and came to me." By then, my memories were quite fuzzy. I didn't recall anything after that.

"And that's how Jane found you two," Tyson said with a nod. Then he breathed a long, slow breath. "I'm glad Petra got her revenge on the man."

Colt at the door grunted. "Yeah."

I felt horrible that I hadn't been able to finish the job. If I had, I might have saved Petra some trauma. Still, I'd fought Tank to a stand-still and that was fucking right-eous. I hadn't known, until that moment, if holding my own against Tank was possible, but now I did.

"What are you going to do?" I asked Tyson.

He shrugged. "Nothing." Then he looked at Colt and me. "I'll need to tell Jane, and the three of us should keep an eye on Petra and see how she's doing over the next little while, if she needs anything, but what's done is done, and frankly, I think Tank got off easy."

I nodded. But still, these two hadn't seen what I had, the sheer savagery and ferociousness of the woman. She'd been completely inhuman. I mean, it was warranted, given what Tank had put her through, I'd just never thought she had *that* in her. Hell, it had scared me.

"Anything else?" Tyson asked.

I shook my head. "No." Only Petra and I would know the full truth of that event.

"Then rest." He rose and left with Colt. Once outside, I heard Tyson sigh and say, "Time to get to work."

I did rest, and I didn't know how much later it was when Jane came to see me. I woke to her gentle calls, smiling up at her once my vision brought her into focus.

"Hey," I said.

"Hey, yourself." Her smile held just a touch of concern. "How are you doing?"

I still ached all over, like I'd been hit by a bus, but most of the stinging pains of the slashes I'd received from Tank were gone. "Better, still in pain, but recovering."

"I'm glad," she whispered, leaning down to kiss me softly. With her face still close, she breathed out her worries. "I don't know what I would have done if I'd lost you."

"You'd still have Tyson and Colt."

"It wouldn't be the same. I need you, Bronn. We *all* need you. I don't think you know how much. Tyson's the brains, and Colt is the heart, but you're the soul of us. You bind us all together. Without you, we'd be directionless, a bit too cold and lost, I think.

"And what does that make you?" I asked.

She gave a breath of a laugh. "I'm the body?" She didn't sound convinced.

"And a sexy body it is."

Another laugh. "I bring us together... physically?"

"You do more than that."

"It's not a perfect analogy, okay? Just know we all need you."

"I know now."

She kissed me softly. I drank in a long sip from her lips and a healthy helping of her scent, which grounded me. She was my rock, my home, my mate.

"I'll get you some food, but there's someone else here to see you, okay?"

I furrowed my brow. "Who?"

She rose and looked toward the door. "Doctor, the patient is all yours."

Debbie Coles walked in, slowly, looking like she felt completely out of place. "It's so dark down here!"

The guest room had a small, high window, but it didn't provide a lot of light.

"Thank you for this," Jane said and left while Debbie sat on the edge of the bed.

"How are you?" she asked.

"Alive, thanks to you. That's what they tell me." I quickly added, "Thank you."

She rolled her eyes. "Can you be more specific? Oh, and you're welcome."

I listed off how I felt and she nodded. After that, she closed her eyes and began a low chant.

It unnerved me a little. Shifters and witches weren't supposed to get along, and chants were usually bad things for us, but I kept my mouth shut and waited.

She passed her hands over me, head to foot, then stopped the chant and nodded. "You'll be fine. I wasn't sure if you might need another dose of healing. You were pretty far gone and I couldn't do a lot. I brought you back from the brink, but your own healing has done a lot since, it seems. Good." Her tone was analytical.

"You don't know how much this means," I whispered.

"I think I can take a guess," she said with a knowing smile.

"I'm so very grateful. If you ever need anything — *anything* — you just call and I'll come. I owe you my life, and I'll repay that debt if I can."

"Really, it's okay."

"But that's not what I meant," I pushed on. "You don't know what this means for *all of us*. If you — a witch — can help me — a shifter — then... it means things *can* change. They can be *different*. Maybe we *can* be the good people we're trying to be, with Jane's help."

"Oh," she said softly. Then she drew a breath and nodded. "I hope you can." She rose as Jane returned with a tray of food. "Keep the bites small and do mostly liquids for another day or so. He's a bit... tender inside."

"I will, thanks," Jane said. The two women shared a look, then Debbie left.

I let Jane feed me, trying not to complain about how slow the whole process was. And when she was done, she kissed me again and told me to rest.

As I drifted off, I finally began to accept that the path ahead was truly one of hope and change. Jane had done it. She'd brought together shifters and witches and fae.

If she could do that, she could do anything. The future was full of possibilities.

JANE

THE DAY AFTER THE ATTACK, NO ONE QUESTIONED ME
directly, but investigators were crawling all over our
community with warrants to search our property. Sheds
were emptied and examined. It seemed the claim of a
wolf attack wasn't entirely believed and they were looking
for weapons. Obviously, they found nothing, but
everyone was still tense with so many outsiders filling our
community.

At the same time, a few reporters showed up, looking
for more information and trying to question the police.
The officers said it was an ongoing investigation and no
one in the community wanted to talk. So the media left
without much of a story.

I tried to ignore the various strangers roaming around
our street when I went to see Bree. She and Parker were
back from the hospital, and since she hadn't been at our
little community meeting last night, I thought she
deserved to know more.

I knocked and pulled my jacket tighter around myself. A cooler wind had settled in, and even though I didn't feel it as much as a human would, I was also feeling just a bit of an anxious chill. I wasn't looking forward to talking to my long-time friend about... all of this.

Bree opened the door, looking haggard. "Jane?" She smiled first, but it faded quickly. It was clear she didn't see me the same as she had before.

"How's Parker?" I asked, genuinely concerned.

She gave a weary smile. "They said it's not a bad wound. He should be up and about in a few weeks." Her voice was tight. Did she blame me for this?

"That's good," I said, not sure how to go on from there. "Can... I... come in?"

Another hesitation, then a heavy sigh. "Yes, of course. Sorry for making you stand out in the cold." She let me in and closed the door.

"The cold doesn't bother me as much as it used to," I said, hoping to use that as a segue into talking about shifters. But Bree just stared at me, not inviting me any farther into her house. I pushed on. "Ah... I thought... well, I spoke to the rest of the community last night explaining everything and I wanted to talk to you, now that you're back."

"Yes, of course, ah... come in...," she said reluctantly. "Well, you're... already in. I guess..."

She was scattered and not thinking straight. I couldn't blame her. She probably hadn't gotten much sleep last night worrying about Parker.

Slowly, I moved toward her living room and sat. She

followed and sat opposite me, still a little robotic in her movements, and I almost wanted to offer her a cup of tea or something, even though this wasn't my house.

"I can... come back later, if now's not good?" I offered.

She blinked. "No, sorry, I'm just tired and... and..." She shivered. "I don't know if I want to know what happened yesterday. It all seems so... surreal, and I'm still not sure of anything."

"Well, I can help with that part, though, I don't know if you'll like what I have to say."

"It's all real?" she said slowly.

"Yes, depending on what you mean by 'all.' But what you saw was real enough." I drew a breath. "There isn't an easy way to say this, so I'll just say it. I'm a werewolf, so are all those guests I have in my house. We prefer to be called shifters. Those men yesterday were working for a small group of other shifters who didn't like that I was trying to reform the rest of them. I'm... so sorry for all of that. It wasn't my fault, but it was caused by things I'd done, if that makes sense?"

"I think so, yes," Bree said as she tried to smile. "So, those three hotties you're hooking up with, they're wolves? Like some paranormal romance?"

I nodded, smiling. "Yup, like that. Only one is a wolf, one is a bear, and one is a lion."

"Lions and wolves and bears? Oh my." She laughed a little at her joke. I joined her, happy to see a little life in her usually jovial features, but it faded quickly. "It was the lion who saved Parker and me. That beautiful Black man?"

"Yes."

"And you're certain he's taken?"

I laughed. "Yeah, sorry."

"He got any brothers?"

"Not that I know of."

"Oh." She sighed. "Well, if any come along, you tell me, okay?"

"I will."

She was silent for a moment. I guessed she was still processing all of this. "Wait... and you said you're a werewolf too? Have you always been?" Her involuntary flinch back told me that thought scared her.

"No. I only became one a couple of weeks ago. I had to, in order to take control of the pack."

"You... control them?"

"Yes, well, I'm their leader."

"Oh?"

So, I told her the full story, explaining everything. She took it surprisingly well, considering how fragile she seemed at the moment. She kept comparing it to some novel or other she'd read. I'd never thought my life worthy of writing about, but then... things had gotten a lot more interesting these last two weeks.

I ended with, "Now that you know the truth, you can't tell anyone. Everyone on the street knows now, but we've all agreed it's better to keep it a secret." That reminded me. "Oh, and have you heard? The Pearsons and Jacobses are moving out."

She raised her brows. "No. Do you think that's wise?"

"I can't stop them, but... what do you mean?"

"Well, if they're not here anymore, then couldn't they tell someone about you or what happened?"

"I don't think they would. People would think they were crazy." But... it was something to think about. I'd have to talk to them and make sure they understood they couldn't tell anyone ever.

Bree nodded.

Silence hung between us for a long moment as I got up the courage to ask, "Does this change anything between us? Are we still friends?"

Bree blinked and smiled. "Of course we are! I mean, I'm jealous as hell that you got three sexy shifters and I'm still stuck with my *personal massagers*, but you being a shifter, that doesn't really change anything, I don't think."

It changed one thing. "It means we all have to be a bit more careful around blood. The disease is transmitted through blood, so if one of us shifters get hurt, don't get too close, okay? Let your boys know."

She nodded. "And Milo, he's not...?"

"No, it's safe for Calvin and Milo to play together."

She nodded. "Good, and thanks for taking Calvin in last night."

"Of course, any time."

She sighed. "Well, thanks for stopping by Jane, it's good to know... all the details, even if I don't believe half of them... yet. But now I'm kicking you out, I need to get some sleep."

I nodded. "Of course." She showed me out and we hugged briefly before I left.

I hadn't realized how much the dread of that talk had been weighing on me. I felt practically weightless as I left. But the sight of all the people prowling around our neighborhood brought me back down to earth like a stone.

Since I was already out of the house, I decided to visit the Jacobses and the Pearsons. Might as well get all the things I was dreading out of the way at once.

My talk with the Jacobses actually went well. They just wanted to put all of this behind them and forget about anything abnormal. I believed them and wished them well. They were already packing. They'd be out of the house by the end of the week, going to stay with family as they house-hunted.

Then I went to the Pearsons'.

Mr. Pearson almost slammed the door in my face, but I stuck my foot in the opening and insisted I only needed a moment of his time and didn't need to come in. He glared at me, partially hidden behind his door as I spoke.

"Why would I want to tell anyone about you?" he snapped after I'd mentioned it. "Everyone would think I'm crazy."

"I'm glad you see it that way," I said. "But I also know you don't like those I've taken in. I'm hoping we can trust you with this, even if you don't trust us."

"Of course, whatever, are we done?"

"It's just that... if you *did* talk, and someone *did* believe you and word got out... Well, it might not be *us* that you'd be pissing off. My pack aren't the only shifters out there." I didn't know this for certain, but it seemed a logical assumption. "And as much as *we've* turned over a new leaf, *others* haven't. And *they* probably wouldn't like to be exposed. So... just think about that, if you ever contemplate changing your mind about keeping our secret."

He grumbled. "Fine, yes, got it. Is that all?"

"Yes, have a nice day, sir." I removed my foot.

The door closed.

The faster they were gone, the better.

Like the Jacobses, they were gone by the end of that week. Which meant, things began to change for our pack.

JANE

Slowly, things settled. The investigation hit a dead end and by the next Saturday, no one came around anymore. The Pearsons and Jacobses had moved out, and that meant it was time to consider Mrs. Khan's offer.

I was hesitant. The pack's funds were *very* limited. We wouldn't even be able to *begin* paying down the loan until I had a full-time job again. I'd been looking but hadn't found any employment nearby, and I wasn't willing to move.

It was Kira who convinced me to finally take the plunge.

"We're too many people crammed in here," she said after pulling me aside for a private conversation. "Even just one of those houses would make a huge difference. The pack would be out of your hair for the most part. You'd have your privacy back."

I hedged for a moment. My privacy wasn't that big of a concern for me these days. I kind of liked having the pack around to help with things. Kira seemed to sense this.

"If not for you, then do it for any number of us who have little to no privacy at the moment. We're all crammed into your basement and it's not easy for us."

That was very true.

"Fine, maybe just one house?"

Kira sighed. "Think for a moment, Jane." She gave me a hard look. "Do you want someone new moving into the neighborhood? Right now, everyone knows about our secret and is fine with it. That's better than we could have ever hoped for. But if someone new comes? Frankly, I'm certain Mrs. Khan thought of that too. Why would she sell to anyone? The house will just sit empty anyway. Why not take it, and work that much harder to make the money we need to repay it?"

She was right.

"Fine! Both!" I threw up my hands, not knowing how we'd afford any of this.

Kira smiled. "We'll get there, don't worry."

And so began the exodus from my house. The Pearsons' place was larger, with four rooms, if the den was made into a bedroom. The Juarez family, along with Cassie and Jake, moved in there. Kira, Rita, Petra, and Winnie moved into the Jacobses' three-bedroom house. Kira gave the other's rooms and turned a portion of the basement into a bedroom for herself. Brutus stayed at my place... as a dog most of the time, and of course, my betas — my mates — stayed with me.

Bronn had healed well, not quite a hundred percent,

but getting there. The inspector had come and taken his statement but had left unsatisfied and not returned since.

The guys had told me about Petra killing Tank. What surprised me wasn't Petra's fury — that made complete sense to me — no, it had been the fact that Petra had found the courage to fight Tank to begin with. If anything, it made me proud of her. But having had my own experience with killing and not feeling comfortable about it, I thought I should talk to her, so we went for a walk down the road on a chilly November day.

It had rained that morning and the clouds remained heavy above us, moisture in the air, making everything feel colder than it was. Even being super-heated shifters, we'd still bundled up.

I hadn't mentioned any reason for the walk to Petra, and after having walked in silence for more than ten minutes, she finally asked.

"Is this about... Tank?" It sounded like, even now, the name was difficult for her to say.

"Yeah," I admitted. "Is that okay?"

She nodded, seeming her usual quiet and withdrawn self today. With a heavy scarf bundled around her neck and chin, she almost seemed to be sinking down into that woolen safety.

When she didn't elaborate right away, I began. "I don't know if it's the same or not, but... when I was fighting Brick and the others, I... I didn't want to kill them. I didn't want to... do what I did to them. But a part of me knew if we let them live, they'd always be coming after us. Still, I found the whole thing... sickening. Yet my beast was mostly indifferent to the carnage. Was that what it was like for you?"

She shook her head. "No." her voice was hushed but hard. "I *wanted* to kill him."

I nodded. Given what he'd done to her, I didn't blame her. I waited for her to go on.

"For *months* I've wanted him to die. I hoped someone else might do it, or an accident. I'd never have fought him on my own, especially with Brick and the others around."

She didn't say anything after that for several minutes, the crunch of our boots on the gravel at the side of the road and the wind in the trees the only sounds.

"I'd dreamed of different ways to kill him, but they were only dreams, and a part of me knew I'd never go through with them." She gave a trembling sigh. "Then, when I saw Bronn fighting Tank, I hoped he'd tear the bastard apart. Bronn had been treated almost as badly as I had, and for far longer. But then Tank struck him down and..." Petra shuddered through her breath. "He was weak, already torn up by Bronn. And no one else was around. I... I snapped. I didn't even fully realize what I was doing. My beast took over, but I was fully on board."

She gave a weird, breathy laugh, and I looked over at her. There was a wildness in her usually soft blue eyes. Her voice was low, but almost excited, her gaze distant as she recounted the events.

"He saw me coming. He *knew* it was me. I'm glad for that. He even laughed. He didn't think I could do it, but I did. I hit him so hard, I knocked him over and I didn't stop after that. Oh, he hit me a few times, but he was weak and I was... unstoppable. I barely felt it. Then everything turned red and warm and..." another manic giggle. "It was better than any of my fantasies. It was better still when he shifted back to human. I'd thought myself done, but when I saw his face... I couldn't let any part of him remain. I did to his body what he'd done to my life, my soul." Her voice trembled as tears traced her cheeks.

I stepped in and embraced her with one arm, side on. *Jesus!* I couldn't imagine what this woman must have gone through to feel that level of rage.

"But..." Petra whispered, on the verge of breaking down. She stopped, hands raised to her face, body shaking. "I thought he'd go away, that the pain would... But it's *still there*. He's still in my soul, tormenting me!" And that broke her.

I caught her as she went slack, her strength gone. I lowered her gently, then sat on the ground with her head in my lap, letting her cry.

So, it wasn't killing him that bothered her, it was that it hadn't been enough to get rid of his stain on her. I'd dealt with some sleaze-bag men in my time, but never anything like what Petra must have endured. I had no clue what to say or how to support her. Would that horrid man's influence on her life ever go away?

I desperately hoped it would, for her sake.

I whispered, "Whatever you need, whenever you need it, just let me know. I'm here for you. We're all here for you."

She nodded, still sobbing. "Thank you, alpha."

"Please just call me Jane." I stroked her hair. "I hope you consider me to be a friend, not just your alpha."

"I do." She seemed to be coming to the end of her tears, at least for now. She sat up slowly, then surprised me by pulling me into a hug. "Thank you, Jane."

I wrapped my arms around her. "Anytime."

"No," she said through her sniffles. "I mean thank you for killing Harley and... and ending all of that."

"Oh." I was definitely not going to say "anytime" to that. So, I settled for, "I'm glad I could help."

And I was, truly. I hated that I'd had to kill that man. However, as strange as my life had become since then, in many ways, it had only gotten better. I had three gorgeous men who wanted me and thought I was beautiful and smart and sexy. I had a pack I could lean on for support, even as I supported them, and I had a community that had come together around all of us.

Yes, I'd lost my job and I had no clue how I was going to pay for *anything*, but I had a network of people willing to help me now, and that made the burden feel a little lighter.

The two of us sat there for some time, simply holding each other, before we eventually got up and went home.

As I dropped Petra off at her new house, a curious group of people headed toward me: Iris and Fern, Debbie Coles, Melody Khan, and Terry Cooper.

"Jane!" Melody Khan shouted. "Just the woman we were looking for!"

Something was up, but not a bad something. They all looked a little too excited, bursting at the seams, and I felt like they were about to pull me into some wild scheme.

And that got me very curious and a little excited too.

JANE

We were closest to Debbie's house, so the group asked me to join them there. Once inside, I sat, as did Terry, but the other four women were so agitated and excited they remained standing, shifting and pacing, bursting with energy.

"Okay, out with it. What's up?" I asked, feeling a little giddy myself. I glanced at Terry — who was smiling broadly — before returning my gaze to the others.

"We have an idea," Mrs. Khan said.

"A plan. A series of plans? A series of ideas that form a plan?" Fern burst out.

"Yes, all of that," Mrs. Khan said, glaring at the others, who hushed a little so she could speak. Then she looked back at me. "We would like to form a sort of collective."

"All working together, helping each other!" Iris exploded and got another stare from Melody.

"Yes, now please let me explain everything!" Mrs. Khan went into full lawyer mode and there was no arguing against her.

Debbie laughed at the Rosses' excitement. "I'm going to go get something," she said and hurried off.

Melody looked to see if there were going to be any more outbursts, then turned back to me. "Your... ah... pack... is it? Yes, well, they've been working so hard, trying to get various businesses up and running to help themselves and help you, and we thought, why stop there? Why can't the whole community pitch in and help out? We all have something to offer, don't we, ladies?"

Fern and Iris nodded as one.

Melody waited a moment before saying, "You can talk now, tell them your ideas."

"Oh!" Fern said. "Good, yes, well, you see, Iris and I have been working on several things for some time now, lots of little projects, but they've only been for us, and we thought, perhaps it was time to expand and share them with all of you."

"And the world!" Iris proclaimed.

"Yes, exactly!" Fern gave Iris a warm look, which spoke volumes about their love for each other. "We have so many things to share! We have the exotic plants we grow in our green house, and the healthy candies we make, and several herbal mixtures which are good for everything from cuts to colds."

"Even a mixture that increases the female sex drive," Iris added excitedly. "We love that one, and I think it could be a big seller."

"Yes, all of that, plus we have our cannabis crop and—"

"So you *are* growing weed! I knew it!" I shouted. It had been a bit of a joke around the community for as long as the two had been there. But no one could find any plants in their house, nor their greenhouse. "Where do you grow it?"

"Wild, in the forest, it's everywhere, most people walk right past it. It's all natural and very high quality."

"Isn't that illegal in West Virginia?" I asked.

"I'm sure we can find some legal loophole to jump through," Mrs. Khan said with a wave of her hand.

"I'm surprised you're okay with this," I said to the ex-lawyer.

She shrugged. "The stuff is mostly harmless and does have medicinal value. We just have to wait for laws to catch up with reality. Until then, these ladies have other things to sell too."

"Exactly!" Fern said.

"Oh, and I thought I'd take your advice," Debbie said returning with a bottle of champagne and several crystal glasses. "I'm going to try selling some of my art. And I can do all the marketing for the collective."

"Between Sanjay and I, we can handle any legal items," Melody added.

"Then you and your folk can do what you're doing as well, and we can all join together to help each other!" Iris said.

"And others might want to do their own thing," Fern added. "Elena Herrera does quilts and knitting. Maybe that Holt boy would like to fix up old cars or something?"

I was more than a little overwhelmed by all of this. I'd never have imagined, in a thousand years, that my neighbors would come together like this. I turned to Terry. "And what is your part in this?"

"I'm the financial backer. I'll loan out start-up money as needed to get things going and help support anyone who needs it while they get their feet under them."

Support anyone who needs it... like me. "Oh, Terry, no, I can't—"

"Nonsense. Your pack has some good ideas and talents to share. Why shouldn't I help them make it work?"

Something in how he said *them* made me realize he wasn't doing this for me. He was doing it for *Petra* and *her* pack, of which I just happened to be a member. As a friend, I may have factored into his kindness, but I got the feeling Petra was a much larger factor in this equation.

"Also, you wouldn't need his support," Melody said with a sly grin. "You'd have a job in this collective too. You'd be our accountant, taking care of the money side of things."

"Wouldn't that be Terry's thing?" I asked.

He held up his hands. "Oh, no, I'm retired and perfectly happy with my day-trading. I'll supply the funds, but I don't want to worry about it after that."

"How much are we talking?" I asked, looking from him to the others.

"No clue!" Fern said, excited still.

Terry chuckled. "We hadn't worked out the details yet, but I'm assuming I'll be investing heavily in this community for a while. I know that investment will pay off, though."

"Terry," I said, voice hushed, which did nothing, they could all still hear me. "How much?"

He shrugged. "I figure maybe a couple million a year

for a few years, then we should be seeing a strong return."

My eyes and mouth went wide. I'd known Terry was well off, but... "Can you afford that? What about your kids and college and...?"

He laughed. "Jane, I think I've mentioned I came from a ridiculously wealthy family. I never *had* to work, but I liked doing it. I won't be touching any of my own funds, this is all coming from what I inherited from my father."

I blinked, still gaping a little.

Iris moved over to slap my arm playfully. "The man wants to be generous and help us! Let him! We all want to be a part of this and help you and those dear folks who saved our community."

I turned my gape to her. Those *dear folks* were shifters, the mortal enemy of fae, or so I'd thought. But... I didn't want to say anything here. I knew Debbie was aware of what Iris and Fern were but didn't know how much Melody knew. Iris caught my discreet glance at Mrs. Khan and shook her head slightly. Then her voice spoke directly into my head, which caused me to gape even more.

She doesn't know yet. We'll tell her everything eventually, but let's take it slow, yes?

I nodded. To Melody it would look like I was just coming to terms with this wild plan.

Slowly I got ahold of myself. "Wow." I drew in a deep breath. "Thank you so much for this. You don't know what it means."

"We can guess," Melody said softly. "You've done so much to help those poor folks get safe and settled. Then they helped us, because you helped them. Now we're helping you, because they helped us. Just accept it."

"I do, thank you, all of you!"

Debbie popped the cork on the champagne.

"To the Woodside Business Cooperative!" Melody offered a toast and we all clinked glasses and drank.

"Is *that* the name we're using?" Fern hedged.

"We'll work out all the details in the coming days," Debbie said to appease Fern. Then to me she added, "Don't fret. Just accept it. Go home and tell your three hot guys the good news."

"Does everyone know I'm with all of them?" I asked, shocked.

"It's sort of obvious, given how the four of you look at each other," Melody said, taking another swig of champagne.

Oh.

I downed my glass and let that sink in, let *all of it* sink in. Only a few minutes ago on the road with Petra I'd been thinking how well everything was going *except* for money and career. But now that was taken care of and I had nothing to complain about.

And suddenly I wanted *very much* to get home and celebrate!

JANE

Before I left, I made plans with Terry to have Milo sleep over with Danny that night. And when I got home, I asked Izzy if she'd like to go stay at the "girls" place with Winnie and Petra and the others for a night. She got the hint and accepted my offer. I called Kira to confirm the plan then got my kids safely out the door.

By the time I closed the door behind them, my three guys had gotten the hint about what was about to happen and assembled in my front room.

My blood boiled. It had been ages since I'd been with Tyson and our bond was stretched taut between us. It had been a busy week and I hadn't spent much quality time with any of them. But now here they were, Bronn was healed, the other two excited, and I had great news to share.

"You'll never guess what happened just now!" I said, then took a few steps toward them.

"Something good?" Colt asked with a grin, as he drew

near. He bent to kiss my cheek then slid behind me, the heat from his body warming mine.

"I like good news," Bronn said placing himself on my left, his lips kissing where Colt had a moment before.

"Don't leave us in suspense," Tyson whispered as he took up position on my right, a kiss to my other cheek.

The intensity of my need for him washed through my mind for a moment, making me forget everything.

"Hmm? What?" I mumbled as I drank in their combined scents and felt the close press of their bodies.

It was just a bit too much, overwhelming my senses and fritzing my brain. I swam in an ocean of pleasant aromas: leather and sweet apples from Colt, Tyson's smokey bacon and brisk sea air. Then there was Bronn's heady cedar and tangy oranges with more than a hint of dark chocolate at the moment. I just wanted to bite into these three and savor their flavors.

But then my brain regained itself after that prolonged sense-induced hiccup.

"Yeah, good news. The community wants to buy into your businesses and create a collective with other new ventures, supporting each other."

"Whoa," Colt breathed, "Really?"

"Yeah! Even the fae want to help... no, actually, they're *excited and eager* to help!"

"Amazing. And all because of you," Bronn whispered, his hot breath on my neck sending an expectant thrill through me.

Tyson smiled, happy at my news, but also staring at me like I was a cold glass of water and he'd just crossed a desert, parched and so very thirsty.

Wow... I was starting to lose my train of thought again, so I pushed on quickly. "I'll be working for the collective, and there should be more than enough money to support us all and..." I was rambling now, a bit too hot, caught up in all the glorious sensations my guys were inducing around me. "It's going to be great!" I said, my voice sounding a bit dreamy. "So, I thought we should celebrate."

Colt swept my hair aside and kissed my neck, the opposite side from Bronn. "And how does our alpha want to celebrate?" he whispered.

Colt's question snagged in my mind for a moment. I knew the answer. I wanted my guys to fuck my brains out, but it was more than that. "I want you to love me, show me how much you love me," I breathed.

Because right now, being here with them felt different than all the times we'd been together before. That first week, they'd soothed me, and helped me cope with being a wolf. Last week they'd proven we were meant to be together, partners in life. I believed it now in a way I hadn't before.

I didn't know if it was finally being done with Brick's looming threat, or the community cooperative idea, or just how much my guys had supported me and my kids and the community, but for the first time, I felt... free!

We'd finally moved past the awkward getting-to-know-you phase in our relationship and were at the divine place where we didn't need to talk to know what each other needed. We were connected, in sync in a way I'd never felt with any man before in my life. And what I wanted right now, was for them to simply revel in that connection with me.

Colt chuckled. "Oh, we can do that."

"And with the house empty, we can do it anywhere we please," Tyson added.

Oh! That hadn't occurred to me before, but as soon as he said it, I *wanted* it. My ex had always been a little sex-obsessed, but his idea of "changing things up" was doing me from behind. I knew Tyson, Colt, and Bronn would be far more creative. I wanted them to make me scream on the dining table, the kitchen counter, on the couch, on the stairs, up against a wall. All of it. All of those fantasies flooded my mind and I simply moaned to let them know how much I agreed with that idea.

"I think that's a yes," Bronn said as he turned my head and his lips found mine.

I moaned again, unabashedly. I wanted to let him know exactly how I felt. Bronn shivered as he sucked it down. I slid my hand over his body to grasp the bulge in his jeans, needing to feel how I affected him.

"So. Fucking. Hot!" Tyson said, still watching.

"Gorgeous," Colt whispered against my ear, before nibbling on my lobe.

My heart pounded like a drummer making the most of an epic solo. I was steaming hot and so very ready, and none of us were even out of our clothes yet.

From the corner of my eye, I caught Tyson's warm smile. There was a hunger to it, but now, also, a softness, and my heart clenched to see it.

That right there was exactly what I needed from him.

That softness mixed with his power and intensity meant I could fall into him and always know he'd catch me gently then devour me and thrill me until I could barely breathe.

"I love you, Jane," he whispered and I lost sight of him as he knelt. My anticipation spiked, wondering what he had planned, but I quickly forgot about him as Colt's teeth raked hard over my neck.

I let out a whine.

Bronn left my lips to translate my desire.

"Bite her," he whispered to Colt.

Colt licked the area, then, with a flash of pain, his teeth sank into my flesh, a true bite, breaking skin, claiming me. And the wolf in me submitted to him. I tilted my head, giving him room as his hands clasped my arms, holding me tight. Colt had complete control and I had complete trust in him. He savored the moment with a guttural sigh, then pulled away, licking the area again to soothe me.

I whined and trembled, my body viscerally reacting, submitting, consumed with desire.

Hell yes! I want more of that!

I wasn't sure why or where this desperate need had come from. My wolf must really like that claiming pain.

I broke away from Bronn. "Bite me," I told him. Then I added. "All of you, bite me and I want to bite you!"

"Hmmm, yeah," Colt said, still licking where he'd claimed me.

"My teeth are sharper," Bronn warned.

"Do it," I breathed.

He tilted my head the other way and kissed my pulse before shifting a little lower over my shoulder. He had to undo a few buttons of my blouse, sliding it off my shoulder, and like Colt, he licked me first.

The sting of his teeth thrilled through me, surging a desperate need in my core so powerful I almost came. I whine-gasped then made that same sound again, but up an octave as Tyson opened my slacks and slid them and my panties slowly over my hips.

Bronn lingered in his bite, shivering and moaning, and his cock, still grasped in my hand through his pants, seemed to swell even larger.

My breath became short and shallow, as he drew back and licked the wound, and my world contracted to these two new points of pain which blasted me with pleasure.

Tyson slid my pants to my knees, and I fully expected to feel his hands or lips on my folds, but his hands stayed gripping my legs as he kissed my hip, then slid his lips down and sank his teeth into the soft flesh of my thigh.

I lost all control. It *must* be a wolf thing, because being bit was somehow my new favorite thing and fucking orgasmic. I bucked and shook as I came, but my guys held me firm as they licked their marks on me. Tyson slid a hand up to cup my core, pressing hard without moving, which was *exactly* what I wanted. I slowly relaxed into his hold as I gushed on his fingers.

I was so relaxed and limp with bliss that, when the three of them were done soothing and cleaning their marks, Colt had to carry me over to the couch, laying me down.

Only now — perhaps just a little too late — Bronn

closed all the curtains of the front room. Thankfully, we were all still dressed... mostly. I was the only one with my pants around my knees.

My guys drew close, Colt at my feet, helping me out of my pants, then massaging my calves and feet with wonderfully strong fingers. Tyson knelt by my head, stroking my hair and kissing my face lightly, which left Bronn my mid-section. He knelt next to the couch and bent to kiss my stomach and hips below my shirt.

"Is... is biting a shifter thing?" I asked, when I was recovered enough to speak, although I was still in a semi-delirious state after that primal orgasm.

Tyson nodded, drawing back a little. "Yes. Many animals bite when mating. For shifters, there is a slightly different thrill to it. It's a way of claiming someone, a bond for life, their mark on you forever. And, if that someone *wants* that mark, it tends to increase their libido and desire for the one marking them."

"Oh yeah, it did," I said with a satisfied sigh. My head lolled back on a pillow, my gaze a bit unfocused on the ceiling. "I mean, it was strange and painful, but also every tooth marking me felt like a thousand dicks inside me and it was... beyond description." I rolled my head to look at Tyson again. "And if I bite you?"

"Probably a similar reaction, though... we'd only have one bite each, so perhaps not quite as intense." His brow furrowed in thought. "Though, as our alpha, your bite might have a greater impact on us. I... don't know."

"You're going to find out," I whispered, voice husky and heavy with intent.

Tyson gave a feral grin, laden with his own anticipation. "Yes, alpha," he whispered.

That obedience, combined with the bonfire of desire behind his eyes sent a thrill through me, and suddenly I was full of energy and ready for the next round.

COLT

I felt the shift in Jane, the languid peace slipping away, replaced by a hard-stoked heat.

"You three are wearing far too much," Jane said, voice low and heated. "But you always strip so fast. I want you to take it slow this time."

"It's a shifter thing. We're used to getting out of our clothes quickly," Tyson said as he stood and took a step back.

I rose and pushed the coffee table out of the way. Bronn got up and the three of us stood before her. It was a good thing the curtains were closed, because the three of us were facing that large bay window. Anyone outside would have gotten the same show Jane was about to get if the curtains had been open.

"Slowly," Jane reminded us as she slid a finger down her body and between her legs.

Gods, just seeing that made me want to rip off my clothes and help. I loved that Jane wasn't afraid to take charge of her own arousal.

I ran my gaze up her stunning figure until it was locked on hers, making her my entire world, tuning out everything else as I slowly began to strip. I had my shirt up over my abs, when I had a brilliant idea. It wouldn't be slow, but I figured it would still be something special for her.

I slid my shirt back down again, this would be the "slow" part, me keeping it on just a little longer.

Jane's gaze — sliding over the three of us — caught mine with a hint of confusion. I smiled, running my hands up my body over my shirt, to the collar. Slowly, I curled my fingers under the collar and... I could have lifted it off from there, but instead. I waited another anticipatory moment, then jerked my hands to the sides, ripping open the collar. I slowly tore it open down the front, then shrugged out of the sleeves and let it fall away.

"Oh!" Jane gasped and squirmed on the couch.

That had been the reaction I'd hoped for.

Her gaze jumped down to my jeans and the bulge of my cock before flicking back up to my eyes.

I chuckled. "T-shirts are cheap, jeans aren't," I said.

She pushed her lip out in a pout and gave me the largest eyes I'd ever seen. I almost gave in to that look... but then she laughed.

"Fine," she giggled, "then your punishment is to leave them on until I tell you."

"Yes, alpha." But she hadn't said anything about what I could do while they were on, so I reached down into my jeans and stroked myself, straightening my strained and painful cock so the tip of it poked up out of the waistband.

Jane bit her lip. "Tease."

Yeah, like she wasn't the most massive tease in the world, laying there rubbing herself with her shirt still on but half-open.

I checked on Tyson and Bronn who were just finishing their striptease. We didn't wear much: T-shirts and jeans... and nothing underneath. Their cocks were out and twitching, Tyson's knot swollen and getting larger.

"I have an idea I think you'll like," Tyson said to Jane.

"By all means," she purred.

He turned to Bronn. "Go sit in one of the dining chairs."

Bronn nodded and went to the dining area. He grabbed a chair and turned it around to face us, then sat, his cock towering in his lap.

"And is *he* supposed to be *my* seat?" Jane asked.

"That's the idea," Tyson said, helping Jane up.

She kissed him, drawing his face down to hers in a long, open, hungry kiss. Then she stepped to me and did the same. Her tongue dove into my mouth and I swirled mine around inside her, tasting her slowly.

Breathless, she broke away, grabbed my arms in her small hands, and positioned me to face Bronn. Then she turned and pressed her back against me and shifted back and forth over my rigid cock.

Who was the tease now?

"Take off my shirt, slowly," she said to me, but her gaze was locked on Bronn.

So, this was meant to be a show for him. Fine, I didn't mind. I was pretty sure I'd enjoy it too.

I slid my hands up her arms and over her shoulders to her neck, holding her slender throat, clasped between my palms. She gave a shivering-moan, suddenly writhing and trembling. I realized I'd pressed on both my bite mark and Bronn's.

"So... sensitive," she breathed, shaking with arousal.

Her body had flushed a dark pink, searingly hot to the touch. I let my hands linger there for a moment longer, before slowly caressing down her front.

I undid one button, which, from my angle, revealed all of her luscious cleavage to me, then slid my hands away from the buttons and grasped her breasts firmly, massaging them through her shirt and bra for a long moment as she moaned and writhed against me.

Bronn, for his part, looked like he was enduring some mild torture. He kept his hands away from his cock, not touching himself, and gripped the chair hard, but his hips were giving subtle shifting thrusts and the dark skin of his cock looked practically purple.

Tyson had moved to one side, leaning on the fridge to get a full view of this tease. He was stroking his cock and grinning, eyes devouring Jane.

"Tell Bronn how much you want his cock," Tyson whispered.

"Fuck," Jane hissed. "Yes, I want your thick cock buried deep inside my pussy while I ride you like a stallion."

Fuck that was hot. As much as she'd be with another guy, that didn't matter. It was imagining seeing Jane in the throes of passion that got me wet, and I didn't want to wait to see that.

I quickly undid the rest of the buttons on her blouse and pulled it off, leaving her bra. I slid my hands up her sides, under her arms, and took another long feel of her full tits and that lacy bra, before following her bra strap around back and undoing the clasp. She let the fabric fall away as she strode over to Bronn and mounted him, hands on his shoulders as she lowered herself onto his thick dick. Slowly, she rocked over him, her head tilted back, hair falling in waves as she moaned unashamedly.

She reached out an arm toward Tyson and curled her finger for him to come to her side. His cock would be roughly at a level for her to take into her mouth.

But Tyson shook his head. "No Jane, take Colt."

"He's being punished for not ripping off his jeans," she said through her gasps as she slowly trembled on Bronn, bliss clearly elevated in her voice.

"When I put my cock inside you, I'm not going to be able to resist. I *am* going to knot you and I don't think you want that in your mouth."

She whined and pouted but relented. "Fine!" she said, then looked back over her shoulder at me.

"Come!" she demanded.

Fuck. That particular word, in that tone, from my alpha, and I almost did come. Luckily, with my cock trapped in my jeans, it was easier to quell my arousal.

I moved to her side while she rode Bronn, who feasted on her glorious tits. They both looked like they would explode with rapture any moment.

Jane looked up at me, then flicked the tip of my dick — still poking out from the top of my waistband — with a finger, making me flinch and groan.

"What *shall* I do with *you*?" she said between gasps and groans.

Then her eyes lit up and her lips curled in a feral smile. "I know." But she didn't elaborate. Instead, she just flicked my dick again, saying, "Take it out and fuck my mouth."

How could I resist that?

I had my jeans undone and pushed down below my balls in an instant. Jane grabbed my twitching cock and lowered it to her lips, sucking hard as she guided her mouth over my length. Few women could take me fully in their mouths, but Jane was a miracle and, with the tip of my cock pressed tight, deep in her throat, her lips slid up to my base.

Fuck! That felt good.

Softly, I put a hand on the side of her head, not urging just caressing her hair, and she slid a hand around my leg, digging her nails into my ass. She kept me close as she drove her mouth over me, fucking her face over my cock with aggressive abandon.

"Fuck," I moaned.

My cock swelled, on the verge of release, choking her more. But before I could come, she stopped and drew back, gasping for a moment and regaining her breath. Hot strands of saliva covered me, dripping off my length, and when she looked up at me, there was that same mischievous look...

What was she planning?

She let her wolf take her, skillfully navigating the shift so only her teeth changed, lengthening, sharp.

Oh... fuck!

Then, slowly, she pressed those piercing points down into my cock, not hard, not deep, just enough to draw blood.

She claimed me. And the force of that bond nearly overwhelmed me.

I let out an inhuman roar as ecstasy exploded within me, a rapture so intense it caused my heart to skip and my brain to shut down.

"Fuck, fuck, fuck, fuck!" I shouted, shooting cum into Jane's mouth so hard it spurted out around my cock, running off her chin in rivulets.

I convulsed in that involuntary release for what seemed like an eternity, until my balls were tight and extremely painful. Then, I stumbled back, catching myself on another chair.

Jane smiled and chuckled. "Now you're mine," she breathed.

And I was, fully, completely. She'd marked me in the most painfully intense and pleasurable way. And given how marks worked, every time my cock was inside her, I'd feel that thrill and remember this.

She turned to Bronn, wiping my cum off her chin, body flushed and shaking.

"Your turn, my lion," she breathed, then leaned forward to sink her teeth into his shoulder, roughly where he'd marked her.

Bronn grunted and his eyes went wide. He cried out as his body twitched. His hands slid to her hips, clamping her in place as he gave a final thrust. Then he licked his bite on her, and Jane joined him in a mutual orgasm which looked like it crashed through them in waves of intense bliss.

Tyson came up beside me and slapped my back. "Well, was it worth it? Saving a pair of jeans to have a cock that's going to be super sensitive every time she touches it?

I chuckled. "Hell yeah!"

Then I slumped down into a chair, spent and deliriously happy.

TYSON

MY FATED BOND WITH JANE WRENCHED AT MY SOUL WITH painful urgency. And seeing her claim Colt and Bronn in her own powerful and sexy way, I was just shy of an orgasm myself. Hell, I felt like I was *having* an orgasm, just not coming yet. It was intense and amazing and pure agony without Jane locked around my knot, but I knew I'd still take my time with her... *if* that's what she wanted.

And I'd have to wait a moment longer as she and Bronn descended from whatever level of heaven they'd just visited.

But when Jane lifted her head from Bronn's shoulder and looked over at me with a raging hunger in her eyes, I knew I wouldn't have to wait too long. It seemed her last orgasm had only made her desperate for more.

Still, she took Bronn's chin in her hand and lifted his head to crash her lips down on his in a long, devouring kiss before she broke away, breathless. Then, she slowly rose from his lap, shivering and mewling a little when his cock slipped out of her.

I went to Jane, helping her stand, since her legs seemed weak, and she leaned against me for a moment, breathing hard, head resting on my shoulder.

"My body says rest," she breathed. "But my bond with you says I need your cock in my pussy right, fucking, now!"

"Which are you listening to?" I asked, as I slowly turned her in my arms.

"Guess," she whispered, her hand grasping my knot and squeezing.

I let out a long, pained grunt, doubling over, legs giving way and falling to my knees, which pulled my cock out of her grasp. I had to stay there for a moment, panting and working to regain myself. That orgasm I was in the middle of had just spiked to unimaginable levels, but I knew I wouldn't come until I was knot deep inside her.

"Fuck," I whispered.

She gave an apologetic little laugh. "Oh... sorry. I forgot you hadn't had any yet. It must be... agony."

"It is. Heavenly agony," I said, slowly standing, breathing hard. "And if what you want is hard and fast, I am so very ready for that. But if you want slow and soft, I can make that work too."

She ran her hands over my chest, up to my shoulders, then around my neck. "My dangerous wolf is so patient and self-sacrificing," she whispered. "Thank you." She drew my head down for a soft kiss. "What do *you* want?" she breathed.

"I want to be knot deep inside you while you bite me." I had no flowery words, only an aching need.

"Yeah, me too," she said with a contented sigh. "But first, can you give me nice hard fucking. You don't get to thrust once we're locked and I really want to feel you fucking me, if that's okay?"

She said it like she was asking to pass the salt. Yet every word set my world on fire.

"Yes alpha," I breathed and plucked her up.

She wrapped her legs around me as I carried her to the kitchen counter and set her ass down on the edge, which put her at exactly the right height for me to give her all the thrusting she wanted. But my cock was trapped between us, so she released her legs around me, opening them out to the sides. It would be awkward for her to remain like that, so I slid my arms down to her thighs, clamping them there, so she wouldn't have to do any of the work to keep herself positioned.

Jane gasped and writhed, whining, and I realized I was gripping where I'd bitten her. I didn't move my hand, but massaged my palm over the spot as I swept my hips back, then plunged my cock into her wet pussy.

"Fucking God, yes! Fuck!" she cried out as I slammed my knot against her clit.

"You want thrusting?" I asked but didn't wait for an answer.

I gave it to her, hard and fast and relentless, bashing my knot against her pussy over and over, my cock swollen and tight inside her gripping sheath. It was an epic feat of restraint to keep from knotting her, but she was my alpha and the woman I adored, and her command — her desires — trumped mine every time.

She bucked and writhed and spewed a long string of words with no real meaning before shifting to guttural grunts and whines and sounds of rapturous desperation.

And for me... it was the same sweetest torture. My own persistent orgasm raged through me, pounding with my racing pulse, filling my cock with expectant swelling, painful yet deliciously pleasurable. I knew as soon as I knotted her, we'd both explode, but I drew out that heavenly moment.

Then she let out a long mewling sound, and suddenly used her arms around my neck to pull herself up, biting my jaw.

Something bright and blinding exploded inside me.

Now! I had to have her. *Now!*

I scooped her up, arms under her thighs, hands on her ass, and moved us to the side to slam her back against the fridge. I planted my hands against the cold metal, her knees over my elbows and slammed my knot into her. She hadn't released my chin and when I knotted her, her teeth sank deeper as she locked around me.

And I did explode, we both did.

Releasing my jaw, she smashed her lips to mine. I licked into her mouth... and she bit my tongue too.

She'd claimed me a second time and the raw euphoria that elicited made me lose all sense.

I spun in a glorious world of shifting colors, each a perfect expression of my ecstasy and love for this glorious woman.

When I finally regained awareness, I found myself kneeling on the floor.

We'd slid down the fridge, still locked together, still trembling through the throes of our combined orgasm, her teeth still claiming my tongue.

She finally released my tongue, then swept hers over and under it repeatedly soothing the bite. Then she pulled back with a sigh of utter contentment and delight. "That was amazing."

"You bit my tongue," I said, not quite believing it. My voice a little slurred from the temporary pain.

"You bit my thigh." She shrugged. "Consider it incentive."

"Incentive?" I didn't understand.

"For you to run your bite over mine."

And... lick her thigh.

Gods. My brain hitched on that thought, breaking for a moment as I imagined it and the delicious spike of bliss we'd both receive.

I chuckled. "Incentive it is."

When my knot finally diminished, I drew out of her, and glanced around. Bronn and Colt must have left while I'd been bathing in the bliss of being locked with my mate.

"They went to the bedroom," she said. "To get things ready for round... three?"

"Four for you, two for the rest of us," I corrected.

She chuckled. "Does it ever bother you that I get three times the orgasms you do?"

I smiled. "Nope. It's what you deserve."

"And you don't deserve more?"

"I won't turn them down, but I'm happy if you're

happy. So, if someone else you love makes you come, I won't complain."

"Good," she said, then tried to rise. She couldn't. And when I discovered I was so exhausted I couldn't either, we both started laughing and couldn't stop.

BRONN

THE WILD GIGGLES FROM THE KITCHEN DREW ME OUT OF the bedroom. Colt and I had lit some candles and laid a spare sheet over the bed so if we made a mess, it wasn't on the usual comforter. We wanted this last joining to be special, slow, sensual, and relaxing, to make sure Jane slept soundly tonight.

When I got to the front room, I had to step around the dining table to see the two of them. They rolled on the floor, laughing so hard they were having trouble breathing.

I stood there for a moment, unsure what was so funny, then found myself giggling just watching them.

"We can't... stand up!" Jane managed to gasp between giggles.

Ah.

I went to Tyson first, helping him up, then supporting him. I half carried the still laughing man into the bedroom and set him on the bed, then went back for Jane.

She, however, was a bit of a mess. Whenever she and Tyson locked, they always made a rather substantial mess when they came apart. I lifted her, carrying her to the bathroom, not the bedroom.

"Jane needs a shower," I called to the others. "We'll join you in a moment." I set her down in the tub.

"I'm a mess," she said, still smiling so wide it looked like it hurt. She also seemed a little tipsy, love-drunk. She blinked up at me. "Are you going to join me and clean me up?"

I knelt next to the tub. "Yeah, after I clean up that mess in the kitchen. Get the water going, as hot as you like."

She slid forward in the tub to the taps and began fiddling. I left her there and returned to the kitchen, getting a cloth and small bucket to wipe down the floor. Once done, I returned to the bathroom. Jane had the shower on, but reclined in the tub, seemingly unable to stand. She'd half pulled the shower curtain and all I could see was her head leaning against the back of the tub, hair wet, eyes closed.

When I got to her, I peeked around the curtain. The spray from the shower was hitting her chest, slowly cleansing her as it ran down her body.

"Do you still want company?" I asked.

"Mmm, yes please." She blinked her eyes open and beamed at me. "Wash me!"

I couldn't help but grin at that offer. Getting into the shower, I adjusted the head down so the spray hit her hips and legs, because once I was behind her, she'd be farther down the tub and I didn't want it in her face.

Then I carefully sat, shifting her forward so I could sit where she'd been.

She squirmed, leaning back on my chest. "There's something big and hard against my back," she said playfully.

"Keep squirming and it'll only get bigger and harder," I warned.

"Promise?"

"Oh, definitely." Then I grabbed a loofa and some bodywash, squirting the goo on her chest before starting to scrub. "Now... you wanted a wash, yes?"

"I'd rather you were squirting something else on my chest," she purred.

Wow, I was surprised she'd gone there. Jane wasn't usually that sexually suggestive.

"*That* wouldn't get you cleaner." I laughed.

"So?" Her tone was playful and provocative.

I knew then, she was going to be trouble. She proved me right a moment later when — soapy and slippery — she managed to turn herself around, then slide down my body, and lick her tongue up my cock from root to tip.

It felt *really* good, but it wouldn't get her clean.

"Now my back," she said and dipped her head on my cock again.

I tried not to think about what her mouth was doing as I leaned forward to scrub her back, but I could only reach so far.

"You need to stop that and sit up a little so I can finish washing you," I said, voice strained from the amazingly slow and sexy blow job I was getting.

"You sure?" she asked, popping off the end of my cock.

I gave her a stern look. "We have things planned for you in the bedroom."

She kept her gaze locked on mine as she slowly put my cock back in her mouth, then slid down until I was tight in her throat with her lips around my base. She swallowed a few times, milking my cock, then slowly drew back.

"You sure?" she asked again.

Fucking hell!

Nope, not anymore, I wasn't.

"Jane," I forced out, although I didn't know if I was about to rebuke her or encourage her.

She grinned. "Fine, you win... or... lose, I'm not sure which."

Both, definitely both.

She propped herself up until she was kneeling. In this position, the shower spray hit the top of her head and covered her in cascading rivulets. She looked like some goddess of rain or rivers as she tilted her head back, eyes closed, and let the water pour over her.

I could have watched that mesmerizing display for a lifetime, but I roused myself and quickly finished soaping and scrubbing her down. Then, I had to press myself against her, reaching an arm past her, to turn the water off.

That left us wet and plastered together.

She bent and kissed her mark on my shoulder, which made me shiver with bliss.

"I'm going to make you come so hard," she whispered, her hot breath caressing my ear and cheek.

"You already have," I replied.

"Then I'll do it again."

Shivering with anticipation, I quickly got us up and toweled off, then carried her into the bedroom.

"Ravish me!" she moaned as I laid her on the bed.

She was already dopey with contentment and squirmed a little as she eyed the three of us.

That had all three of us — even the recently spent Tyson — with cocks hard and ready to do as she'd demanded. Despite that, we were going to take our time and make sure our alpha — our mate, our love — was fully satisfied.

We crawled onto the bed with her, Tyson moving between her legs. They both shivered and moaned when he licked his bite on her thigh. With a groan, he clamped his mouth over her pussy and she squirmed with mounting bliss.

Colt and I reached our places to either side of her. He was slightly lower and began to pleasure her breasts with hands and mouth. I had the honor of watching her rapturous face and kissing her slender lips. I didn't rush it, kissing her softly, brushing my lips over hers. That was until one of her hands came up to slide over my shaved head and demand deeper. Even still, with my mouth pressed to hers, I took my time exploring, savoring every moment.

When we finally broke apart, she was near to breathless. "You're all being so soft and patient and giving."

"Is that bad?" I asked with a smile.

"No, it's wonderful," she breathed, smiling, eyes heavily lidded, tremors of bliss rolling through her in waves.

"You wanted us to show you how much we love you," I whispered. "We showed you our heat and passion first, now you're seeing the true depth of our affection and devotion."

She gave a soft smile, tears teasing the edges of her eyes, overjoyed.

"Everything we do, we do for you," I told her. "We do... *with* you. Partners and guides and lovers and fathers. You make us want to be all those things and just... better people. That's why we worship you. We elevate you, so we can aspire to be more like you. But we know you're human, just like the rest of us." I gave a quick laugh. "So we're also there for you and standing beside you every step of the way."

Wow. I'd surprised myself with those words. I wasn't usually anywhere near that eloquent.

"Exactly," Colt whispered.

"Bronn said it perfectly," Tyson added.

Jane, still shivering with pleasant arousal, blinked at me, then looked at the others. "Wow," she breathed. She looked like she wanted to say more, but didn't or couldn't, completely choked up with emotion.

"Cat got your tongue?" Tyson asked with a chuckle before diving back down to her folds.

Jane gasped at his attention. "No," she managed through her trembling breaths. Then her gaze caught mine. "But he will in a moment."

Now that was an invitation I wasn't going to refuse.

Except before I returned to her lips, I kissed her cheek and nibbled on her ear.

"I love you," Jane breathed.

I knew she didn't mean just me, but I also knew I was included in that love. *Me*, broken and messed up as I was, the lost lion who'd been torn from his pride, who'd never felt at home in this pack until now.

Jane had done that. She'd made this pack a place of acceptance, a family. I finally had a home and a loving mate, and it was the most wonderful feeling in the world.

And I was going to show my love just how much I loved her back.

We all were.

JANE

THIS EVENING HAD FAR SURPASSED MY EXPECTATIONS. Every passing moment brought me even greater joy and made me feel even more loved and adored.

Watching my guys strip had been playful and fun and *very* sexy.

Then, riding Bronn, with Colt in my mouth — as punishment for not ripping off his jeans — I'd felt powerful and sexy. I'd claimed them with my bite and they'd responded with explosive passion.

And Tyson had given me all of the hard and heated love I'd needed before I'd claimed him, too. Then we'd locked and I'd claimed him again, which had been a moment of pure and radiant bliss, stunning both of us.

Afterward, we'd laughed, so free and joyful. I hadn't thought it possible to be happier than that, but my sexy shower with Bronn had only elevated my mood even more.

And now my guys were showering me with affection. Bronn's perfect words a moment ago had filled my heart with such grateful love and pure delight that tears of pure joy traced my cheeks.

There were no words for how I felt.

No words other than… "I love you."

All three men stopped what they were doing, taking in everything I'd put into those words. Then, they resumed their pleasuring, and I let myself simply bask in this warmth and love and attention.

The next tear that escaped my eye, Bronn kissed away.

His lips brushed mine again, just as Tyson slid two thick fingers inside me. I gasped into Bronn's mouth as this new sensation mixed rapture with my joy and shot it through the roof.

When Tyson curled his fingers, licking my clit, and Colt flicked his tongue over the nipple he'd sucked into his mouth, and Bronn pressed his lips to mine with passion once more, a billowing, pleasant warmth saturated my being.

I felt like I'd lit up, glowing, as I squirmed through a wonderous orgasm. More tears escaped as I shuddered and wriggled and moaned, letting my guys know how they were making me feel.

When I could speak again, I gasped out, "Dicks!"

That caused all three of them to rumble with deep laughter.

"I think we can make that happen," Bronn said through his soft chuckles.

"Yes, alpha," Colt murmured, kissing my chest once again before the three of them began to move.

Colt rolled on top of me, the head of his massive cock

teasing and playing in the soaked mess that was my well-fucked core.

"Not you," I said with playfully scolding. "You didn't rip off your pants so no pussy for you."

I fully expected him to be contrite or beg or come up with some profession of love which would sway me, but instead he grinned wide. "Then I guess I get your ass."

My eyes went wide as he rolled off me again. My gaze followed him as he reached for my nightstand and opened the drawer to pull out a bottle of lube. God, he meant it!

My mind broke just a little trying to comprehend Colt's monster cock in my ass. In all the times my guys had been with me, it had only ever been Bronn who'd taken me there. He was the smallest of the three of them — even if no woman would *ever* call him small — and he'd filled me so completely. Colt would ruin me.

And a part of me cried out for exactly that.

"I think you broke her," Tyson said, caressing me with his hands and lips.

Yup, broken. I couldn't do anything other than watch Colt squirt lube over his long cock and massage it in.

The strangest thought occurred to me then. The part of me that so desperately wanted Colt to punish my ass... wasn't new. I'd forgotten until now, but long ago I'd been rather sexually adventurous. I'd perfected the blowjob as a teen hoping to "save my virginity for the right man."

But then, once I'd gone to college, I'd gotten a little freaky. I'd tried all sorts of things. It had been my adventurous nature that had brought me and my ex together. Though, looking back, I could see I'd wanted to experiment far more than he had. He'd liked that I was up for anything, but mostly, he'd just wanted to get his dick wet.

Even after we'd gotten married and had kids, I'd still wanted something adventurous, but hadn't had as much time for sex. My ex wanted sex all the time, but when we were together, he'd just get off, then pull out and fall asleep. He'd wanted quantity, I'd wanted quality, and we'd both been unsatisfied.

When he'd left, I'd just assumed that was it, no more fun down there for me.

But now these three men had brought my sexuality to life once more. They not only cared for me and my kids, helping with every aspect of my life, but they desired me too, and wanted to please me in all the fun and unusual ways I — had once — longed for.

Colt laughed. "Oh man, you guys should see her face. She went from stunned to starving."

I smiled at that, then finally turned my head away from Colt, more and more excited for what was to come. Finding new energy, I pushed Tyson onto his back and climbed on top of him.

To no one in particular, I said, "Better lube my ass too, just in case." I wiggled my ass a little, which meant I was gyrating my core over Tyson's cock.

He grunted.

"You really going to do this?" Tyson asked.

I grinned. "I am. I've remembered who I am, the fun and flirty side of me. And I want more of that. So... yeah."

"I like fun and flirty," Tyson said, sliding his hands through my hair, capturing a handful, and pulling me down to claim my lips.

Which meant he got the full gasp-in-mouth experience as someone squirted chilly wetness on my ass and began to massage it into my puckered entrance. It must have been Bronn because I was fairly certain Colt had still been lubing himself at the side of the bed.

I gasped again when Bronn slid first one, then two slick fingers inside me, to spread the lube around. Fuck, that felt good. I couldn't wait to have Colt inside me.

"Here I come, gorgeous," Colt whispered near my shoulder, then the two fingers left me and something massive pressed on the same spot.

I let out a long moan, rising in pitch as that huge cock pushed harder and slipped around in all that lube before Colt's thick tip penetrated me.

I tore my lips away from Tyson's and lifted my head to shout, "Holy fucking fuuuuck!" I drew out that last word as Colt teased himself slowly deeper into my ass.

Every time I thought *he can't go deeper, that has to be it*, he'd slip another inch inside me and I'd unleash another string of profanities. Then I simply stopped speaking all together, eyes wide and mouth gaping as he just... kept... *going!*

And when, finally, his hips pressed against my ass cheeks, he let out a long grunting sigh. "So. Fucking. Tight!" he hissed.

I grunted in agreement. He stretched me to my limit, so deep, it felt like he was practically in my stomach. I couldn't imagine what it would feel like when he began thrusting.

"Gods! Your bite!" Colt's voice rose an octave. Given

how hard I was squeezing him, I couldn't imagine what my mark on his cock must be doing to him.

"I think you broke her again," Tyson said, as he kissed my neck and chin.

I trembled so hard I couldn't control myself. This felt amazing and impossible.

Colt's strong hands slid down my sides, then under me, pulling me up slowly. Yet every minor movement shifted his cock inside me and spiked my bliss to new levels. And when he had my back pressed to his chest, he slid his hands up to massage my tits, pulling, plucking and playing.

I didn't know what I must have looked like, but I knew I felt like jelly: just firm enough to stay upright, but all wobbly and limp and loose.

"Bronn," Tyson hissed with restrained passion. "Get in here," he slid out from under me. "If I go now, I'll knot her again."

The thought of his knot in my pussy, pressed against the monster shaft in my ass broke my mind for a moment, and by the time I blinked back to reality, Bronn was shuffling in, kneeling before me.

"Jane?" he asked, tentative. "You want this?"

Again, I must have looked completely delirious, he was being so careful. I couldn't speak so I just nodded. I was fairly certain that as soon as Bronn slid into me, I'd come... hard.

The beautiful lion shifter didn't rush in, though. He reached down first to massage my drenched folds. My eyes rolled back and I convulsed with a contraction of bliss at his firm attention. I didn't come, but I was certainly ready to. I was experiencing all of the radiant ecstasy of an orgasm, just without the release.

"Fuck," Colt hissed behind me as I clamped down on his cock. "She's so fucking close!"

Then Bronn's hand slipped away and his cock slid inside me in one slow but firm motion.

I lost it. I didn't have much control in this position, but I did what I could, wrapping my arms around Bronn and pulling him tight to me. I wanted to feel all his hardness against all my softness and have something to grind my clit against as I writhed and wriggled through this momentous orgasm.

"Fuck!" Bronn hissed as he began long slow thrusts. "Gods Jane, you're so fucking wet, but still squeezing my cock. It's divine!"

"Squeezing *your* cock, you should feel what she's doing to mine!" Colt sounded like he was in the most exquisite, blissful agony.

And yet still, he hadn't moved an inch, planted deep inside me but not thrusting. It was making me mad with anticipation.

"Too much!" Bronn hissed as his pace quickened, thrusting hard into my gushing pussy. "Yes!" he cried out. "Fuck!" His fingers dug into my hips as he drove himself into me harder and harder.

And my orgasm only lengthened and heightened, pounding through me so hard I was nearly insensate. My mind stopped working, going completely by feel.

And there was *so much* to feel! I wanted Bronn to come, wanted to feel the pulse of his cock as he filled me with his heat. I'd asked for dicks and I'd gotten them, though I would never have imagined this level of mind-blowing ecstasy.

"Come!" I managed to shout, voice ragged and raw. To my ears it hadn't even sounded like a word, but Bronn seemed to understand.

"Yes, sweetness," he breathed as he panted, redoubling his assault on me.

Then, with a final hard slam of his cock inside me, which smashed my clit in all the right ways, Bronn stiffened and came.

I raked my nails up his back until my hands found the back of his head and I crashed our faces together in a messy kiss of raw, mindless passion. Then, as if one mind, we separated and tilted our heads to the other's shoulder and sucked on our marks there. Bronn's powerful heat surged inside me as I exploded around him.

And through all of this, Colt didn't shift an inch. He hadn't so much as tried a shallow thrust into my ass, he was solid and stiff behind me. I couldn't see him and couldn't fathom what he was feeling or thinking. One distant part of my mind, that wasn't in the highest of heavens, wondered why he hadn't come with Bronn and me.

But then, as Bronn shook and drew back, pulling out of me, and Tyson quickly took his place, I knew.

Colt was waiting... for this.

For Tyson's knot and my lock and all of the clenching fury which would happen in just a moment.

Bronn shifted to the side, but remained kneeling at my level and our faces crashed together once more as Tyson drew close and slid his cock inside me.

Yet, when his knot pressed to my pussy, he didn't push it in right away. Instead, he ground it over my clit and drove me higher into this extended rapture. My head tilted back, eyes to the heavens, mouth open in a silent prayer of utter, maddening, bliss.

"Fuck," Tyson hissed, thrusting and smashing his knot against me, which was purely divine.

Perhaps he couldn't fit? Maybe Colt had stretched me too much and I was too tight for Tyson's knot? I didn't know, I was certainly well lubricated and ready after that last gushing orgasm.

Then Colt began pulling out, a long slow process, and I felt every inch of his thick, veined shaft, since I gripped him so tightly.

"Now," Colt hissed to Tyson. Tyson tried again, his knot pressing on my folds for a moment before slipping inside.

I instantly locked around that glorious knot and the untold heights of bliss I reached, completely broke me. I lost all sense and thought.

Then, I was slammed back into awareness when Colt began his hard, long thrusts into my ass.

I made very unladylike noises then, perhaps inhuman noises as I experienced pure euphoria. Every slam of Colt's cock into me jarred me over Tyson's swollen knot, bashing my bliss to oblivion and beyond.

"Fuck! I can't! Your mark!" Colt bellowed. Then, with a final ass-punishing thrust, drove deep and came.

That caused Tyson to lose it. I was already lost. We came together in a festival of bliss.

Fireworks blossomed behind my eyes.

Stars exploded.

I exploded.

We all exploded.

Nothing left but panting, wheezing, parched and burning lungs in bodies wracked with uncontrollable tremors.

It was eerily quiet. Then Bronn whispered, "Fucking hell, that looks intense."

I blinked, returning to myself from whatever galaxy of pure pleasure I'd just visited.

Tyson and Colt still pulsed inside me, filling me with every drop of their love. I shifted to look at Bronn, a little sad that he'd been left out of this. He was furiously stroking his cock.

"So... fucking... hot!" he hissed, then his fist gripped his tip and he shuddered.

No. I didn't want him to come and not be inside me. I couldn't speak, but I opened my mouth, curling my tongue to beckon him. He understood.

He stood on the bed and slid his cock through his fist between my lips. Hot streams of cum hit the back of my throat, and I drank him down, sucking him dry until he fell back on the bed, huffing and swearing. Not long later, Tyson and Colt finally finished and the three of us collapsed into a heap with Bronn.

JANE

I WOKE LATER THAT NIGHT TO FIND WE'D ALL FALLEN ASLEEP like that, still entwined and mingled.

All the candles had burned out and I smiled in the darkness.

It would be two more years until Izzy went to college. Another two more until Milo left. Four years. I'd be forty-eight. That was still young-ish, wasn't it? Some folks kept up their sex life into their elder years. I had lots of years of kinky, mind-blowing sex ahead of me. And between those sessions, I'd have three amazing men as my partners in life, and a community coming together to support me as well.

After I'd shot Harley — and found out about packs and alphas — I could remember thinking how much my life would change. And it had. What I couldn't have imagined then, was that it would be better now than before.

I wasn't some washed-up old maid. My life was far from over. And I wasn't plain Jane Myers. I was a mother, a leader, a wolf, an alpha, and a damned-sexy bitch.

That's what I'd learned from these men, my pack, my family, and the neighbors around me. And with that thought, I slid into a contented sleep.

You'd think after a prolong night of sex, sex, and more sex, I'd wake up sore. But this wolf's body of mine healed quickly and I woke feeling refreshed and invigorated. I also woke to the amazing smell of bacon.

At first, I thought it was just Tyson's scent... but no, I could hear the distant sizzling from the kitchen and the smell of coffee.

Slowly, I disengaged from Tyson and Colt's slumbering forms, noticing that Bronn wasn't in bed. I found a house coat and put it on as I made my way out to the kitchen.

Bronn was buck naked and cooking. If there was anything sexier than a buff Black man, naked and cooking I didn't know what that was. And with the kids out of the house and most of the pack gone, he could be naked as much as he wanted this morning.

He turned to me and smiled. "Hey, sweetness."

I came up behind him and wrapped my arms around his waist, kissing my mark on his shoulder. He shivered in response.

"Hey, none of that, I'm trying to cook!"

"Can I help?" I asked. It was a trick question, but he still answered as I'd hoped.

"No, you go sit and relax. I've got it handled."

"Right answer," I said, then, just for fun, kissed my mark again. This time his shiver was harder and lasted longer.

"Stop that!" he hissed playfully.

I giggled as I slipped off him to grab a cup of coffee, which he'd already brewed. I stirred in a bit of sugar, but didn't add any cream, I wanted it black, like the man in my kitchen. Then I leaned on the counter and sipped it as I watched him work.

I could get used to this.

Then Izzy came bursting through the front door in a rush. "Hey Mom, I need to grab some... *Bronn*!"

I smiled, because the way she'd said his name was with all of the disgusted loathing of a teenager seeing her *father* naked. She could just as easily have been saying *Dad* the same way.

"Sorry, Izzy," Bronn said, turning away, though that meant she still had a full view of his butt. She tore her gaze away from that rigid roundness and back to me.

"I'm just grabbing a few things. Terry's taking us shopping for furniture for the new houses. Petra, Dana, Cassie, Jake and I are going. Is that okay?"

"Yup," I said easily. Then I made a point of looking at Bronn before saying, "Take your time."

"Ewwww, *Mom*!" There was that same tone again. "Fine, I'm staying out all day. Call me when you and the trini-dads are done with your *alone time*." Then she ran to her room, rummaged around for a moment, then ran out again.

I had a silly smile plastered on my face. "Trini-dads?" I said, sounding out the word, laughing.

Bronn shrugged. "It fits."

It did... very well. And it seemed Izzy was adapting far better than I'd hoped, especially after running away two weeks ago. Things really were settling into a new normal.

"How do you like your bacon?" Bronn asked. A perfectly normal question, and perhaps it was because of that, that my smile grew wider still.

I couldn't help myself. "Nice and firm, rigid. I don't like floppy meat."

Bronn chuckled, giving me some side-eye with a raised brow.

"Didn't get enough last night?" he asked.

How best to answer that? "I have three incredibly sexy, younger men with the stamina of stallions and ten years of parched pussy to make up for." I sipped my coffee after saying that and watched his reaction.

His cock twitched and rose, beginning to swell and lengthen.

It was a start, but not quite what I'd hoped for. So, I put my coffee down, hiked myself up onto the counter, and opened my legs until my robe was pushed back to my hips. I wasn't wearing any underwear, giving him a perfect view of my pussy. Bronn couldn't take his eyes off me, but still refused to leave the bacon. So, I licked my finger, slowly slipping it in and out of my mouth, before lowering it to play with my clit.

"Fuck it, bacon's done!" he said, quickly taking the pan off the heat and dumping the bacon onto a plate he'd prepared with paper towels. "You're too fucking sexy for your own good, you know that?" he whispered, clamping his hand behind my neck to pull me forward for a long kiss. And when he pulled back, he knelt next to the counter and pulled my finger aside so he could take its place with his mouth and hands.

"Yes, I am," I purred, one hand on the back of his

head, leaning my head back against the cupboards. Then I reached over with my other hand and plucked one of the pieces of bacon off the plate and brought it to my lips. It was perfect, firm and crisp and salty and smokey and so very good.

Best breakfast ever!

TERRY CALLED BEFORE HE LEFT WITH THE LADIES. MILO and Danny were going over to the Longs to play with Calvin for the day. That meant I had no familial responsibilities for the first time in a long time. So, we took it easy all day, lounging and playing, teasing and tempting and talking. It was wonderful.

Mrs. Khan called at one point to set up an official meeting of the Woodside Business Cooperative, but other than that, we were undisturbed until dinner time. Even then, I was told to shower and relax, while the guys took care of everything.

By the time I'd dressed, my kids were home and I could hear them excitedly talking about their days to the guys. I left my room and paused. Something scratched at the back door, and I went and opened it to find Brutus in his wolf form outside.

"You could shift and let yourself in, you know."

Brutus sat there and gave the wolfen equivalent of a shrug.

"You really like it as a wolf, don't you?"

The snaggle-toothed wolf, with his tongue lolling out, nodded.

I looked around the yard, then wondered, "Have you been outside all night and all day?"

Another nod.

"Did you mind?"

A shake of the head.

"You... were giving us some privacy?"

Another nod.

"Thanks, Brutus, come on in." I let him past and he even wiped his paws on the back mat before continuing.

Then the two of us joined the others in the dining room.

"Brutus!" Milo shouted. He jumped off his chair and hugged the rough looking wolf around the neck. Brutus leaned into it, clearly loving it. "Thanks for looking out for me last night."

That caught my attention. "What's that?" I asked,

Milo looked up, eyes sparkling. "When we left this morning Brutus was lying on the front step of Terry's house. I think he was there all night, sort of keeping an eye on me."

Oh...

"Thank you, Brutus," I said and knelt to pet the dog... wolf... shifter, whatever. I ruffled his fur, then turned to Izzy. "How was shopping?"

"Terry has good taste. I like the furniture they're getting better than ours. And he's got it bad for Petra, everyone knows it now and the two of them are so cute together."

"And you and Jake?" I asked, curious.

She blushed. "Ah... we're... cool." Then she rolled her eyes. "He's *terrified* of pissing off the alpha, so he's taking it super slow. I said it was okay if he wanted to kiss me, but he wanted to get your permission first."

Permission... for a kiss? I liked that boy more and more.

"I'm not going to ask what *you* did all day," Izzy said. "Don't want to make myself sick before dinner."

I hid a smile as we all sat down to eat. The guys had cooked up steak and hamburgers, with baked potatoes and a big Caesar salad. It was delicious. We talked and laughed and ate, enjoying the food and the company.

I couldn't stop smiling. Before bikers and wolves had come into my life, my table had never been this lively. Milo and Izzy and I might have talked, but we'd have been subdued. Life had been flat, dull, monotonous. Which meant, this wasn't just a new normal for all of us, this was a better life, a full life.

So much had changed, and the best change was, I could now say I was *truly* happy. Only one thing would make me happier, and during a lull in the conversation, I figured, why not ask for it.

"Bronn, Colt, and Tyson... will you marry me?"

The answer, of course, was a three-fold, resounding, "Yes!"

EPILOGUE

PETRA

"A bridesmaid?" I asked, stunned. One of my hands drifted up and began rubbing my belly, it had become a habit, and Jane caught the movement.

"The wedding's not till the spring, you'll have had your baby by then."

But that really wasn't why I'd been shocked to be asked. Jane was an amazing woman. She'd stepped in and saved the pack and saved my life in so many ways.

I owed her everything.

But I wasn't anything special. Why would this amazing woman, my alpha, want *me* standing up with her on her wedding day?

Yet here she was, beaming, practically vibrating with life and joy. "Just say yes," she begged.

"Yes," I tried as hard as I could not to make that sound like a question.

"Thank you!" she squealed and hugged me tightly. "Bree... ah Breanna Long, is the maid of honor. She'll be getting ahold of you for some stuff, but mostly all you have to do is show up and look beautiful, which should be a breeze for you."

I hugged Jane back, so very thankful for her, and everything she'd done. "Thank you," I said and meant it.

She pulled back, holding me at arm's length. Somberness tempered the joy on her features when she asked, "How are *you* doing?"

Physically, I was well enough. I didn't like hospitals, so I'd gotten up the courage to ask the fae ladies to do a "check-up" on me and the baby. They said we were both strong and healthy, with no concerns.

But... my issues weren't physical.

"I'm... okay," I said, honestly. I'd made it through the night last night without a single nightmare, at least none that I remembered in the morning. "Some days are better than others. Today is a good day."

Jane smiled. "I'm glad. Remember, I'm here if you need anything at all."

I nodded. Her generosity of spirit boggled my mind. She'd already given me the greatest gift of all: killing Harley and getting me away from Tank. I'd never be able to repay her for that. There were no words, no gifts, no actions which would ever match what she'd done.

She leaned in and hugged me again quickly before pulling back with a deep breath. "Now I need to find Cassie and ask her!"

That brilliant smile of hers returned as she left and headed for the house that the Juarez family and Cassie and Jake now shared.

I felt restless after that and needed to do something.

"I'm going for a walk!" I called to my housemates. There were several calls of acknowledgment from other parts of the house as I put on a light jacket and headed out.

It was November, and a chilly day, but being a shifter and with a bun in the oven, I barely felt the chill these days.

Jane had gotten distracted in her quest to cross the street and was chatting with Debbie Coles next door. I waved to them, still shocked that a witch had accepted us shifters so easily. Just another minor miracle for our alpha.

Debbie waved back.

I turned in the other direction and headed up the street. Lucas Juarez was helping Erik Holt with his car, their heads buried under the hood. Milo and Danny were out playing tag with Calvin Long on his front lawn, being watched over by Parker Long, who was hobbling around on crutches.

At the top of the street, I crossed over and went to knock on Mrs. Khan's door.

We'd start work on her kitchen tomorrow.

She answered quickly. She had an apron on and I could see her kitchen was a disaster behind her. It looked like she was doing some last-minute cooking while cleaning out her cupboards all at once.

"Oh, hello, dearie," she said. "Don't worry, we'll be all

cleaned out and ready for your crew to come in and start taking it all down, tomorrow."

"Need any help?" I wasn't sure why I offered other than this woman had done a lot for our pack recently. She was starting to feel like a sort of mother figure.

"Oh, no, we're good. Thank you for offering."

We stood there awkwardly for a moment before I broke things off with, "See you tomorrow at eight, then."

"Yes, tomorrow at eight. Good night, dearie." Mrs. Khan closed the door.

I ambled past Jane's house. My acute hearing picked up what sounded like Colt training Izzy in self-defense in the basement.

And that... brought me to Terry's door.

A part of me had known I'd end up here, but I'd told myself I was just walking around the neighborhood, nothing more.

I raised my hand to press the doorbell as I glanced over at the Herreras' place, where Niko and Mr. Herrera were chatting on the lawn between their two houses. It was good to see the pack integrating so well with these folks.

The door in front of me opened. I was caught, stunned, my hand still poised over the doorbell.

"Hey," Terry said, leaning on the doorframe. "I saw you approach from the front window. Want to come in?"

Yes, I did.

No, I didn't.

Why was this so hard?

But I knew why. The same reason why *everything* in my life was hard. I was messed up inside because of Tank.

Even that thought made me want to run from the kind-hearted man in front of me. Run so I wouldn't get close to him, so he'd never want to... to kiss me or touch me. If we just talked, I could imagine us being together. He was so kind and funny and handsome and everything I'd ever wanted in a man. But then his hand would brush my arm and I'd flinch away, or he'd lean a little too close and I'd panic and squirm. I didn't want it to happen, but it did. I couldn't help myself.

"Or..." Terry drew out the word with a shrug, smiling the whole time. "We could stand here and talk. Whatever you're comfortable with." And there he was, being so perfect, again!

"Thank you for buying us furniture," I blurted. Wow, yeah, that was smooth and didn't make me sound like a pity case at all.

His smile softened a little. "You can take it out of the cost of my renovation if you like," he suggested.

If I did, we'd be doing it for free. He'd bought the pack two houses' worth of furniture!

"I... should go," I whispered, turning.

He reached out to stop me — he didn't even touch me — and still I flinched.

His hand froze.

I froze, feeling ashamed and stupid and... broken.

"Please," he pleaded in the barest of whispers. "Stay."

And I wanted to, desperately.

"I can stand across the room, if you like, but please. I'd... like to talk some more."

Sometimes it was so easy to talk to him and I didn't even think about it, but other times...

I closed my eyes, feeling tears leave them and wet my cheeks. I wiped them away and took a long breath, nodding. "Okay," I whispered.

I turned back and he held the door open for me, standing back. I crept in and he closed the door... not quite all the way. It would let in the cool autumn air... but it also gave me a symbolic way out.

He was always doing little things like that, so considerate. Why couldn't I get over myself and be near him?

I sat on one end of a couch and he kept to his word, leaning on the wall on the far side of the long front room, like Jane's house.

Terry's house was a bit larger than Jane's, the front room more spacious. It was also flipped, with the kitchen on the left side and the living room on the right. And since it was a bit deeper, the dining room wasn't so much in the middle as closer to the front on the right side.

And there he was, more than thirty feet away, as far as he could get across the front room.

This was silly.

"You could... sit... on the couch, if you want," I said, halting and slow. Even my voice betrayed me.

He made his way over slowly, like I was a wounded animal — which I guess I was — and sat on the far end of the couch opposite me.

Silence hung between us.

I used to know how to talk to people, have casual conversations, but that had been... before. And even though that had been only eight months ago, it felt like a whole other me, a previous life.

"I have... two brothers, twins actually," he began,

speaking in a calm and easy way. "Have I mentioned that?"

We'd chatted a few times now, and honestly, I couldn't remember much of what we'd talked about. I'd just been dazzled by his green eyes and kind smile and the fact that he looked at me like I was precious. I couldn't fathom how any man could look at me like that. Especially one who had any clue what I was and what I'd gone through. I was a monster, a broken and used up monster.

"Maybe," I said trying to smile. "But tell me again."

"Their names are Nick and Nate. After me, my mom had really wanted a girl, one of each, you know, but instead she got the terror twins, two more boys."

I realized my hand had been rubbing my belly again. I stopped, pushing that hand down to my lap.

"Do you know...?" He stopped himself. "Sorry. Ah... back to my family."

"A girl," I said quickly.

I didn't really know yet, but I was praying for a girl. It had to be a girl, because if it wasn't, I didn't know what I'd do. I'd promised myself I'd keep this child, claim it, make it mine, because I'd always wanted kids. It didn't matter who the father had been, this child would be a blessing, a new life for me to care for and look after... or so I hoped.

In truth, I was terrified. If it was a boy, I was worried I'd take one look and see Tank. I didn't know what I'd do then.

It was just another messed up part of me. I was trying to be strong and make my life my own. I knew Tank was dead, I'd made *very* sure of that. But it hadn't been enough to erase his mark on me.

Terry started talking again. "My mother is a tenacious woman. She had to be, to put up with we three boys... and my father. He—"

"Kiss me!" I blurted, stunning myself.

Terry blinked. "Are... you sure?"

Nope. I didn't even know where that had come from. Though, as I sat there thinking about it... I began to understand. I couldn't stop thinking about Tank and just conversation wasn't doing it for me. I needed more.

I patted the couch next to me, an invitation.

He got up and moved over. Even then he didn't sit right next to me, giving me space. So, I went to him, inching across the couch until the fabric of our clothes over hips and legs touched... and I didn't pull away.

"Kiss me, please," I repeated, I raised a hand to his face, that kind and soft face with those sparkling green eyes.

He reached up slowly, carefully, and swept his hand back through my long bangs on the left side, lightly.

Gods! It felt so good to have someone touch me so gently, lovingly.

I leaned in slowly and he did the same. I wouldn't close my eyes, I needed to see him, even if it was far too close and his features would be all blurred. That didn't matter. I needed to see it was him, not... anyone else.

I trembled like a leaf as our lips touched. I prayed he'd be gentle and soft, and he was. He didn't push or press. He yielded to me, letting my lips brush his, no more. One pass, then another, and I drew back.

Gods! It had been wonderful, not a savage thing, but soft and caring.

"Thank you," I breathed, shaking so hard I thought I might come apart. Yet the steady gaze of those calm green eyes helped to still me.

"Whatever you need," he whispered. "I'm here."

The door flew open.

I jumped up.

"Hey, Dad, I'm home! Oh, hi Petra!" Danny called as he returned from playing. He sprinted through the main room and was gone down the back hall in an instant.

"That... was... a surprise," Terry said.

I couldn't help it, I laughed. I laughed so hard that Terry began laughing with me. I laughed so hard I fell back down onto the couch. All my pent-up tension had snapped in that instant and now I could do nothing but let it out with laughter.

And yet, eventually, my wild laughter turned to heaving sobs and Terry bundled me in his arms. I put my head on his shoulder, staining his shirt with a river of tears. He simply held me, carefully, tenderly, tight enough to be comforting without being possessive.

And when my tears stopped, when I was exhausted and red-eyed and empty of emotion — for now — Terry still held me.

I drew back, needing to see his kind face. His soft, soothing smile melted my heart. I must have looked awful, but he still gazed at me like I was the most cherished thing in the world.

"Feel better?" he asked.

I nodded.

"Good. If... if you ever need to cry on my shoulder again... I'm here for that too."

Those words, that look, caused a crack to form in the sturdy walls I'd built up around my heart. This man had just seen me manic then despondent and still I got the feeling he wouldn't want to be anywhere else in the world but by my side.

For the first time in a long time, I found myself smiling, a genuine smile, not forced at all. Because as of that moment, I started to believe that maybe, just maybe, this relationship could work.

Find out more about Petra and Terry (and his brothers) in the next series: **Mama Bear and the Millionaires.**

OTHER BOOKS BY TESSA COLE

NEPHILIM'S DESTINY

Destined Shadows, prequel story

Destined Darkness, book 1

Destined Blood, book 2

Destined Fire, book 3

Destined Storm, book 4

Destined Radiance, book 5

ANGEL'S FATE

Fated Bonds, book 1

Fated Winter, book 2

Fated Fear, book 3

Fated Despair, book 4

Fated Resolve, book 5

Fated Heart, book 6

ENSNARED BY THE PACK

Wolf Deceived, book 1

Wolf Denied, book 2

Wolf Desired, book 3

Wolf Distressed, book 4

OTHER BOOKS BY CLARA WILS

THE GRECIAN GODDESS TRILOGY

Co-written with Tessa Cole

Kiss of the Goddess, book 1

Power of the Goddess, book 2

Bonds of the Goddess, book 3

THE MISTS OF ELISTA TRILOGY

Bonds and Blood, book 1

Shape and Shadows, book 2

Form and Fury, book 3

SISTER SPIRITS

Double Discover, book 1

Double Danger, book 2

Double Disaster, book 3

Double Doom, book 4

Double Destiny, book 5

THE SECRETS GODS KEEP

Co-written with Tessa Cole

Craving Demons, book 1

Chaos Demons, book 2

www.ingramcontent.com/pod-product-compliance
Lightning Source LLC
Chambersburg PA
CBHW020330180626
46812CB00001B/129